# CRUCIAL INSTANCES

## SANCTUARY

She had meant to wait for him on the Terrace.

# CRUCIAL INSTANCES

## SANCTUARY

BY

EDITH WHARTON

NEW YORK
CHARLES SCRIBNER'S SONS
1914

CRUCIAL INSTANCES
COPYRIGHT, 1901, BY CHARLES SCRIBNER'S SONS

---

SANCTUARY
COPYRIGHT, 1903, BY CHARLES SCRIBNER'S SONS

# TABLE OF CONTENTS

## *CRUCIAL INSTANCES*

### I
*The Duchess at Prayer* . . . . . . . . 1

### II
*The Angel at the Grave* . . . . . . . 35

### III
*The Recovery* . . . . . . . . . . 65

### IV
*"Copy": A Dialogue* . . . . . . . 99

### V
*The Rembrandt* . . . . . . . . . 123

### VI
*The Moving Finger* . . . . . . . . 153

### VII
*The Confessional* . . . . . . . . . 181

---

## *SANCTUARY*

243

# CRUCIAL INSTANCES

# THE DUCHESS AT PRAYER

HAVE you ever questioned the long shuttered front of an old Italian house, that motionless mask, smooth, mute, equivocal as the face of a priest behind which buzz the secrets of the confessional? Other houses declare the activities they shelter; they are the clear expressive cuticle of a life flowing close to the surface; but the old palace in its narrow street, the villa on its cypress-hooded hill, are as impenetrable as death. The tall windows are like blind eyes, the great door is a shut mouth. Inside there may be sunshine, the scent of myrtles, and a pulse of life through all the arteries of the huge frame; or a mortal solitude, where bats lodge in the disjointed stones and the keys rust in unused doors. . .

## II

FROM the loggia, with its vanishing frescoes, I looked down an avenue barred by a ladder of cypress-shadows to the ducal escutcheon and mutilated vases of the gate. Flat noon lay on the gardens, on fountains, porticoes and grottoes. Below the terrace, where a chrome-colored lichen had sheeted the balustrade as with fine *laminæ* of gold, vineyards stooped to the rich valley clasped in hills. The lower slopes were

# THE DUCHESS AT PRAYER

strewn with white villages like stars spangling a summer dusk; and beyond these, fold on fold of blue mountain, clear as gauze against the sky. The August air was lifeless, but it seemed light and vivifying after the atmosphere of the shrouded rooms through which I had been led. Their chill was on me and I hugged the sunshine.

"The Duchess's apartments are beyond," said the old man.

He was the oldest man I had ever seen; so sucked back into the past that he seemed more like a memory than a living being. The one trait linking him with the actual was the fixity with which his small saurian eye held the pocket that, as I entered, had yielded a *lira* to the gate-keeper's child. He went on, without removing his eye:

"For two hundred years nothing has been changed in the apartments of the Duchess."

"And no one lives here now?"

"No one, sir. The Duke goes to Como for the summer season."

I had moved to the other end of the loggia. Below me, through hanging groves, white roofs and domes flashed like a smile.

"And that's Vicenza?"

"*Proprio!*" The old man extended fingers as lean as the hands fading from the walls behind us. "You see

# THE DUCHESS AT PRAYER

the palace roof over there, just to the left of the Basilica? The one with the row of statues like birds taking flight? That's the Duke's town palace, built by Palladio."

"And does the Duke come there?"

"Never. In winter he goes to Rome."

"And the palace and the villa are always closed?"

"As you see—always."

"How long has this been?"

"Since I can remember."

I looked into his eyes: they were like tarnished metal mirrors reflecting nothing. "That must be a long time," I said involuntarily.

"A long time," he assented.

I looked down on the gardens. An opulence of dahlias overran the box-borders, between cypresses that cut the sunshine like basalt shafts. Bees hung above the lavender; lizards sunned themselves on the benches and slipped through the cracks of the dry basins. Everywhere were vanishing traces of that fantastic horticulture of which our dull age has lost the art. Down the alleys maimed statues stretched their arms like rows of whining beggars; faun-eared terms grinned in the thickets, and above the laurustinus walls rose the mock ruin of a temple, falling into real ruin in the bright disintegrating air. The glare was blinding.

"Let us go in," I said.

# THE DUCHESS AT PRAYER

The old man pushed open a heavy door, behind which the cold lurked like a knife.

"The Duchess's apartments," he said.

Overhead and around us the same evanescent frescoes, under foot the same scagliola volutes, unrolled themselves interminably. Ebony cabinets, with inlay of precious marbles in cunning perspective, alternated down the room with the tarnished efflorescence of gilt consoles supporting Chinese monsters; and from the chimney-panel a gentleman in the Spanish habit haughtily ignored us.

"Duke Ercole II.," the old man explained, "by the Genoese Priest."

It was a narrow-browed face, sallow as a wax effigy, high-nosed and cautious-lidded, as though modelled by priestly hands; the lips weak and vain rather than cruel; a quibbling mouth that would have snapped at verbal errors like a lizard catching flies, but had never learned the shape of a round yes or no. One of the Duke's hands rested on the head of a dwarf, a simian creature with pearl ear-rings and fantastic dress; the other turned the pages of a folio propped on a skull.

"Beyond is the Duchess's bedroom," the old man reminded me.

Here the shutters admitted but two narrow shafts of light, gold bars deepening the subaqueous gloom. On a dais the bedstead, grim, nuptial, official, lifted its baldachin; a yellow Christ agonized between the curtains,

# THE DUCHESS AT PRAYER

and across the room a lady smiled at us from the chimney-breast.

The old man unbarred a shutter and the light touched her face. Such a face it was, with a flicker of laughter over it like the wind on a June meadow, and a singular tender pliancy of mien, as though one of Tiepolo's lenient goddesses had been busked into the stiff sheath of a seventeenth century dress!

"No one has slept here," said the old man, "since the Duchess Violante."

"And she was—?"

"The lady there—first Duchess of Duke Ercole II."

He drew a key from his pocket and unlocked a door at the farther end of the room. "The chapel," he said. "This is the Duchess's balcony." As I turned to follow him the Duchess tossed me a sidelong smile.

I stepped into a grated tribune above a chapel festooned with stucco. Pictures of bituminous saints mouldered between the pilasters; the artificial roses in the altar-vases were gray with dust and age, and under the cobwebby rosettes of the vaulting a bird's nest clung. Before the altar stood a row of tattered arm-chairs, and I drew back at sight of a figure kneeling near them.

"The Duchess," the old man whispered. "By the Cavaliere Bernini."

It was the image of a woman in furred robes and spreading fraise, her hand lifted, her face addressed to

# THE DUCHESS AT PRAYER

the tabernacle. There was a strangeness in the sight of that immovable presence locked in prayer before an abandoned shrine. Her face was hidden, and I wondered whether it were grief or gratitude that raised her hands and drew her eyes to the altar, where no living prayer joined her marble invocation. I followed my guide down the tribune steps, impatient to see what mystic version of such terrestrial graces the ingenious artist had found—the Cavaliere was master of such arts. The Duchess's attitude was one of transport, as though heavenly airs fluttered her laces and the love-locks escaping from her coif. I saw how admirably the sculptor had caught the poise of her head, the tender slope of the shoulder; then I crossed over and looked into her face—it was a frozen horror. Never have hate, revolt and agony so possessed a human countenance. . .

The old man crossed himself and shuffled his feet on the marble.

"The Duchess Violante," he repeated.

"The same as in the picture?"

"Eh—the same."

"But the face—what does it mean?"

He shrugged his shoulders and turned deaf eyes on me. Then he shot a glance round the sepulchral place, clutched my sleeve and said, close to my ear: "It was not always so."

# THE DUCHESS AT PRAYER

"What was not?"

"The face—so terrible."

"The Duchess's face?"

"The statue's. It changed after—"

"After?"

"It was put here."

"The statue's face *changed*—?"

He mistook my bewilderment for incredulity and his confidential finger dropped from my sleeve. "Eh, that's the story. I tell what I've heard. What do I know?" He resumed his senile shuffle across the marble. "This is a bad place to stay in—no one comes here. It's too cold. But the gentleman said, *I must see everything!*"

I let the *lire* sound. "So I must—and hear everything. This story, now—from whom did you have it?"

His hand stole back. "One that saw it, by God!"

"That saw it?"

"My grandmother, then. I'm a very old man."

"Your grandmother? Your grandmother was—?"

"The Duchess's serving girl, with respect to you."

"Your grandmother? Two hundred years ago?"

"Is it too long ago? That's as God pleases. I am a very old man and she was a very old woman when I was born. When she died she was as black as a miraculous Virgin and her breath whistled like the wind in a keyhole. She told me the story when I was a little boy. She told it to me out there in the garden, on a bench

# THE DUCHESS AT PRAYER

by the fish-pond, one summer night of the year she died. It must be true, for I can show you the very bench we sat on..."

### III

NOON lay heavier on the gardens; not our live humming warmth but the stale exhalation of dead summers. The very statues seemed to drowse like watchers by a death-bed. Lizards shot out of the cracked soil like flames and the bench in the laurustinus-niche was strewn with the blue varnished bodies of dead flies. Before us lay the fish-pond, a yellow marble slab above rotting secrets. The villa looked across it, composed as a dead face, with the cypresses flanking it for candles...

### IV

. . . . . . . . .

"IMPOSSIBLE, you say, that my mother's mother should have been the Duchess's maid? What do I know? It is so long since anything has happened here that the old things seem nearer, perhaps, than to those who live in cities... But how else did she know about the statue then? Answer me that, sir! That she saw with her eyes, I can swear to, and never smiled again, so she told me, till they put her first child in her arms . . . for she was taken to wife

## THE DUCHESS AT PRAYER

by the steward's son, Antonio, the same who had carried the letters. . . But where am I? Ah, well . . . she was a mere slip, you understand, my grandmother, when the Duchess died, a niece of the upper maid, Nencia, and suffered about the Duchess because of her pranks and the funny songs she knew. It's possible, you think, she may have heard from others what she afterward fancied she had seen herself? How that is, it's not for an unlettered man to say; though indeed I myself seem to have seen many of the things she told me. This is a strange place. No one comes here, nothing changes, and the old memories stand up as distinct as the statues in the garden. . .

"It began the summer after they came back from the Brenta. Duke Ercole had married the lady from Venice, you must know; it was a gay city, then, I'm told, with laughter and music on the water, and the days slipped by like boats running with the tide. Well, to humor her he took her back the first autumn to the Brenta. Her father, it appears, had a grand palace there, with such gardens, bowling-alleys, grottoes and casinos as never were; gondolas bobbing at the water-gates, a stable full of gilt coaches, a theatre full of players, and kitchens and offices full of cooks and lackeys to serve up chocolate all day long to the fine ladies in masks and furbelows, with their pet dogs and their blackamoors and their *abates*. Eh! I know it all

# THE DUCHESS AT PRAYER

as if I'd been there, for Nencia, you see, my grandmother's aunt, travelled with the Duchess, and came back with her eyes round as platters, and not a word to say for the rest of the year to any of the lads who'd courted her here in Vicenza.

"What happened there I don't know—my grandmother could never get at the rights of it, for Nencia was mute as a fish where her lady was concerned—but when they came back to Vicenza the Duke ordered the villa set in order; and in the spring he brought the Duchess here and left her. She looked happy enough, my grandmother said, and seemed no object for pity. Perhaps, after all, it was better than being shut up in Vicenza, in the tall painted rooms where priests came and went as softly as cats prowling for birds, and the Duke was forever closeted in his library, talking with learned men. The Duke was a scholar; you noticed he was painted with a book? Well, those that can read 'em make out that they're full of wonderful things; as a man that's been to a fair across the mountains will always tell his people at home it was beyond anything *they'll* ever see. As for the Duchess, she was all for music, play-acting and young company. The Duke was a silent man, stepping quietly, with his eyes down, as though he'd just come from confession; when the Duchess's lap-dog yapped at his heels he danced like a man in a swarm of hornets; when the Duchess

# THE DUCHESS AT PRAYER

laughed he winced as if you'd drawn a diamond across a window-pane. And the Duchess was always laughing.

"When she first came to the villa she was very busy laying out the gardens, designing grottoes, planting groves and planning all manner of agreeable surprises in the way of water-jets that drenched you unexpectedly, and hermits in caves, and wild men that jumped at you out of thickets. She had a very pretty taste in such matters, but after a while she tired of it, and there being no one for her to talk to but her maids and the chaplain—a clumsy man deep in his books—why, she would have strolling players out from Vicenza, mountebanks and fortune-tellers from the market-place, travelling doctors and astrologers, and all manner of trained animals. Still it could be seen that the poor lady pined for company, and her waiting women, who loved her, were glad when the Cavaliere Ascanio, the Duke's cousin, came to live at the vineyard across the valley—you see the pinkish house over there in the mulberries, with a red roof and a pigeon-cote?

"The Cavaliere Ascanio was a cadet of one of the great Venetian houses, *pezzi grossi* of the Golden Book. He had been meant for the Church, I believe, but what! he set fighting above praying and cast in his lot with the captain of the Duke of Mantua's *bravi*, himself a Venetian of good standing, but a little at odds with the law. Well, the next I know, the Cava-

# THE DUCHESS AT PRAYER

liere was in Venice again, perhaps not in good odor on account of his connection with the gentleman I speak of. Some say he tried to carry off a nun from the convent of Santa Croce; how that may be I can't say; but my grandmother declared he had enemies there, and the end of it was that on some pretext or other the Ten banished him to Vicenza. There, of course, the Duke, being his kinsman, had to show him a civil face; and that was how he first came to the villa.

"He was a fine young man, beautiful as a Saint Sebastian, a rare musician, who sang his own songs to the lute in a way that used to make my grandmother's heart melt and run through her body like mulled wine. He had a good word for everybody, too, and was always dressed in the French fashion, and smelt as sweet as a bean-field; and every soul about the place welcomed the sight of him.

"Well, the Duchess, it seemed, welcomed it too; youth will have youth, and laughter turns to laughter; and the two matched each other like the candlesticks on an altar. The Duchess—you've seen her portrait—but to hear my grandmother, sir, it no more approached her than a weed comes up to a rose. The Cavaliere, indeed, as became a poet, paragoned her in his song to all the pagan goddesses of antiquity; and doubtless these were finer to look at than mere women; but so, it seemed, was she; for, to believe my grandmother,

# THE DUCHESS AT PRAYER

she made other women look no more than the big French fashion-doll that used to be shown on Ascension days in the Piazza. She was one, at any rate, that needed no outlandish finery to beautify her; whatever dress she wore became her as feathers fit the bird; and her hair did n't get its color by bleaching on the housetop. It glittered of itself like the threads in an Easter chasuble, and her skin was whiter than fine wheaten bread and her mouth as sweet as a ripe fig. . .

"Well, sir, you could no more keep them apart than the bees and the lavender. They were always together, singing, bowling, playing cup and ball, walking in the gardens, visiting the aviaries and petting her grace's trick-dogs and monkeys. The Duchess was as gay as a foal, always playing pranks and laughing, tricking out her animals like comedians, disguising herself as a peasant or a nun (you should have seen her one day pass herself off to the chaplain as a mendicant sister), or teaching the lads and girls of the vineyards to dance and sing madrigals together. The Cavaliere had a singular ingenuity in planning such entertainments and the days were hardly long enough for their diversions. But toward the end of the summer the Duchess fell quiet and would hear only sad music, and the two sat much together in the gazebo at the end of the garden. It was there the Duke found them one day when he drove out from Vicenza in his gilt coach. He came but

# THE DUCHESS AT PRAYER

once or twice a year to the villa, and it was, as my grandmother said, just a part of her poor lady's ill-luck to be wearing that day the Venetian habit, which uncovered the shoulders in a way the Duke always scowled at, and her curls loose and powdered with gold. Well, the three drank chocolate in the gazebo, and what happened no one knew, except that the Duke, on taking leave, gave his cousin a seat in his carriage; but the Cavaliere never returned.

"Winter approaching, and the poor lady thus finding herself once more alone, it was surmised among her women that she must fall into a deeper depression of spirits. But far from this being the case, she displayed such cheerfulness and equanimity of humor that my grandmother, for one, was half-vexed with her for giving no more thought to the poor young man who, all this time, was eating his heart out in the house across the valley. It is true she quitted her gold-laced gowns and wore a veil over her head; but Nencia would have it she looked the lovelier for the change and so gave the Duke greater displeasure. Certain it is that the Duke drove out oftener to the villa, and though he found his lady always engaged in some innocent pursuit, such as embroidery or music, or playing games with her young women, yet he always went away with a sour look and a whispered word to the chaplain. Now as to the chaplain, my grandmother owned there had

# THE DUCHESS AT PRAYER

been a time when her grace had not handled him overwisely. For, according to Nencia, it seems that his reverence, who seldom approached the Duchess, being buried in his library like a mouse in a cheese—well, one day he made bold to appeal to her for a sum of money, a large sum, Nencia said, to buy certain tall books, a chest full of them, that a foreign pedlar had brought him; whereupon the Duchess, who could never abide a book, breaks out at him with a laugh and a flash of her old spirit—'Holy Mother of God, must I have more books about me? I was nearly smothered with them in the first year of my marriage;' and the chaplain turning red at the affront, she added: 'You may buy them and welcome, my good chaplain, if you can find the money; but as for me, I am yet seeking a way to pay for my turquoise necklace, and the statue of Daphne at the end of the bowling-green, and the Indian parrot that my black boy brought me last Michaelmas from the Bohemians—so you see I've no money to waste on trifles;' and as he backs out awkwardly she tosses at him over her shoulder: 'You should pray to Saint Blandina to open the Duke's pocket!' to which he returned, very quietly, 'Your excellency's suggestion is an admirable one, and I have already entreated that blessed martyr to open the Duke's understanding.'

"Thereat, Nencia said (who was standing by), the

# THE DUCHESS AT PRAYER

Duchess flushed wonderfully red and waved him out of the room; and then 'Quick!' she cried to my grandmother (who was too glad to run on such errands), 'Call me Antonio, the gardener's boy, to the box-garden; I've a word to say to him about the new clove-carnations. . .'

"Now I may not have told you, sir, that in the crypt under the chapel there has stood, for more generations than a man can count, a stone coffin containing a thigh-bone of the blessed Saint Blandina of Lyons, a relic offered, I've been told, by some great Duke of France to one of our own dukes when they fought the Turk together; and the object, ever since, of particular veneration in this illustrious family. Now, since the Duchess had been left to herself, it was observed she affected a fervent devotion to this relic, praying often in the chapel and even causing the stone slab that covered the entrance to the crypt to be replaced by a wooden one, that she might at will descend and kneel by the coffin. This was matter of edification to all the household and should have been peculiarly pleasing to the chaplain; but, with respect to you, he was the kind of man who brings a sour mouth to the eating of the sweetest apple.

"However that may be, the Duchess, when she dismissed him, was seen running to the garden, where she talked earnestly with the boy Antonio about the new clove-carnations; and the rest of the day she sat in-

# THE DUCHESS AT PRAYER

doors and played sweetly on the virginal. Now Nencia always had it in mind that her grace had made a mistake in refusing that request of the chaplain's; but she said nothing, for to talk reason to the Duchess was of no more use than praying for rain in a drought.

"Winter came early that year, there was snow on the hills by All Souls, the wind stripped the gardens, and the lemon-trees were nipped in the lemon-house. The Duchess kept her room in this black season, sitting over the fire, embroidering, reading books of devotion (which was a thing she had never done) and praying frequently in the chapel. As for the chaplain, it was a place he never set foot in but to say mass in the morning, with the Duchess overhead in the tribune, and the servants aching with rheumatism on the marble floor. The chaplain himself hated the cold, and galloped through the mass like a man with witches after him. The rest of the day he spent in his library, over a brazier, with his eternal books. . .

"You'll wonder, sir, if I'm ever to get to the gist of the story; and I've gone slowly, I own, for fear of what's coming. Well, the winter was long and hard. When it fell cold the Duke ceased to come out from Vicenza, and not a soul had the Duchess to speak to but her maid-servants and the gardeners about the place. Yet it was wonderful, my grandmother said, how she kept her brave colors and her spirits; only it was

## THE DUCHESS AT PRAYER

remarked that she prayed longer in the chapel, where a brazier was kept burning for her all day. When the young are denied their natural pleasures they turn often enough to religion; and it was a mercy, as my grandmother said, that she, who had scarce a live sinner to speak to, should take such comfort in a dead saint.

"My grandmother seldom saw her that winter, for though she showed a brave front to all she kept more and more to herself, choosing to have only Nencia about her and dismissing even her when she went to pray. For her devotion had that mark of true piety, that she wished it not to be observed; so that Nencia had strict orders, on the chaplain's approach, to warn her mistress if she happened to be in prayer.

"Well, the winter passed, and spring was well forward, when my grandmother one evening had a bad fright. That it was her own fault I won't deny, for she'd been down the lime-walk with Antonio when her aunt fancied her to be stitching in her chamber; and seeing a sudden light in Nencia's window, she took fright lest her disobedience be found out, and ran up quickly through the laurel-grove to the house. Her way lay by the chapel, and as she crept past it, meaning to slip in through the scullery, and groping her way, for the dark had fallen and the moon was scarce up, she heard a crash close behind her, as though someone had dropped from a window of the chapel. The young fool's heart

# THE DUCHESS AT PRAYER

turned over, but she looked round as she ran, and there, sure enough, was a man scuttling across the terrace; and as he doubled the corner of the house my grandmother swore she caught the whisk of the chaplain's skirts. Now that was a strange thing, certainly; for why should the chaplain be getting out of the chapel window when he might have passed through the door? For you may have noticed, sir, there's a door leads from the chapel into the saloon on the ground floor; the only other way out being through the Duchess's tribune.

"Well, my grandmother turned the matter over, and next time she met Antonio in the lime-walk (which, by reason of her fright, was not for some days) she laid before him what had happened; but to her surprise he only laughed and said, 'You little simpleton, he wasn't getting out of the window, he was trying to look in'; and not another word could she get from him.

"So the season moved on to Easter, and news came the Duke had gone to Rome for that holy festivity. His comings and goings made no change at the villa, and yet there was no one there but felt easier to think his yellow face was on the far side of the Apennines, unless perhaps it was the chaplain.

"Well, it was one day in May that the Duchess, who had walked long with Nencia on the terrace, rejoicing at the sweetness of the prospect and the pleasant scent of the gilly-flowers in the stone vases, the Duchess

# THE DUCHESS AT PRAYER

toward midday withdrew to her rooms, giving orders that her dinner should be served in her bed-chamber. My grandmother helped to carry in the dishes, and observed, she said, the singular beauty of the Duchess, who in honor of the fine weather had put on a gown of shot-silver and hung her bare shoulders with pearls, so that she looked fit to dance at court with an emperor. She had ordered, too, a rare repast for a lady that heeded so little what she ate — jellies, game-pasties, fruits in syrup, spiced cakes and a flagon of Greek wine; and she nodded and clapped her hands as the women set it before her, saying again and again, 'I shall eat well to-day.'

"But presently another mood seized her; she turned from the table, called for her rosary, and said to Nencia: 'The fine weather has made me neglect my devotions. I must say a litany before I dine.'

"She ordered the women out and barred the door, as her custom was; and Nencia and my grandmother went down-stairs to work in the linen-room.

"Now the linen-room gives on the court-yard, and suddenly my grandmother saw a strange sight approaching. First up the avenue came the Duke's carriage (whom all thought to be in Rome), and after it, drawn by a long string of mules and oxen, a cart carrying what looked like a kneeling figure wrapped in death-clothes. The strangeness of it struck the girl dumb and

# THE DUCHESS AT PRAYER

the Duke's coach was at the door before she had the wit to cry out that it was coming. Nencia, when she saw it, went white and ran out of the room. My grandmother followed, scared by her face, and the two fled along the corridor to the chapel. On the way they met the chaplain, deep in a book, who asked in surprise where they were running, and when they said, to announce the Duke's arrival, he fell into such astonishment and asked them so many questions and uttered such ohs and ahs, that by the time he let them by the Duke was at their heels. Nencia reached the chapel-door first and cried out that the Duke was coming; and before she had a reply he was at her side, with the chaplain following.

"A moment later the door opened and there stood the Duchess. She held her rosary in one hand and had drawn a scarf over her shoulders; but they shone through it like the moon in a mist, and her countenance sparkled with beauty.

"The Duke took her hand with a bow. 'Madam,' he said, 'I could have had no greater happiness than thus to surprise you at your devotions.'

"'My own happiness,' she replied, 'would have been greater had your excellency prolonged it by giving me notice of your arrival.'

"'Had you expected me, Madam,' said he, 'your appearance could scarcely have been more fitted to the

[ 21 ]

# THE DUCHESS AT PRAYER

"'It is my semblance, not the sculptor's work, I desire to conceal.'

"'If you are fit for my house, Madam, you are fit for God's, and entitled to the place of honor in both. Bring the statue forward, you dawdlers!' he called out to the men.

"The Duchess fell back submissively. 'You are right, sir, as always; but I would at least have the image stand on the left of the altar, that, looking up, it may behold your excellency's seat in the tribune.'

"'A pretty thought, Madam, for which I thank you; but I design before long to put my companion image on the other side of the altar; and the wife's place, as you know, is at her husband's right hand.'

"'True, my lord — but, again, if my poor presentment is to have the unmerited honor of kneeling beside yours, why not place both before the altar, where it is our habit to pray in life?'

"'And where, Madam, should we kneel if they took our places? Besides,' says the Duke, still speaking very blandly, 'I have a more particular purpose in placing your image over the entrance to the crypt; for not only would I thereby mark your special devotion to the blessed saint who rests there, but, by sealing up the opening in the pavement, would assure the perpetual preservation of that holy martyr's bones, which hitherto have been too thoughtlessly exposed to sacrilegious attempts.'

# THE DUCHESS AT PRAYER

"'What attempts, my lord?' cries the Duchess. 'No one enters this chapel without my leave.'

"'So I have understood, and can well believe from what I have learned of your piety; yet at night a malefactor might break in through a window, Madam, and your excellency not know it.'

"'I'm a light sleeper,' said the Duchess.

"The Duke looked at her gravely. 'Indeed?' said he. 'A bad sign at your age. I must see that you are provided with a sleeping-draught.'

"The Duchess's eyes filled. 'You would deprive me, then, of the consolation of visiting those venerable relics?'

"'I would have you keep eternal guard over them, knowing no one to whose care they may more fittingly be entrusted.'

"By this the image was brought close to the wooden slab that covered the entrance to the crypt, when the Duchess, springing forward, placed herself in the way.

"'Sir, let the statue be put in place to-morrow, and suffer me, to-night, to say a last prayer beside those holy bones.'

"The Duke stepped instantly to her side. 'Well thought, Madam; I will go down with you now, and we will pray together.'

"'Sir, your long absences have, alas! given me the

# THE DUCHESS AT PRAYER

habit of solitary devotion, and I confess that any presence is distracting.'

"'Madam, I accept your rebuke. Hitherto, it is true, the duties of my station have constrained me to long absences; but henceforward I remain with you while you live. Shall we go down into the crypt together?'

"'No; for I fear for your excellency's ague. The air there is excessively damp.'

"'The more reason you should no longer be exposed to it; and to prevent the intemperance of your zeal I will at once make the place inaccessible.'

"The Duchess at this fell on her knees on the slab, weeping excessively and lifting her hands to heaven.

"'Oh,' she cried, 'you are cruel, sir, to deprive me of access to the sacred relics that have enabled me to support with resignation the solitude to which your excellency's duties have condemned me; and if prayer and meditation give me any authority to pronounce on such matters, suffer me to warn you, sir, that I fear the blessed Saint Blandina will punish us for thus abandoning her venerable remains!'

"The Duke at this seemed to pause, for he was a pious man, and my grandmother thought she saw him exchange a glance with the chaplain; who, stepping timidly forward, with his eyes on the ground, said, 'There is indeed much wisdom in her excellency's words, but I would suggest, sir, that her pious wish

# THE DUCHESS AT PRAYER

might be met, and the saint more conspicuously honored, by transferring the relics from the crypt to a place beneath the altar.'

"'True!' cried the Duke, 'and it shall be done at once.'

"But thereat the Duchess rose to her feet with a terrible look.

"'No,' she cried, 'by the body of God! For it shall not be said that, after your excellency has chosen to deny every request I addressed to him, I owe his consent to the solicitation of another!'

"The chaplain turned red and the Duke yellow, and for a moment neither spoke.

"Then the Duke said, 'Here are words enough, Madam. Do you wish the relics brought up from the crypt?'

"'I wish nothing that I owe to another's intervention!'

"'Put the image in place then,' says the Duke furiously; and handed her grace to a chair.

"She sat there, my grandmother said, straight as an arrow, her hands locked, her head high, her eyes on the Duke, while the statue was dragged to its place; then she stood up and turned away. As she passed by Nencia, 'Call me Antonio,' she whispered; but before the words were out of her mouth the Duke stepped between them.

# THE DUCHESS AT PRAYER

"'Madam,' says he, all smiles now, 'I have travelled straight from Rome to bring you the sooner this proof of my esteem. I lay last night at Monselice and have been on the road since daybreak. Will you not invite me to supper?'

"'Surely, my lord,' said the Duchess. 'It shall be laid in the dining-parlor within the hour.'

"'Why not in your chamber and at once, Madam? Since I believe it is your custom to sup there.'

"'In my chamber?' says the Duchess, in disorder.

"'Have you anything against it?' he asked.

"'Assuredly not, sir, if you will give me time to prepare myself.'

"'I will wait in your cabinet,' said the Duke.

"At that, said my grandmother, the Duchess gave one look, as the souls in hell may have looked when the gates closed on our Lord; then she called Nencia and passed to her chamber.

"What happened there my grandmother could never learn, but that the Duchess, in great haste, dressed herself with extraordinary splendor, powdering her hair with gold, painting her face and bosom, and covering herself with jewels till she shone like our Lady of Loreto; and hardly were these preparations complete when the Duke entered from the cabinet, followed by the servants carrying supper. Thereupon the Duchess dismissed Nencia, and what follows my grandmother

# THE DUCHESS AT PRAYER

learned from a pantry-lad who brought up the dishes and waited in the cabinet; for only the Duke's body-servant entered the bed-chamber.

"Well, according to this boy, sir, who was looking and listening with his whole body, as it were, because he had never before been suffered so near the Duchess, it appears that the noble couple sat down in great good humor, the Duchess playfully reproving her husband for his long absence, while the Duke swore that to look so beautiful was the best way of punishing him. In this tone the talk continued, with such gay sallies on the part of the Duchess, such tender advances on the Duke's, that the lad declared they were for all the world like a pair of lovers courting on a summer's night in the vineyard; and so it went till the servant brought in the mulled wine.

"'Ah,' the Duke was saying at that moment, 'this agreeable evening repays me for the many dull ones I have spent away from you; nor do I remember to have enjoyed such laughter since the afternoon last year when we drank chocolate in the gazebo with my cousin Ascanio. And that reminds me,' he said, 'is my cousin in good health?'

"'I have no reports of it,' says the Duchess. 'But your excellency should taste these figs stewed in malmsey—'

"'I am in the mood to taste whatever you offer,' said

# THE DUCHESS AT PRAYER

he; and as she helped him to the figs he added, 'If my enjoyment were not complete as it is, I could almost wish my cousin Ascanio were with us. The fellow is rare good company at supper. What do you say, Madam? I hear he's still in the country; shall we send for him to join us?'

"'Ah,' said the Duchess, with a sigh and a languishing look, 'I see your excellency wearies of me already.'

"'I, Madam? Ascanio is a capital good fellow, but to my mind his chief merit at this moment is his absence. It inclines me so tenderly to him that, by God, I could empty a glass to his good health.'

"With that the Duke caught up his goblet and signed to the servant to fill the Duchess's.

"'Here's to the cousin,' he cried, standing, 'who has the good taste to stay away when he's not wanted. I drink to his very long life — and you, Madam?'

"At this the Duchess, who had sat staring at him with a changed face, rose also and lifted her glass to her lips.

"'And I to his happy death,' says she in a wild voice; and as she spoke the empty goblet dropped from her hand and she fell face down on the floor.

"The Duke shouted to her women that she had swooned, and they came and lifted her to the bed. . . She suffered horribly all night, Nencia said, twisting herself like a heretic at the stake, but without a word

# THE DUCHESS AT PRAYER

escaping her. The Duke watched by her, and toward daylight sent for the chaplain; but by this she was unconscious and, her teeth being locked, our Lord's body could not be passed through them.

. . . . . . .

"The Duke announced to his relations that his lady had died after partaking too freely of spiced wine and an omelet of carp's roe, at a supper she had prepared in honor of his return; and the next year he brought home a new Duchess, who gave him a son and five daughters. . ."

## V

THE sky had turned to a steel gray, against which the villa stood out sallow and inscrutable. A wind strayed through the gardens, loosening here and there a yellow leaf from the sycamores; and the hills across the valley were purple as thunder-clouds.

. . . . . . .

"And the statue—?" I asked.

"Ah, the statue. Well, sir, this is what my grandmother told me, here on this very bench where we're sitting. The poor child, who worshipped the Duchess as a girl of her years will worship a beautiful kind mistress, spent a night of horror, you may fancy, shut out from her lady's room, hearing the cries that came from it, and seeing, as she crouched in her corner, the women

[ 31 ]

# THE DUCHESS AT PRAYER

rush to and fro with wild looks, the Duke's lean face in the door, and the chaplain skulking in the antechamber with his eyes on his breviary. No one minded her that night or the next morning; and toward dusk, when it became known the Duchess was no more, the poor girl felt the pious wish to say a prayer for her dead mistress. She crept to the chapel and stole in unobserved. The place was empty and dim, but as she advanced she heard a low moaning, and coming in front of the statue she saw that its face, the day before so sweet and smiling, had the look on it that you know—and the moaning seemed to come from its lips. My grandmother turned cold, but something, she said afterward, kept her from calling or shrieking out, and she turned and ran from the place. In the passage she fell in a swoon; and when she came to her senses, in her own chamber, she heard that the Duke had locked the chapel door and forbidden any to set foot there. . . The place was never opened again till the Duke died, some ten years later; and then it was that the other servants, going in with the new heir, saw for the first time the horror that my grandmother had kept in her bosom. . ."

"And the crypt?" I asked. "Has it never been opened?"

"Heaven forbid, sir!" cried the old man, crossing himself. "Was it not the Duchess's express wish that the relics should not be disturbed?"

# THE ANGEL AT THE GRAVE

# THE ANGEL AT THE GRAVE

THE House stood a few yards back from the elm-shaded village street, in that semi-publicity sometimes cited as a democratic protest against old-world standards of domestic exclusiveness. This candid exposure to the public eye is more probably a result of the gregariousness which, in the New England bosom, oddly coexists with a shrinking from direct social contact; most of the inmates of such houses preferring that furtive intercourse which is the result of observations through shuttered windows and a categorical acquaintance with the neighboring clothes-lines. The House, however, faced its public with a difference. For sixty years it had written itself with a capital letter, had self-consciously squared itself in the eye of an admiring nation. The most searching inroads of village intimacy hardly counted in a household that opened on the universe; and a lady whose door-bell was at any moment liable to be rung by visitors from London or Vienna was not likely to flutter up-stairs when she observed a neighbor "stepping over."

The solitary inmate of the Anson House owed this induration of the social texture to the most conspicuous accident in her annals: the fact that she was the only granddaughter of the great Orestes Anson. She had

# THE ANGEL AT THE GRAVE

been born, as it were, into a museum, and cradled in a glass case with a label; the first foundations of her consciousness being built on the rock of her grandfather's celebrity. To a little girl who acquires her earliest knowledge of literature through a *Reader* embellished with fragments of her ancestor's prose, that personage necessarily fills an heroic space in the foreground of life. To communicate with one's past through the impressive medium of print, to have, as it were, a footing in every library in the country, and an acknowledged kinship with that world-diffused clan, the descendants of the great, was to be pledged to a standard of manners that amazingly simplified the lesser relations of life. The village street on which Paulina Anson's youth looked out led to all the capitals of Europe; and over the roads of intercommunication unseen caravans bore back to the elm-shaded House the tribute of an admiring world.

Fate seemed to have taken a direct share in fitting Paulina for her part as the custodian of this historic dwelling. It had long been secretly regarded as a "visitation" by the great man's family that he had left no son and that his daughters were not "intellectual." The ladies themselves were the first to lament their deficiency, to own that nature had denied them the gift of making the most of their opportunities. A profound veneration for their parent and an unswerving faith in **his** doctrines had not amended their congenital inca-

# THE ANGEL AT THE GRAVE

pacity to understand what he had written. Laura, who had her moments of mute rebellion against destiny, had sometimes thought how much easier it would have been if their progenitor had been a poet; for she could recite, with feeling, portions of *The Culprit Fay* and of the poems of Mrs. Hemans; and Phœbe, who was more conspicuous for memory than imagination, kept an album filled with "selections." But the great man was a philosopher; and to both daughters respiration was difficult on the cloudy heights of metaphysic. The situation would have been intolerable but for the fact that, while Phœbe and Laura were still at school, their father's fame had passed from the open ground of conjecture to the chill privacy of certitude. Dr. Anson had in fact achieved one of those anticipated immortalities not uncommon at a time when people were apt to base their literary judgments on their emotions, and when to affect plain food and despise England went a long way toward establishing a man's intellectual pre-eminence. Thus, when the daughters were called on to strike a filial attitude about their parent's pedestal, there was little to do but to pose gracefully and point upward; and there are spines to which the immobility of worship is not a strain. A legend had by this time crystallized about the great Orestes, and it was of more immediate interest to the public to hear what brand of tea he drank, and whether he took off his boots in the

# THE ANGEL AT THE GRAVE

hall, than to rouse the drowsy echo of his dialectic. A great man never draws so near his public as when it has become unnecessary to read his books and is still interesting to know what he eats for breakfast.

As recorders of their parent's domestic habits, as pious scavengers of his waste-paper basket, the Misses Anson were unexcelled. They always had an interesting anecdote to impart to the literary pilgrim, and the tact with which, in later years, they intervened between the public and the growing inaccessibility of its idol, sent away many an enthusiast satisfied to have touched the veil before the sanctuary. Still it was felt, especially by old Mrs. Anson, who survived her husband for some years, that Phœbe and Laura were not worthy of their privileges. There had been a third daughter so unworthy of hers that she had married a distant cousin, who had taken her to live in a new Western community where the *Works of Orestes Anson* had not yet become a part of the civic consciousness; but of this daughter little was said, and she was tacitly understood to be excluded from the family heritage of fame. In time, however, it appeared that the traditional penny with which she had been cut off had been invested to unexpected advantage; and the interest on it, when she died, returned to the Anson House in the shape of a granddaughter who was at once felt to be what Mrs. Anson called a "compensation." It was Mrs. Anson's

# THE ANGEL AT THE GRAVE

firm belief that the remotest operations of nature were governed by the centripetal force of her husband's greatness and that Paulina's exceptional intelligence could be explained only on the ground that she was designed to act as the guardian of the family temple.

The House, by the time Paulina came to live in it, had already acquired the publicity of a place of worship; not the perfumed chapel of a romantic idolatry but the cold clean empty meeting-house of ethical enthusiasms. The ladies lived on its outskirts, as it were, in cells that left the central fane undisturbed. The very position of the furniture had come to have a ritual significance: the sparse ornaments were the offerings of kindred intellects, the steel engravings by Raphael Morghen marked the Via Sacra of a European tour, and the black-walnut desk with its bronze inkstand modelled on the Pantheon was the altar of this bleak temple of thought.

To a child compact of enthusiasms, and accustomed to pasture them on the scanty herbage of a new social soil, the atmosphere of the old house was full of floating nourishment. In the compressed perspective of Paulina's outlook it stood for a monument of ruined civilizations, and its white portico opened on legendary distances. Its very aspect was impressive to eyes that had first surveyed life from the jig-saw "residence" of a raw-edged Western town. The high-ceilinged rooms,

# THE ANGEL AT THE GRAVE

with their panelled walls, their polished mahogany, their portraits of triple-stocked ancestors and of ringleted "females" in crayon, furnished the child with the historic scenery against which a young imagination constructs its vision of the past. To other eyes the cold spotless thinly-furnished interior might have suggested the shuttered mind of a maiden-lady who associates fresh air and sunlight with dust and discoloration; but it is the eye which supplies the coloring-matter, and Paulina's brimmed with the richest hues.

Nevertheless, the House did not immediately dominate her. She had her confused out-reachings toward other centres of sensation, her vague intuition of a heliocentric system; but the attraction of habit, the steady pressure of example, gradually fixed her roving allegiance and she bent her neck to the yoke. Vanity had a share in her subjugation; for it had early been discovered that she was the only person in the family who could read her grandfather's works. The fact that she had perused them with delight at an age when (even presupposing a metaphysical bias) it was impossible for her to understand them, seemed to her aunts and grandmother sure evidence of predestination. Paulina was to be the interpreter of the oracle, and the philosophic fumes so vertiginous to meaner minds would throw her into the needed condition of clairvoyance. Nothing could have been more genuine

# THE ANGEL AT THE GRAVE

than the emotion on which this theory was based. Paulina, in fact, delighted in her grandfather's writings. His sonorous periods, his mystic vocabulary, his bold flights into the rarefied air of the abstract, were thrilling to a fancy unhampered by the need of definitions. This purely verbal pleasure was supplemented later by the excitement of gathering up crumbs of meaning from the rhetorical board. What could have been more stimulating than to construct the theory of a girlish world out of the fragments of this Titanic cosmogony? Before Paulina's opinions had reached the stage when ossification sets in their form was fatally predetermined.

The fact that Dr. Anson had died and that his apotheosis had taken place before his young priestess's induction to the temple, made her ministrations easier and more inspiring. There were no little personal traits —such as the great man's manner of helping himself to salt, or the guttural cluck that started the wheels of speech—to distract the eye of young veneration from the central fact of his divinity. A man whom one knows only through a crayon portrait and a dozen yellowing tomes on free-will and intuition is at least secure from the belittling effects of intimacy.

Paulina thus grew up in a world readjusted to the fact of her grandfather's greatness; and as each organism draws from its surroundings the kind of nourish-

# THE ANGEL AT THE GRAVE

ment most needful to its growth, so from this somewhat colorless conception she absorbed warmth, brightness and variety. Paulina was the type of woman who transmutes thought into sensation and nurses a theory in her bosom like a child.

In due course Mrs. Anson "passed away"—no one died in the Anson vocabulary—and Paulina became more than ever the foremost figure of the commemorative group. Laura and Phœbe, content to leave their father's glory in more competent hands, placidly lapsed into needlework and fiction, and their niece stepped into immediate prominence as the chief "authority" on the great man. Historians who were "getting up" the period wrote to consult her and to borrow documents; ladies with inexplicable yearnings begged for an interpretation of phrases which had "influenced" them, but which they had not quite understood; critics applied to her to verify some doubtful citation or to decide some disputed point in chronology; and the great tide of thought and investigation kept up a continuous murmur on the quiet shores of her life.

An explorer of another kind disembarked there one day in the shape of a young man to whom Paulina was primarily a kissable girl, with an after-thought in the shape of a grandfather. From the outset it had been impossible to fix Hewlett Winsloe's attention on Dr. Anson. The young man behaved with the innocent

# THE ANGEL AT THE GRAVE

profanity of infants sporting on a tomb. His excuse was that he came from New York, a Cimmerian outskirt which survived in Paulina's geography only because Dr. Anson had gone there once or twice to lecture. The curious thing was that she should have thought it worth while to find excuses for young Winsloe. The fact that she did so had not escaped the attention of the village; but people, after a gasp of awe, said it was the most natural thing in the world that a girl like Paulina Anson should think of marrying. It would certainly seem a little odd to see a man in the House, but young Winsloe would of course understand that the Doctor's books were not to be disturbed, and that he must go down to the orchard to smoke—. The village had barely framed this *modus vivendi* when it was convulsed by the announcement that young Winsloe declined to live in the House on any terms. Hang going down to the orchard to smoke! He meant to take his wife to New York. The village drew its breath and watched.

Did Persephone, snatched from the warm fields of Enna, peer half-consentingly down the abyss that opened at her feet? Paulina, it must be owned, hung a moment over the black gulf of temptation. She would have found it easy to cope with a deliberate disregard of her grandfather's rights; but young Winsloe's unconsciousness of that shadowy claim was as much a

# THE ANGEL AT THE GRAVE

natural function as the falling of leaves on a grave. His love was an embodiment of the perpetual renewal which to some tender spirits seems a crueller process than decay.

On women of Paulina's mould this piety toward implicit demands, toward the ghosts of dead duties walking unappeased among usurping passions, has a stronger hold than any tangible bond. People said that she gave up young Winsloe because her aunts disapproved of her leaving them; but such disapproval as reached her was an emanation from the walls of the House, from the bare desk, the faded portraits, the dozen yellowing tomes that no hand but hers ever lifted from the shelf.

II

AFTER that the House possessed her. As if conscious of its victory, it imposed a conqueror's claims. It had once been suggested that she should write a life of her grandfather, and the task from which she had shrunk as from a too-oppressive privilege now shaped itself into a justification of her course. In a burst of filial pantheism she tried to lose herself in the vast ancestral consciousness. Her one refuge from scepticism was a blind faith in the magnitude and the endurance of the idea to which she had sacrificed her life, and with a passionate instinct of self-preservation she labored to fortify her position.

# THE ANGEL AT THE GRAVE

The preparations for the *Life* led her through by-ways that the most scrupulous of the previous biographers had left unexplored. She accumulated her material with a blind animal patience unconscious of fortuitous risks. The years stretched before her like some vast blank page spread out to receive the record of her toil; and she had a mystic conviction that she would not die till her work was accomplished.

The aunts, sustained by no such high purpose, withdrew in turn to their respective divisions of the Anson "plot," and Paulina remained alone with her task. She was forty when the book was completed. She had travelled little in her life, and it had become more and more difficult to her to leave the House even for a day; but the dread of entrusting her document to a strange hand made her decide to carry it herself to the publisher. On the way to Boston she had a sudden vision of the loneliness to which this last parting condemned her. All her youth, all her dreams, all her renunciations lay in that neat bundle on her knee. It was not so much her grandfather's life as her own that she had written; and the knowledge that it would come back to her in all the glorification of print was of no more help than, to a mother's grief, the assurance that the lad she must part with will return with epaulets.

She had naturally addressed herself to the firm which had published her grandfather's works. Its founder, a

# THE ANGEL AT THE GRAVE

personal friend of the philosopher's, had survived the Olympian group of which he had been a subordinate member, long enough to bestow his octogenarian approval on Paulina's pious undertaking. But he had died soon afterward; and Miss Anson found herself confronted by his grandson, a person with a brisk commercial view of his trade, who was said to have put "new blood" into the firm.

This gentleman listened attentively, fingering her manuscript as though literature were a tactile substance; then, with a confidential twist of his revolving chair, he emitted the verdict: "We ought to have had this ten years sooner."

Miss Anson took the words as an allusion to the repressed avidity of her readers. "It has been a long time for the public to wait," she solemnly assented.

The publisher smiled. "They haven't waited," he said.

She looked at him strangely. "Haven't waited?"

"No—they've gone off; taken another train. Literature's like a big railway-station now, you know: there's a train starting every minute. People are not going to hang round the waiting-room. If they can't get to a place when they want to they go somewhere else."

The application of this parable cost Miss Anson several minutes of throbbing silence. At length she said:

# THE ANGEL AT THE GRAVE

"Then I am to understand that the public is no longer interested in — in my grandfather?" She felt as though heaven must blast the lips that risked such a conjecture.

"Well, it's this way. He's a name still, of course. People don't exactly want to be caught not knowing who he is; but they don't want to spend two dollars finding out, when they can look him up for nothing in any biographical dictionary."

Miss Anson's world reeled. She felt herself adrift among mysterious forces, and no more thought of prolonging the discussion than of opposing an earthquake with argument. She went home carrying the manuscript like a wounded thing. On the return journey she found herself travelling straight toward a fact that had lurked for months in the background of her life, and that now seemed to await her on the very threshold: the fact that fewer visitors came to the House. She owned to herself that for the last four or five years the number had steadily diminished. Engrossed in her work, she had noted the change only to feel thankful that she had fewer interruptions. There had been a time when, at the travelling season, the bell rang continuously, and the ladies of the House lived in a chronic state of "best silks" and expectancy. It would have been impossible then to carry on any consecutive work; and she now saw that the silence which had gathered round her task had been the hush of death.

## THE ANGEL AT THE GRAVE

Not of *his* death! The very walls cried out against the implication. It was the world's enthusiasm, the world's faith, the world's loyalty that had died. A corrupt generation that had turned aside to worship the brazen serpent. Her heart yearned with a prophetic passion over the lost sheep straying in the wilderness. But all great glories had their interlunar period; and in due time her grandfather would once more flash full-orbed upon a darkling world.

The few friends to whom she confided her adventure reminded her with tender indignation that there were other publishers less subject to the fluctuations of the market; but much as she had braved for her grandfather she could not again brave that particular probation. She found herself, in fact, incapable of any immediate effort. She had lost her way in a labyrinth of conjecture where her worst dread was that she might put her hand upon the clue.

She locked up the manuscript and sat down to wait. If a pilgrim had come just then the priestess would have fallen on his neck; but she continued to celebrate her rites alone. It was a double solitude; for she had always thought a great deal more of the people who came to see the House than of the people who came to see her. She fancied that the neighbors kept a keen eye on the path to the House; and there were days when the figure of a stranger strolling past

## THE ANGEL AT THE GRAVE

the gate seemed to focus upon her the scorching sympathies of the village. For a time she thought of travelling; of going to Europe, or even to Boston; but to leave the House now would have seemed like deserting her post. Gradually her scattered energies centred themselves in the fierce resolve to understand what had happened. She was not the woman to live long in an unmapped country or to accept as final her private interpretation of phenomena. Like a traveller in unfamiliar regions she began to store for future guidance the minutest natural signs. Unflinchingly she noted the accumulating symptoms of indifference that marked her grandfather's descent toward posterity. She passed from the heights on which he had been grouped with the sages of his day to the lower level where he had come to be "the friend of Emerson," "the correspondent of Hawthorne," or (later still) "the Dr. Anson" mentioned in their letters. The change had taken place as slowly and imperceptibly as a natural process. She could not say that any ruthless hand had stripped the leaves from the tree: it was simply that, among the evergreen glories of his group, her grandfather's had proved deciduous.

She had still to ask herself why. If the decay had been a natural process, was it not the very pledge of renewal? It was easier to find such arguments than to be convinced by them. Again and again she tried to

# THE ANGEL AT THE GRAVE

drug her solicitude with analogies; but at last she saw that such expedients were but the expression of a growing incredulity. The best way of proving her faith in her grandfather was not to be afraid of his critics. She had no notion where these shadowy antagonists lurked; for she had never heard of the great man's doctrine being directly combated. Oblique assaults there must have been, however, Parthian shots at the giant that none dared face; and she thirsted to close with such assailants. The difficulty was to find them. She began by re-reading the *Works;* thence she passed to the writers of the same school, those whose rhetoric bloomed perennial in *First Readers* from which her grandfather's prose had long since faded. Amid that clamor of far-off enthusiasms she detected no controversial note. The little knot of Olympians held their views in common with an early-Christian promiscuity. They were continually proclaiming their admiration for each other, the public joining as chorus in this guileless antiphon of praise; and she discovered no traitor in their midst.

What then had happened? Was it simply that the main current of thought had set another way? Then why did the others survive? Why were they still marked down as tributaries to the philosophic stream? This question carried her still farther afield, and she pressed on with the passion of a champion whose re-

# THE ANGEL AT THE GRAVE

luctance to know the worst might be construed into a doubt of his cause. At length—slowly but inevitably—an explanation shaped itself. Death had overtaken the doctrines about which her grandfather had draped his cloudy rhetoric. They had disintegrated and been re-absorbed, adding their little pile to the dust drifted about the mute lips of the Sphinx. The great man's contemporaries had survived not by reason of what they taught, but of what they were; and he, who had been the mere mask through which they mouthed their lesson, the instrument on which their tune was played, lay buried deep among the obsolete tools of thought.

The discovery came to Paulina suddenly. She looked up one evening from her reading and it stood before her like a ghost. It had entered her life with stealthy steps, creeping close before she was aware of it. She sat in the library, among the carefully-tended books and portraits; and it seemed to her that she had been walled alive into a tomb hung with the effigies of dead ideas. She felt a desperate longing to escape into the outer air, where people toiled and loved, and living sympathies went hand in hand. It was the sense of wasted labor that oppressed her; of two lives consumed in that ruthless process that uses generations of effort to build a single cell. There was a dreary parallel between her grandfather's fruitless toil and her own un-

# THE ANGEL AT THE GRAVE

profitable sacrifice. Each in turn had kept vigil by a corpse.

## III

THE bell rang—she remembered it afterward—with a loud thrilling note. It was what they used to call the "visitor's ring"; not the tentative tinkle of a neighbor dropping in to borrow a sauce-pan or discuss parochial incidents, but a decisive summons from the outer world.

Miss Anson put down her knitting and listened. She sat up-stairs now, making her rheumatism an excuse for avoiding the rooms below. Her interests had insensibly adjusted themselves to the perspective of her neighbors' lives, and she wondered—as the bell re-echoed—if it could mean that Mrs. Heminway's baby had come. Conjecture had time to ripen into certainty, and she was limping toward the closet where her cloak and bonnet hung, when her little maid fluttered in with the announcement: "A gentleman to see the house."

"The *House?*"

"Yes, m'm. I don't know what he means," faltered the messenger, whose memory did not embrace the period when such announcements were a daily part of the domestic routine.

Miss Anson glanced at the proffered card. The name it bore—*Mr. George Corby*—was unknown to her, but

# THE ANGEL AT THE GRAVE

the blood rose to her languid cheek. "Hand me my Mechlin cap, Katy," she said, trembling a little, as she laid aside her walking stick. She put her cap on before the mirror, with rapid unsteady touches. "Did you draw up the library blinds?" she breathlessly asked.

She had gradually built up a wall of commonplace between herself and her illusions, but at the first summons of the past filial passion swept away the frail barriers of expediency.

She walked down-stairs so hurriedly that her stick clicked like a girlish heel; but in the hall she paused, wondering nervously if Katy had put a match to the fire. The autumn air was cold and she had the reproachful vision of a visitor with elderly ailments shivering by her inhospitable hearth. She thought instinctively of the stranger as a survivor of the days when such a visit was a part of the young enthusiast's itinerary.

The fire was unlit and the room forbiddingly cold; but the figure which, as Miss Anson entered, turned from a lingering scrutiny of the book-shelves, was that of a fresh-eyed sanguine youth clearly independent of any artificial caloric. She stood still a moment, feeling herself the victim of some anterior impression that made this robust presence an insubstantial thing; but the young man advanced with an air of genial assurance which rendered him at once more real and more reminiscent.

# THE ANGEL AT THE GRAVE

"Why this, you know," he exclaimed, "is simply immense!"

The words, which did not immediately present themselves as slang to Miss Anson's unaccustomed ear, echoed with an odd familiarity through the academic silence.

"The room, you know, I mean," he explained with a comprehensive gesture. "These jolly portraits, and the books—that's the old gentleman himself over the mantelpiece, I suppose?—and the elms outside, and—and the whole business. I do like a congruous background —don't you?"

His hostess was silent. No one but Hewlett Winsloe had ever spoken of her grandfather as "the old gentleman."

"It's a hundred times better than I could have hoped," her visitor continued, with a cheerful disregard of her silence. "The seclusion, the remoteness, the philosophic atmosphere—there's so little of that kind of flavor left! I should have simply hated to find that he lived over a grocery, you know.—I had the deuce of a time finding out where he *did* live," he began again, after another glance of parenthetical enjoyment. "But finally I got on the trail through some old book on Brook Farm. I was bound I'd get the environment right before I did my article."

Miss Anson, by this time, had recovered sufficient

# THE ANGEL AT THE GRAVE

self-possession to seat herself and assign a chair to her visitor.

"Do I understand," she asked slowly, following his rapid eye about the room, "that you intend to write an article about my grandfather?"

"That's what I'm here for," Mr. Corby genially responded; "that is, if you're willing to help me; for I can't get on without your help," he added with a confident smile.

There was another pause, during which Miss Anson noticed a fleck of dust on the faded leather of the writing-table and a fresh spot of discoloration in the right-hand upper corner of Raphael Morghen's "Parnassus."

"Then you believe in him?" she said, looking up. She could not tell what had prompted her; the words rushed out irresistibly.

"Believe in him?" Corby cried, springing to his feet. "Believe in Orestes Anson? Why, I believe he's simply the greatest—the most stupendous—the most phenomenal figure we've got!"

The color rose to Miss Anson's brow. Her heart was beating passionately. She kept her eyes fixed on the young man's face, as though it might vanish if she looked away.

"You—you mean to say this in your article?" she asked.

# THE ANGEL AT THE GRAVE

"Say it? Why, the facts will say it," he exulted. "The baldest kind of a statement would make it clear. When a man is as big as that he doesn't need a pedestal!"

Miss Anson sighed. "People used to say that when I was young," she murmured. "But now—"

Her visitor stared. "When you were young? But how did they know—when the thing hung fire as it did? When the whole edition was thrown back on his hands?"

"The whole edition—what edition?" It was Miss Anson's turn to stare.

"Why, of his pamphlet—*the* pamphlet—the one thing that counts, that survives, that makes him what he is! For heaven's sake," he tragically adjured her, "don't tell me there isn't a copy of it left!"

Miss Anson was trembling slightly. "I don't think I understand what you mean," she faltered, less bewildered by his vehemence than by the strange sense of coming on an unexplored region in the very heart of her dominion.

"Why, his account of the *amphioxus*, of course! You can't mean that his family didn't know about it—that *you* don't know about it? I came across it by the merest accident myself, in a letter of vindication that he wrote in 1830 to an old scientific paper; but I understood there were journals—early journals; there must be references to it somewhere in the 'twenties. He

[ 56 ]

must have been at least ten or twelve years ahead of Yarrell; and he saw the whole significance of it, too— he saw where it led to. As I understand it, he actually anticipated in his pamphlet Saint Hilaire's theory of the universal type, and supported the hypothesis by describing the notochord of the *amphioxus* as a cartilaginous vertebral column. The specialists of the day jeered at him, of course, as the specialists in Goethe's time jeered at the plant-metamorphosis. As far as I can make out, the anatomists and zoologists were down on Dr. Anson to a man; that was why his cowardly publishers went back on their bargain. But the pamphlet must be here somewhere—he writes as though, in his first disappointment, he had destroyed the whole edition; but surely there must be at least one copy left?"

His scientific jargon was as bewildering as his slang; and there were even moments in his discourse when Miss Anson ceased to distinguish between them; but the suspense with which he continued to gaze on her acted as a challenge to her scattered thoughts.

"The *amphioxus*," she murmured, half-rising. "It's an animal, isn't it—a fish? Yes, I think I remember." She sank back with the inward look of one who retraces some lost line of association.

Gradually the distance cleared, the details started into life. In her researches for the biography she had

## THE ANGEL AT THE GRAVE

patiently followed every ramification of her subject, and one of these overgrown paths now led her back to the episode in question. The great Orestes's title of "Doctor" had in fact not been merely the spontaneous tribute of a national admiration; he had actually studied medicine in his youth, and his diaries, as his granddaughter now recalled, showed that he had passed through a brief phase of anatomical ardor before his attention was diverted to super-sensual problems. It had indeed seemed to Paulina, as she scanned those early pages, that they revealed a spontaneity, a freshness of feeling somehow absent from his later lucubrations—as though this one emotion had reached him directly, the others through some intervening medium. In the excess of her commemorative zeal she had even struggled through the unintelligible pamphlet to which a few lines in the journal had bitterly directed her. But the subject and the phraseology were alien to her and unconnected with her conception of the great man's genius; and after a hurried perusal she had averted her thoughts from the episode as from a revelation of failure. At length she rose a little unsteadily, supporting herself against the writing-table. She looked hesitatingly about the room; then she drew a key from her old-fashioned reticule and unlocked a drawer beneath one of the book-cases. Young Corby watched her breathlessly. With a tremulous hand she turned over

# THE ANGEL AT THE GRAVE

the dusty documents that seemed to fill the drawer. "Is this it?" she said, holding out a thin discolored volume.

He seized it with a gasp. "Oh, by George," he said, dropping into the nearest chair.

She stood observing him strangely as his eye devoured the mouldy pages.

"Is this the only copy left?" he asked at length, looking up for a moment as a thirsty man lifts his head from his glass.

"I think it must be. I found it long ago, among some old papers that my aunts were burning up after my grandmother's death. They said it was of no use — that he'd always meant to destroy the whole edition and that I ought to respect his wishes. But it was something *he* had written; to burn it was like shutting the door against his voice — against something he had once wished to say, and that nobody had listened to. I wanted him to feel that I was always here, ready to listen, even when others hadn't thought it worth while; and so I kept the pamphlet, meaning to carry out his wish and destroy it before my death."

Her visitor gave a groan of retrospective anguish. "And but for me — but for to-day — you would have?"

"I should have thought it my duty."

"Oh, by George — by George," he repeated, subdued afresh by the inadequacy of speech.

# THE ANGEL AT THE GRAVE

She continued to watch him in silence. At length he jumped up and impulsively caught her by both hands.

"He's bigger and bigger!" he almost shouted. "He simply leads the field! You'll help me go to the bottom of this, won't you? We must turn out all the papers—letters, journals, memoranda. He must have made notes. He must have left some record of what led up to this. We must leave nothing unexplored. By Jove," he cried, looking up at her with his bright convincing smile, "do you know you're the granddaughter of a Great Man?"

Her color flickered like a girl's. "Are you—sure of him?" she whispered, as though putting him on his guard against a possible betrayal of trust.

"Sure! Sure! My dear lady—" he measured her again with his quick confident glance. "Don't *you* believe in him?"

She drew back with a confused murmur. "I—used to." She had left her hands in his: their pressure seemed to send a warm current to her heart. "It ruined my life!" she cried with sudden passion. He looked at her perplexedly.

"I gave up everything," she went on wildly, "to keep *him* alive. I sacrificed myself—others—I nursed his glory in my bosom and it died—and left me—left me here alone." She paused and gathered her courage

# THE ANGEL AT THE GRAVE

with a gasp. "Don't make the same mistake!" she warned him.

He shook his head, still smiling. "No danger of that! You're not alone, my dear lady. He's here with you—he's come back to you to-day. Don't you see what's happened? Don't you see that it's your love that has kept him alive? If you'd abandoned your post for an instant—let things pass into other hands—if your wonderful tenderness hadn't perpetually kept guard—this might have been—must have been—irretrievably lost." He laid his hand on the pamphlet. "And then—then he *would* have been dead!"

"Oh," she said, "don't tell me too suddenly!" And she turned away and sank into a chair.

The young man stood watching her in an awed silence. For a long time she sat motionless, with her face hidden, and he thought she must be weeping.

At length he said, almost shyly: "You'll let me come back, then? You'll help me work this thing out?"

She rose calmly and held out her hand. "I'll help you," she declared.

"I'll come to-morrow, then. Can we get to work early?"

"As early as you please."

"At eight o'clock, then," he said briskly. "You'll have the papers ready?"

"I'll have everything ready." She added with a

# THE ANGEL AT THE GRAVE

half-playful hesitancy: "And the fire shall be lit for you."

He went out with his bright nod. She walked to the window and watched his buoyant figure hastening down the elm-shaded street. When she turned back into the empty room she looked as though youth had touched her on the lips.

# THE RECOVERY

# THE RECOVERY

TO the visiting stranger Hillbridge's first question was, "Have you seen Keniston's things?" Keniston took precedence of the colonial State House, the Gilbert Stuart Washington and the Ethnological Museum; nay, he ran neck and neck with the President of the University, a prehistoric relic who had known Emerson, and who was still sent about the country in cotton-wool to open educational institutions with a toothless oration on Brook Farm.

Keniston was sent about the country too: he opened art exhibitions, laid the foundation of academies, and acted in a general sense as the spokesman and apologist of art. Hillbridge was proud of him in his peripatetic character, but his fellow-townsmen let it be understood that to "know" Keniston one must come to Hillbridge. Never was work more dependent for its effect on "atmosphere," on *milieu*. Hillbridge was Keniston's *milieu*, and there was one lady, a devotee of his art, who went so far as to assert that once, at an exhibition in New York, she had passed a Keniston without recognizing it. "It simply didn't want to be seen in such surroundings; it was hiding itself under an incognito," she declared.

It was a source of special pride to Hillbridge that it

# THE RECOVERY

contained all the artist's best works. Strangers were told that Hillbridge had discovered him. The discovery had come about in the simplest manner. Professor Driffert, who had a reputation for "collecting," had one day hung a sketch on his drawing-room wall, and thereafter Mrs. Driffert's visitors (always a little flurried by the sense that it was the kind of house in which one might be suddenly called upon to distinguish between a dry-point and an etching, or between Raphael Mengs and Raphael Sanzio) were not infrequently subjected to the Professor's off-hand inquiry, "By-the-way, have you seen my Keniston?" The visitors, perceptibly awed, would retreat to a critical distance and murmur the usual guarded generalities, while they tried to keep the name in mind long enough to look it up in the Encyclopædia. The name was not in the Encyclopædia; but, as a compensating fact, it became known that the man himself was in Hillbridge. Hillbridge, then, owned an artist whose celebrity it was the proper thing to take for granted! Some one else, emboldened by the thought, bought a Keniston; and the next year, on the occasion of the President's golden jubilee, the Faculty, by unanimous consent, presented him with a Keniston. Two years later there was a Keniston exhibition, to which the art-critics came from New York and Boston; and not long afterward a well-known Chicago collector vainly attempted to buy Professor Driffert's sketch,

# THE RECOVERY

which the art journals cited as a rare example of the painter's first or silvery manner. Thus there gradually grew up a small circle of connoisseurs known in artistic circles as men who collected Kenistons.

Professor Wildmarsh, of the chair of Fine Arts and Archæology, was the first critic to publish a detailed analysis of the master's methods and purpose. The article was illustrated by engravings which (though they had cost the magazine a fortune) were declared by Professor Wildmarsh to give but an imperfect suggestion of the esoteric significance of the originals. The Professor, with a tact that contrived to make each reader feel himself included among the exceptions, went on to say that Keniston's work would never appeal to any but exceptional natures; and he closed with the usual assertion that to apprehend the full meaning of the master's "message" it was necessary to see him in the surroundings of his own home at Hillbridge.

Professor Wildmarsh's article was read one spring afternoon by a young lady just speeding eastward on her first visit to Hillbridge, and already flushed with anticipation of the intellectual opportunities awaiting her. In East Onondaigua, where she lived, Hillbridge was looked on as an Oxford. Magazine writers, with the easy American use of the superlative, designated it as "the venerable Alma Mater," the "antique seat of learning," and Claudia Day had been brought up to regard it as the fountain-head of knowledge, and of that mental distinction which is so much rarer than knowledge. An innate passion for all that was thus distinguished and exceptional made her revere Hillbridge as the native soil of those intellectual amenities that were of such difficult growth in the thin air of East Onondaigua. At the first suggestion of a visit to Hillbridge—whither she went at the invitation of a girl friend who (incredible apotheosis!) had married one of the University professors—Claudia's spirit dilated with the sense of new possibilities. The vision of herself walking under the "historic elms" toward the Memorial Library, standing rapt before the Stuart Washington, or drinking in, from some obscure corner of an academic drawing-room, the President's reminiscences of the Concord group—this vividness of self-projection into the emotions awaiting her made her glad of any delay that prolonged so exquisite a moment.

It was in this mood that she opened the article on Keniston. She knew about him, of course; she was wonderfully "well up," even for East Onondaigua. She had read of him in the magazines; she had met, on a visit to New York, a man who collected Kenistons, and a photogravure of a Keniston in an "artistic" frame hung above her writing-table at home. But Professor Wildmarsh's article made her feel how little she

# THE RECOVERY

really knew of the master; and she trembled to think of the state of relative ignorance in which, but for the timely purchase of the magazine, she might have entered Hillbridge. She had, for instance, been densely unaware that Keniston had already had three "manners," and was showing symptoms of a fourth. She was equally ignorant of the fact that he had founded a school and "created a formula"; and she learned with a thrill that no one could hope to understand him who had not seen him in his studio at Hillbridge, surrounded by his own works. "The man and the art interpret each other," their exponent declared; and Claudia Day, bending a brilliant eye on the future, wondered if she were ever to be admitted to the privilege of that double initiation.

Keniston, to his other claims to distinction, added that of being hard to know. His friends always hastened to announce the fact to strangers—adding after a pause of suspense that they "would see what they could do." Visitors in whose favor he was induced to make an exception were further warned that he never spoke unless he was interested—so that they must n't mind if he remained silent. It was under these reassuring conditions that, some ten days after her arrival at Hillbridge, Miss Day was introduced to the master's studio. She found him a tall listless-looking man, who appeared middle-aged to her youth, and who stood before his own pictures with a vaguely interrogative gaze, leaving the task of their interpretation to the lady who had courageously contrived the visit. The studio, to Claudia's surprise, was bare and shabby. It formed a rambling addition to the small cheerless house in which the artist lived with his mother and a widowed sister. For Claudia it added the last touch to his distinction to learn that he was poor, and that what he earned was devoted to the maintenance of the two limp women who formed a neutral-tinted background to his impressive outline. His pictures of course fetched high prices; but he worked slowly—"painfully," as his devotees preferred to phrase it—with frequent intervals of ill health and inactivity, and the circle of Keniston connoisseurs was still as small as it was distinguished. The girl's fancy instantly hailed in him that favorite figure of imaginative youth, the artist who would rather starve than paint a pot-boiler. It is known to comparatively few that the production of successful pot-boilers is an art in itself, and that such heroic abstentions as Keniston's are not always purely voluntary.

On the occasion of her first visit the artist said so little that Claudia was able to indulge to the full the harrowing sense of her inadequacy. No wonder she had not been one of the few that he cared to talk to; every word she uttered must so obviously have diminished the inducement! She had been cheap, trivial, conven-

# THE RECOVERY

tional; at once gushing and inexpressive, eager and constrained. She could feel him counting the minutes till the visit was over, and as the door finally closed on the scene of her discomfiture she almost shared the hope with which she confidently credited him — that they might never meet again.

## II

MRS. DAVANT glanced reverentially about the studio. "I have always said," she murmured, "that they ought to be seen in Europe."

Mrs. Davant was young, credulous and emotionally extravagant: she reminded Claudia of her earlier self — the self that, ten years before, had first set an awestruck foot on that very threshold.

"Not for *his* sake," Mrs. Davant continued, "but for Europe's."

Claudia smiled. She was glad that her husband's pictures were to be exhibited in Paris. She concurred in Mrs. Davant's view of the importance of the event; but she thought her visitor's way of putting the case a little overcharged. Ten years spent in an atmosphere of Keniston-worship had insensibly developed in Claudia a preference for moderation of speech. She believed in her husband, of course; to believe in him, with an increasing abandonment and tenacity, had become one of the necessary laws of being; but she did not believe

## THE RECOVERY

in his admirers. Their faith in him was perhaps as genuine as her own; but it seemed to her less able to give an account of itself. Some few of his appreciators doubtless measured him by their own standards; but it was difficult not to feel that in the Hillbridge circle, where rapture ran the highest, he was accepted on what was at best but an indirect valuation; and now and then she had a frightened doubt as to the independence of her own convictions. That innate sense of relativity which even East Onondaigua had not been able to check in Claudia Day had been fostered in Mrs. Keniston by the artistic absolutism of Hillbridge, and she often wondered that her husband remained so uncritical of the quality of admiration accorded him. Her husband's uncritical attitude toward himself and his admirers had in fact been one of the surprises of her marriage. That an artist should believe in his potential powers seemed to her at once the incentive and the pledge of excellence: she knew there was no future for a hesitating talent. What perplexed her was Keniston's satisfaction in his achievement. She had always imagined that the true artist must regard himself as the imperfect vehicle of the cosmic emotion—that beneath every difficulty overcome a new one lurked, the vision widening as the scope enlarged. To be initiated into these creative struggles, to shed on the toiler's path the consolatory ray of faith and encouragement, had seemed the chief

## THE RECOVERY

privilege of her marriage. But there is something supererogatory in believing in a man obviously disposed to perform that service for himself; and Claudia's ardor gradually spent itself against the dense surface of her husband's complacency. She could smile now at her vision of an intellectual communion which should admit her to the inmost precincts of his inspiration. She had learned that the creative processes are seldom self-explanatory, and Keniston's inarticulateness no longer discouraged her; but she could not reconcile her sense of the continuity of all high effort to his unperturbed air of finishing each picture as though he had despatched a masterpiece to posterity. In the first recoil from her disillusionment she even allowed herself to perceive that, if he worked slowly, it was not because he mistrusted his powers of expression, but because he had really so little to express.

"It's for Europe," Mrs. Davant vaguely repeated; and Claudia noticed that she was blushingly intent on tracing with the tip of her elaborate sunshade the pattern of the shabby carpet.

"It will be a revelation to them," she went on provisionally, as though Claudia had missed her cue and left an awkward interval to fill.

Claudia had in fact a sudden sense of deficient intuition. She felt that her visitor had something to communicate which required, on her own part, an intelligent co-operation; but what it was her insight failed to suggest. She was, in truth, a little tired of Mrs. Davant, who was Keniston's latest worshipper, who ordered pictures recklessly, who paid for them regally in advance, and whose gallery was, figuratively speaking, crowded with the artist's unpainted masterpieces. Claudia's impatience was perhaps complicated by the uneasy sense that Mrs. Davant was too young, too rich, too inexperienced; that somehow she ought to be warned. — Warned of what? That some of the pictures might never be painted? Scarcely that, since Keniston, who was scrupulous in business transactions, might be trusted not to take any material advantage of such evidence of faith. Claudia's impulse remained undefined. She merely felt that she would have liked to help Mrs. Davant, and that she did not know how.

"You'll be there to see them?" she asked, as her visitor lingered.

"In Paris?" Mrs. Davant's blush deepened. "We must all be there together."

Claudia smiled. "My husband and I mean to go abroad some day—but I don't see any chance of it at present."

"But he *ought* to go—you ought both to go this summer!" Mrs. Davant persisted. "I know Professor Wildmarsh and Professor Driffert and all the other critics think that Mr. Keniston's never having been to

# THE RECOVERY

Europe has given his work much of its wonderful individuality, its peculiar flavor and meaning—but now that his talent is formed, that he has full command of his means of expression," (Claudia recognized one of Professor Driffert's favorite formulas) "they all think he ought to see the work of the *other* great masters—that he ought to visit the home of his ancestors, as Professor Wildmarsh says!" She stretched an impulsive hand to Claudia. "You ought to let him go, Mrs. Keniston!"

Claudia accepted the admonition with the philosophy of the wife who is used to being advised on the management of her husband. "I sha'n't interfere with him," she declared; and Mrs. Davant instantly caught her up with a cry of, "Oh, it's too lovely of you to say that!" With this exclamation she left Claudia to a silent renewal of wonder.

A moment later Keniston entered: to a mind curious in combinations it might have occurred that he had met Mrs. Davant on the door-step. In one sense he might, for all his wife cared, have met fifty Mrs. Davants on the door-step: it was long since Claudia had enjoyed the solace of resenting such coincidences. Her only thought now was that her husband's first words might not improbably explain Mrs. Davant's last; and she waited for him to speak.

He paused with his hands in his pockets before an

# THE RECOVERY

unfinished picture on the easel; then, as his habit was, he began to stroll touristlike from canvas to canvas, standing before each in a musing ecstasy of contemplation that no readjustment of view ever seemed to disturb. Her eye instinctively joined his in its inspection; it was the one point where their natures merged. Thank God, there was no doubt about the pictures! She was what she had always dreamed of being—the wife of a great artist. Keniston dropped into an armchair and filled his pipe. "How should you like to go to Europe?" he asked.

His wife looked up quickly. "When?"

"Now—this spring, I mean." He paused to light the pipe. "I should like to be over there while these things are being exhibited."

Claudia was silent.

"Well?" he repeated after a moment.

"How can we afford it?" she asked.

Keniston had always scrupulously fulfilled his duty to the mother and sister whom his marriage had dislodged; and Claudia, who had the atoning temperament which seeks to pay for every happiness by making it a source of fresh obligations, had from the outset accepted his ties with an exaggerated devotion. Any disregard of such a claim would have vulgarized her most delicate pleasures; and her husband's sensitiveness to it in great measure extenuated the artistic ob-

# THE RECOVERY

tuseness that often seemed to her like a failure of the moral sense. His loyalty to the dull women who depended on him was, after all, compounded of finer tissues than any mere sensibility to ideal demands.

"Oh, I don't see why we shouldn't," he rejoined. "I think we might manage it."

"At Mrs. Davant's expense?" leaped from Claudia. She could not tell why she had said it; some inner barrier seemed to have given way under a confused pressure of emotions.

He looked up at her with frank surprise. "Well, she *has* been very jolly about it—why not? She has a tremendous feeling for art—the keenest I ever knew in a woman." Claudia imperceptibly smiled. "She wants me to let her pay in advance for the four panels she has ordered for the Memorial Library. That would give us plenty of money for the trip, and my having the panels to do is another reason for my wanting to go abroad just now."

"Another reason?"

"Yes; I've never worked on such a big scale. I want to see how those old chaps did the trick; I want to measure myself with the big fellows over there. An artist ought to, once in his life."

She gave him a wondering look. For the first time his words implied a sense of possible limitation; but his easy tone seemed to retract what they conceded.

# THE RECOVERY

What he really wanted was fresh food for his self-satisfaction: he was like an army that moves on after exhausting the resources of the country.

Womanlike, she abandoned the general survey of the case for the consideration of a minor point.

"Are you sure you can do that kind of thing?" she asked.

"What kind of thing?"

"The panels."

He glanced at her indulgently: his self-confidence was too impenetrable to feel the pin-prick of such a doubt.

"Immensely sure," he said with a smile.

"And you don't mind taking so much money from her in advance?"

He stared. "Why should I? She'll get it back — with interest!" He laughed and drew at his pipe. "It will be an uncommonly interesting experience. I shouldn't wonder if it freshened me up a bit."

She looked at him again. This second hint of self-distrust struck her as the sign of a quickened sensibility. What if, after all, he was beginning to be dissatisfied with his work? The thought filled her with a renovating sense of his sufficiency.

# THE RECOVERY

## III

THEY stopped in London to see the National Gallery.

It was thus that, in their inexperience, they had narrowly put it; but in reality every stone of the streets, every trick of the atmosphere, had its message of surprise for their virgin sensibilities. The pictures were simply the summing up, the final interpretation, of the cumulative pressure of an unimagined world; and it seemed to Claudia that long before they reached the doors of the gallery she had some intuitive revelation of what awaited them within.

They moved about from room to room without exchanging a word. The vast noiseless spaces seemed full of sound, like the roar of a distant multitude heard only by the inner ear. Had their speech been articulate their language would have been incomprehensible; and even that far-off murmur of meaning pressed intolerably on Claudia's nerves. Keniston took the onset without outward sign of disturbance. Now and then he paused before a canvas, or prolonged from one of the benches his silent communion with some miracle of line or color; but he neither looked at his wife nor spoke to her. He seemed to have forgotten her presence.

Claudia was conscious of keeping a furtive watch on

## THE RECOVERY

him; but the sum total of her impressions was negative. She remembered thinking when she first met him that his face was rather expressionless; and he had the habit of self-engrossed silences.

All that evening, at the hotel, they talked about London, and he surprised her by an acuteness of observation that she had sometimes inwardly accused him of lacking. He seemed to have seen everything, to have examined, felt, compared, with nerves as finely adjusted as her own; but he said nothing of the pictures. The next day they returned to the National Gallery, and he began to study the paintings in detail, pointing out differences of technique, analyzing and criticising, but still without summing up his conclusions. He seemed to have a sort of provincial dread of showing himself too much impressed. Claudia's own sensations were too complex, too overwhelming, to be readily classified. Lacking the craftsman's instinct to steady her, she felt herself carried off her feet by the rush of incoherent impressions. One point she consciously avoided, and that was the comparison of her husband's work with what they were daily seeing. Art, she inwardly argued, was too various, too complex, dependent on too many inter-relations of feeling and environment, to allow of its being judged by any provisional standard. Even the subtleties of technique must be modified by the artist's changing purpose, as

[ 80 ]

## THE RECOVERY

this in turn is acted on by influences of which he is himself unconscious. How, then, was an unprepared imagination to distinguish between such varied reflections of the elusive vision? She took refuge in a passionate exaggeration of her own ignorance and insufficiency.

After a week in London they went to Paris. The exhibition of Keniston's pictures had been opened a few days earlier; and as they drove through the streets on the way to the station an "impressionist" poster here and there invited them to the display of the American artist's work. Mrs. Davant, who had been in Paris for the opening, had already written rapturously of the impression produced, enclosing commendatory notices from one or two papers. She reported that there had been a great crowd on the first day, and that the critics had been "immensely struck."

The Kenistons arrived in the evening, and the next morning Claudia, as a matter of course, asked her husband at what time he meant to go and see the pictures.

He looked up absently from his guide-book.

"What pictures?"

"Why—yours," she said, surprised.

"Oh, they'll keep," he answered; adding with a slightly embarrassed laugh, "We'll give the other chaps a show first." Presently he laid down his book and proposed that they should go to the Louvre.

# THE RECOVERY

They spent the morning there, lunched at a restaurant near by, and returned to the gallery in the afternoon. Keniston had passed from inarticulateness to an eager volubility. It was clear that he was beginning to co-ordinate his impressions, to find his way about in a corner of the great imaginative universe. He seemed extraordinarily ready to impart his discoveries; and Claudia felt that her ignorance served him as a convenient buffer against the terrific impact of new sensations.

On the way home she asked when he meant to see Mrs. Davant.

His answer surprised her. "Does she know we're here?"

"Not unless you've sent her word," said Claudia, with a touch of harmless irony.

"That's all right, then," he returned simply. "I want to wait and look about a day or two longer. She'd want us to go sight-seeing with her; and I'd rather get my impressions alone."

The next two days were hampered by the necessity of eluding Mrs. Davant. Claudia, under different circumstances, would have scrupled to share in this somewhat shabby conspiracy; but she found herself in a state of suspended judgment, wherein her husband's treatment of Mrs. Davant became for the moment merely a clue to larger meanings.

# THE RECOVERY

They had been four days in Paris when Claudia, returning one afternoon from a parenthetical excursion to the Rue de la Paix, was confronted on her threshold by the reproachful figure of their benefactress. It was not to her, however, that Mrs. Davant's reproaches were addressed. Keniston, it appeared, had borne the brunt of them; for he stood leaning against the mantelpiece of their modest *salon* in that attitude of convicted negligence when, if ever, a man is glad to take refuge behind his wife.

Claudia had however no immediate intention of affording him such shelter. She wanted to observe and wait.

"He's too impossible!" cried Mrs. Davant, sweeping her at once into the central current of her grievance.

Claudia looked from one to the other.

"For not going to see you?"

"For not going to see his pictures!" cried the other nobly.

Claudia colored and Keniston shifted his position uneasily.

"I can't make her understand," he said, turning to his wife.

"I don't care about myself!" Mrs. Davant interjected.

"*I* do, then; it's the only thing I do care about," he hurriedly protested. "I meant to go at once—to write — Claudia wanted to go, but I would n't let her." He looked helplessly about the pleasant red-curtained room, which was rapidly burning itself into Claudia's consciousness as a visible extension of Mrs. Davant's claims.

"I can't explain," he broke off.

Mrs. Davant in turn addressed herself to Claudia.

"People think it's so odd," she complained. "So many of the artists here are anxious to meet him; they've all been so charming about the pictures; and several of our American friends have come over from London expressly for the exhibition. I told every one that he would be here for the opening — there was a private view, you know — and they were so disappointed — they wanted to give him an ovation; and I did n't know what to say. What *am* I to say?" she abruptly ended.

"There's nothing to say," said Keniston slowly.

"But the exhibition closes the day after to-morrow."

"Well, *I* sha'n't close — I shall be here," he declared with an effort at playfulness. "If they want to see me — all these people you're kind enough to mention — won't there be other chances?"

"But I wanted them to see you *among* your pictures — to hear you talk about them, explain them in that wonderful way. I wanted you to interpret each other, as Professor Wildmarsh says!"

# THE RECOVERY

"Oh, hang Professor Wildmarsh!" said Keniston, softening the commination with a smile. "If my pictures are good for anything they oughtn't to need explaining."

Mrs. Davant stared. "But I thought that was what made them so interesting!" she exclaimed.

Keniston looked down. "Perhaps it was," he murmured.

There was an awkward silence, which Claudia broke by saying, with a glance at her husband: "But if the exhibition is to remain open to-morrow, could we not meet you there? And perhaps you could send word to some of our friends."

Mrs. Davant brightened like a child whose broken toy is glued together. "Oh, *do* make him!" she implored. "I'll ask them to come in the afternoon—we'll make it into a little tea—a *five o'clock*. I'll send word at once to everybody!" She gathered up her beruffled boa and sunshade, settling her plumage like a reassured bird. "It will be too lovely!" she ended in a self-consoling murmur.

But in the doorway a new doubt assailed her. "You won't fail me?" she said, turning plaintively to Keniston. "You'll make him come, Mrs. Keniston?"

"I'll bring him!" Claudia promised.

# THE RECOVERY

## IV

WHEN, the next morning, she appeared equipped for their customary ramble, her husband surprised her by announcing that he meant to stay at home.

"The fact is I'm rather surfeited," he said, smiling. "I suppose my appetite isn't equal to such a plethora. I think I'll write some letters and join you somewhere later."

She detected the wish to be alone and responded to it with her usual readiness.

"I shall sink to my proper level and buy a bonnet, then," she said. "I haven't had time to take the edge off that appetite."

They agreed to meet at the Hôtel Cluny at mid-day, and she set out alone with a vague sense of relief. Neither she nor Keniston had made any direct reference to Mrs. Davant's visit; but its effect was implicit in their eagerness to avoid each other.

Claudia accomplished some shopping in the spirit of perfunctoriness that robs even new bonnets of their bloom; and this business despatched, she turned aimlessly into the wide inviting brightness of the streets. Never had she felt more isolated amid that ordered beauty which gives a social quality to the very stones and mortar of Paris. All about her were evidences of an artistic sensibility pervading every form of life like the nervous structure of the huge frame—a sensibility so delicate, alert and universal that it seemed to leave no room for obtuseness or error. In such a medium the faculty of plastic expression must develop as unconsciously as any organ in its normal surroundings; to be "artistic" must cease to be an attitude and become a natural function. To Claudia the significance of the whole vast revelation was centred in the light it shed on one tiny spot of consciousness—the value of her husband's work. There are moments when to the groping soul the world's accumulated experiences are but stepping-stones across a private difficulty.

She stood hesitating on a street corner. It was barely eleven, and she had an hour to spare before going to the Hôtel Cluny. She seemed to be letting her inclination float as it would on the cross-currents of suggestion emanating from the brilliant complex scene before her; but suddenly, in obedience to an impulse that she became aware of only in acting on it, she called a cab and drove to the gallery where her husband's pictures were exhibited.

A magnificent official in gold braid sold her a ticket and pointed the way up the empty crimson-carpeted stairs. His duplicate, on the upper landing, held out a catalogue with an air of recognizing the futility of the offer; and a moment later she found herself in the

## THE RECOVERY

long noiseless impressive room full of velvet-covered ottomans and exotic plants. It was clear that the public ardor on which Mrs. Davant had expatiated had spent itself earlier in the week; for Claudia had this luxurious apartment to herself. Something about its air of rich privacy, its diffusion of that sympathetic quality in other countries so conspicuously absent from the public show-room, seemed to emphasize its present emptiness. It was as though the flowers, the carpet, the lounges, surrounded their visitor's solitary advance with the mute assurance that they had done all they could toward making the thing "go off," and that if they had failed it was simply for lack of co-operation. She stood still and looked about her. The pictures struck her instantly as odd gaps in the general harmony; it was self-evident that they had not co-operated. They had not been pushing, aggressive, discordant: they had merely effaced themselves. She swept a startled eye from one familiar painting to another. The canvases were all there—and the frames—but the miracle, the mirage of life and meaning, had vanished like some atmospheric illusion. What was it that had happened? And had it happened to *her* or to the pictures? She tried to rally her frightened thoughts; to push or coax them into a semblance of resistance; but argument was swept off its feet by the huge rush of a single conviction—the conviction that the pictures were bad.

# THE RECOVERY

There was no standing up against that: she felt herself submerged.

The stealthy fear that had been following her all these days had her by the throat now. The great vision of beauty through which she had been moving as one enchanted was turned to a phantasmagoria of evil mocking shapes. She hated the past; she hated its splendor, its power, its wicked magical vitality. . . She dropped into a seat and continued to stare at the wall before her. Gradually, as she stared, there stole out to her from the dimmed humbled canvases a reminder of what she had once seen in them, a spectral appeal to her faith to call them back to life. What proof had she that her present estimate of them was less subjective than the other? The confused impressions of the last few days were hardly to be pleaded as a valid theory of art. How, after all, did she know that the pictures were bad? On what suddenly acquired technical standard had she thus decided the case against them? It seemed as though it were a standard outside of herself, as though some unheeded inner sense were gradually making her aware of the presence, in that empty room, of a critical intelligence that was giving out a subtle effluence of disapproval. The fancy was so vivid that, to shake it off, she rose and began to move about again. In the middle of the room stood a monumental divan surmounted by a *massif*

# THE RECOVERY

of palms and azaleas. As Claudia's muffled wanderings carried her around the angle of this seat, she saw that its farther side was occupied by the figure of a man, who sat with his hands resting on his stick and his head bowed upon them. She gave a little cry and her husband rose and faced her.

Instantly the live point of consciousness was shifted, and she became aware that the quality of the pictures no longer mattered. It was what *he* thought of them that counted: her life hung on that.

They looked at each other a moment in silence; such concussions are not apt to flash into immediate speech. At length he said simply, "I didn't know you were coming here."

She colored as though he had charged her with something underhand.

"I didn't mean to," she stammered; "but I was too early for our appointment—"

Her words cast a revealing glare on the situation. Neither of them looked at the pictures; but to Claudia those unobtruding presences seemed suddenly to press upon them and force them apart.

Keniston glanced at his watch. "It's twelve o'clock," he said. "Shall we go on?"

# THE RECOVERY

## V

AT the door he called a cab and put her in it; then, drawing out his watch again, he said abruptly: "I believe I'll let you go alone. I'll join you at the hotel in time for luncheon." She wondered for a moment if he meant to return to the gallery; but, looking back as she drove off, she saw him walk rapidly away in the opposite direction.

The cabman had carried her half-way to the Hôtel Cluny before she realized where she was going, and cried out to him to turn home. There was an acute irony in this mechanical prolongation of the quest of beauty. She had had enough of it, too much of it; her one longing was to escape, to hide herself away from its all-suffusing implacable light.

At the hotel, alone in her room, a few tears came to soften her seared vision; but her mood was too tense to be eased by weeping. Her whole being was centred in the longing to know what her husband thought. Their short exchange of words had, after all, told her nothing. She had guessed a faint resentment at her unexpected appearance; but that might merely imply a dawning sense, on his part, of being furtively watched and criticised. She had sometimes wondered if he was never conscious of her observation; there were moments when it seemed to radiate from her in visible

## THE RECOVERY

waves. Perhaps, after all, he was aware of it, on his guard against it, as a lurking knife behind the thick curtain of his complacency; and to-day he must have caught the gleam of the blade.

Claudia had not reached the age when pity is the first chord to vibrate in contact with any revelation of failure. Her one hope had been that Keniston should be clear-eyed enough to face the truth. Whatever it turned out to be, she wanted him to measure himself with it. But as his image rose before her she felt a sudden half-maternal longing to thrust herself between him and disaster. Her eagerness to see him tested by circumstances seemed now like a cruel scientific curiosity. She saw in a flash of sympathy that he would need her most if he fell beneath his fate.

He did not, after all, return for luncheon; and when she came up-stairs from her solitary meal their *salon* was still untenanted. She permitted herself no sensational fears; for she could not, at the height of apprehension, figure Keniston as yielding to any tragic impulse; but the lengthening hours brought an uneasiness that was fuel to her pity. Suddenly she heard the clock strike five. It was the hour at which they had promised to meet Mrs. Davant at the gallery—the hour of the "ovation." Claudia rose and went to the window, straining for a glimpse of her husband in the crowded street. Could it be that he had forgotten her, had gone to the

# THE RECOVERY

gallery without her? Or had something happened—that veiled "something" which, for the last hour, had grimly hovered on the outskirts of her mind?

She heard a hand on the door and Keniston entered. As she turned to meet him her whole being was swept forward on a great wave of pity: she was so sure, now, that he must know.

But he confronted her with a glance of preoccupied brightness; her first impression was that she had never seen him so vividly, so expressively pleased. If he needed her, it was not to bind up his wounds.

He gave her a smile which was clearly the lingering reflection of some inner light. "I didn't mean to be so late," he said, tossing aside his hat and the little red volume that served as a clue to his explorations. "I turned in to the Louvre for a minute after I left you this morning, and the place fairly swallowed me up—I couldn't get away from it. I've been there ever since." He threw himself into a chair and glanced about for his pipe.

"It takes time," he continued musingly, "to get at them, to make out what they're saying—the big fellows, I mean. They're not a communicative lot. At first I couldn't make much out of their lingo—it was too different from mine! But gradually, by picking up a hint here and there, and piecing them together, I've begun to understand; and to-day, by Jove, I got one or

## THE RECOVERY

two of the old chaps by the throat and fairly turned them inside out—made them deliver up their last drop." He lifted a brilliant eye to her. "Lord, it was tremendous!" he declared.

He had found his pipe and was musingly filling it. Claudia waited in silence.

"At first," he began again, "I was afraid their language was too hard for me—that I should never quite know what they were driving at; they seemed to cold-shoulder me, to be bent on shutting me out. But I was bound I wouldn't be beaten, and now, to-day"—he paused a moment to strike a match—"when I went to look at those things of mine it all came over me in a flash. By Jove! it was as if I'd made them all into a big bonfire to light me on my road!"

His wife was trembling with a kind of sacred terror. She had been afraid to pray for light for him, and here he was joyfully casting his whole past upon the pyre!

"Is there nothing left?" she faltered.

"Nothing left? There's everything!" he exulted. "Why, here I am, not much over forty, and I've found out already—already!" He stood up and began to move excitedly about the room. "My God! Suppose I'd never known! Suppose I'd gone on painting things like that forever! Why, I feel like those chaps at revivalist meetings when they get up and say they're saved! Won't somebody please start a hymn?"

## THE RECOVERY

Claudia, with a tremulous joy, was letting herself go on the strong current of his emotion; but it had not yet carried her beyond her depth, and suddenly she felt hard ground underfoot.

"Mrs. Davant—" she exclaimed.

He stared, as though suddenly recalled from a long distance. "Mrs. Davant?"

"We were to have met her—this afternoon—now—"

"At the gallery? Oh, that's all right. I put a stop to that; I went to see her after I left you; I explained it all to her."

"All?"

"I told her I was going to begin all over again."

Claudia's heart gave a forward bound and then sank back hopelessly.

"But the panels—?"

"That's all right too. I told her about the panels," he reassured her.

"You told her—?"

"That I can't paint them now. She doesn't understand, of course; but she's the best little woman and she trusts me."

She could have wept for joy at his exquisite obtuseness. "But that isn't all," she wailed. "It doesn't matter how much you've explained to her. It doesn't do away with the fact that we're living on those panels!"

# THE RECOVERY

"Living on them?"

"On the money that she paid you to paint them. Is n't that what brought us here? And—if you mean to do as you say—to begin all over again—how in the world are we ever to pay her back?"

Her husband turned on her an inspired eye. "There's only one way that I know of," he imperturbably declared, "and that's to stay out here till I learn how to paint them."

"COPY"

## "COPY"

### A DIALOGUE

Mrs. Ambrose Dale—*forty, slender, still young*—*sits in her drawing-room at the tea-table. The winter twilight is falling, a lamp has been lit, there is a fire on the hearth, and the room is pleasantly dim and flower-scented. Books are scattered everywhere*—*mostly with autograph inscriptions "From the Author"*—*and a large portrait of* Mrs. Dale, *at her desk, with papers strewn about her, takes up one of the wall-panels. Before* Mrs. Dale *stands* Hilda, *fair and twenty, her hands full of letters.*

MRS. DALE. Ten more applications for autographs? Isn't it strange that people who'd blush to borrow twenty dollars don't scruple to beg for an autograph?

*Hilda (reproachfully).* Oh—

*Mrs. Dale.* What's the difference, pray?

*Hilda.* Only that *your* last autograph sold for fifty—

*Mrs. Dale (not displeased).* Ah?—I sent for you, Hilda, because I'm dining out to-night, and if there's nothing important to attend to among these letters you needn't sit up for me.

*Hilda.* You don't mean to work?

*Mrs. Dale.* Perhaps; but I sha'n't need you. You'll see that my cigarettes and coffee-machine are in place,

## "COPY"

and that I don't have to crawl about the floor in search of my pen-wiper? That's all. Now about these letters—

*Hilda (impulsively).* Oh, Mrs. Dale—

*Mrs. Dale.* Well?

*Hilda.* I'd rather sit up for you.

*Mrs. Dale.* Child, I've nothing for you to do. I shall be blocking out the tenth chapter of *Winged Purposes* and it won't be ready for you till next week.

*Hilda.* It isn't that—but it's so beautiful to sit here, watching and listening, all alone in the night, and to feel that you're in there *(she points to the study-door)* creating—. *(Impulsively.)* What do I care for sleep?

*Mrs. Dale (indulgently).* Child—silly child!— Yes, I should have felt so at your age—it would have been an inspiration—

*Hilda (rapt).* It is!

*Mrs. Dale.* But you must go to bed; I must have you fresh in the morning; for you're still at the age when one *is* fresh in the morning! *(She sighs.)* The letters? *(Abruptly.)* Do you take notes of what you feel, Hilda—here, all alone in the night, as you say?

*Hilda (shyly).* I have—

*Mrs. Dale (smiling).* For the diary?

*Hilda (nods and blushes).*

*Mrs. Dale (caressingly).* Goose!—Well, to business. What is there?

## "COPY"

*Hilda.* Nothing important, except a letter from Stroud & Fayerweather to say that the question of the royalty on *Pomegranate Seed* has been settled in your favor. The English publishers of *Immolation* write to consult you about a six-shilling edition; Olafson, the Copenhagen publisher, applies for permission to bring out a Danish translation of *The Idol's Feet;* and the editor of the *Semaphore* wants a new serial — I think that's all; except that *Woman's Sphere* and *The Droplight* ask for interviews — with photographs —

*Mrs. Dale.* The same old story! I'm so tired of it all. *(To herself, in an undertone.)* But how should I feel if it all stopped? *(The servant brings in a card.)*

*Mrs. Dale (reading it).* Is it possible? Paul Ventnor? *(To the servant.)* Show Mr. Ventnor up. *(To herself.)* Paul Ventnor!

*Hilda (breathless).* Oh, Mrs. Dale — *the* Mr. Ventnor?

*Mrs. Dale (smiling).* I fancy there's only one.

*Hilda.* The great, great poet? *(Irresolute.)* No, I don't dare —

*Mrs. Dale (with a tinge of impatience).* What?

*Hilda (fervently).* Ask you — if I might — oh, here in this corner, where he can't possibly notice me — stay just a moment? Just to see him come in? To see the meeting between you — the greatest novelist and the greatest poet of the age? Oh, it's too much to ask! It's an historic moment.

## "COPY"

*Mrs. Dale.* Why, I suppose it is. I hadn't thought of it in that light. Well *(smiling)*, for the diary—

*Hilda.* Oh, thank you, *thank you!* I'll be off the very instant I've heard him speak.

*Mrs. Dale.* The very instant, mind. *(She rises, looks at herself in the glass, smooths her hair, sits down again, and rattles the tea-caddy.)* Isn't the room very warm?— *(She looks over at her portrait.)* I've grown stouter since that was painted—. You'll make a fortune out of that diary, Hilda—

*Hilda (modestly).* Four publishers have applied to me already—

*The Servant (announces).* Mr. Paul Ventnor.

*(Tall, nearing fifty, with an incipient stoutness buttoned into a masterly frock-coat, Ventnor drops his glass and advances vaguely, with a short-sighted stare.)*

*Ventnor.* Mrs. Dale?

*Mrs. Dale.* My dear friend! This is kind. *(She looks over her shoulder at Hilda, who vanishes through the door to the left.)* The papers announced your arrival, but I hardly hoped—

*Ventnor (whose short-sighted stare is seen to conceal a deeper embarrassment).* You hadn't forgotten me, then?

*Mrs. Dale.* Delicious! Do *you* forget that you're public property?

*Ventnor.* Forgotten, I mean, that we were old friends?

*Mrs. Dale.* Such old friends! May I remind you that

## "COPY"

it's nearly twenty years since we've met? Or do you find cold reminiscences indigestible?

*Ventnor.* On the contrary, I've come to ask you for a dish of them—we'll warm them up together. You're my first visit.

*Mrs. Dale.* How perfect of you! So few men visit their women friends in chronological order; or at least they generally do it the other way round, beginning with the present day and working back—if there's time—to prehistoric woman.

*Ventnor.* But when prehistoric woman has become historic woman—?

*Mrs. Dale.* Oh, it's the reflection of my glory that has guided you here, then?

*Ventnor.* It's a spirit in my feet that has led me, at the first opportunity, to the most delightful spot I know.

*Mrs. Dale.* Oh, the first opportunity—!

*Ventnor.* I might have seen you very often before; but never just in the right way.

*Mrs. Dale.* Is this the right way?

*Ventnor.* It depends on you to make it so.

*Mrs. Dale.* What a responsibility! What shall I do?

*Ventnor.* Talk to me—make me think you're a little glad to see me; give me some tea and a cigarette; and say you're out to everyone else.

*Mrs. Dale.* Is that all? *(She hands him a cup of tea.)*

## "COPY"

The cigarettes are at your elbow—. And do you think I shouldn't have been glad to see you before?

*Ventnor.* No; I think I should have been too glad to see *you*.

*Mrs. Dale.* Dear me, what precautions! I hope you always wear goloshes when it looks like rain and never by any chance expose yourself to a draught. But I had an idea that poets courted the emotions—

*Ventnor.* Do novelists?

*Mrs. Dale.* If you ask *me*—on paper!

*Ventnor.* Just so; that's safest. My best things about the sea have been written on shore. *(He looks at her thoughtfully.)* But it wouldn't have suited us in the old days, would it?

*Mrs. Dale (sighing).* When we were real people!

*Ventnor.* Real people?

*Mrs. Dale.* Are *you*, now? I died years ago. What you see before you is a figment of the reporter's brain—a monster manufactured out of newspaper paragraphs, with ink in its veins. A keen sense of copyright is *my* nearest approach to an emotion.

*Ventnor (sighing).* Ah, well, yes—as you say, we're public property.

*Mrs. Dale.* If one shared equally with the public! But the last shred of my identity is gone.

*Ventnor.* Most people would be glad to part with theirs on such terms. I have followed your work with

## "COPY"

immense interest. *Immolation* is a masterpiece. I read it last summer when it first came out.

*Mrs. Dale (with a shade less warmth). Immolation* has been out three years.

*Ventnor.* Oh, by Jove—no? Surely not— But one is so overwhelmed—one loses count. *(Reproachfully.)* Why have you never sent me your books?

*Mrs. Dale.* For that very reason.

*Ventnor (deprecatingly).* You know I didn't mean it for you! And *my* first book—do you remember—was dedicated to you.

*Mrs. Dale. Silver Trumpets—*

*Ventnor (much interested).* Have you a copy still, by any chance? The first edition, I mean? Mine was stolen years ago. Do you think you could put your hand on it?

*Mrs. Dale (taking a small shabby book from the table at her side).* It's here.

*Ventnor (eagerly).* May I have it? Ah, thanks. This is *very* interesting. The last copy sold in London for £40, and they tell me the next will fetch twice as much. It's quite *introuvable*.

*Mrs. Dale.* I know that. *(A pause. She takes the book from him, opens it, and reads, half to herself—)*

> *How much we two have seen together,*
> *Of other eyes unwist,*
> *Dear as in days of leafless weather*
> *The willow's saffron mist,*

## "COPY"

*Strange as the hour when Hesper swings*
  *A-sea in beryl green,*
*While overhead on dalliant wings*
  *The daylight hangs serene,*

*And thrilling as a meteor's fall*
  *Through depths of lonely sky,*
*When each to each two watchers call:*
  *I saw it! — So did I.*

*Ventnor.* Thin, thin — the troubadour tinkle. Odd how little promise there is in first volumes!

*Mrs. Dale (with irresistible emphasis).* I thought there was a distinct promise in this!

*Ventnor (seeing his mistake).* Ah — the one you would never let me fulfil? *(Sentimentally.)* How inexorable you were! You never dedicated a book to *me*.

*Mrs. Dale.* I hadn't begun to write when we were — dedicating things to each other.

*Ventnor.* Not for the public — but you wrote for me; and, wonderful as you are, you've never written anything since that I care for half as much as —

*Mrs. Dale (interested).* Well?

*Ventnor.* Your letters.

*Mrs. Dale (in a changed voice).* My letters — do you remember them?

*Ventnor.* When I don't, I reread them.

*Mrs. Dale (incredulous).* You have them still?

## "COPY"

*Ventnor (unguardedly).* You haven't mine, then?

*Mrs. Dale (playfully).* Oh, *you* were a celebrity already. Of course I kept them! *(Smiling.)* Think what they are worth now! I always keep them locked up in my safe over there. *(She indicates a cabinet.)*

*Ventnor (after a pause).* I always carry yours with me.

*Mrs. Dale (laughing).* You—

*Ventnor.* Wherever I go. *(A longer pause. She looks at him fixedly.)* I have them with me now.

*Mrs. Dale (agitated).* You—have them with you—now?

*Ventnor (embarrassed).* Why not? One never knows—

*Mrs. Dale.* Never knows—?

*Ventnor (humorously).* Gad—when the bank-examiner may come round. You forget I'm a married man.

*Mrs. Dale.* Ah—yes.

*Ventnor (sits down beside her).* I speak to you as I couldn't to anyone else—without deserving a kicking. You know how it all came about. *(A pause.)* You'll bear witness that it wasn't till you denied me all hope—

*Mrs. Dale (a little breathless).* Yes, yes—

*Ventnor.* Till you sent me from you—

*Mrs. Dale.* It's so easy to be heroic when one is young! One doesn't realize how long life is going to last afterward. *(Musing.)* Nor what weary work it is gathering up the fragments.

*Ventnor.* But the time comes when one sends for the

china-mender, and has the bits riveted together, and turns the cracked side to the wall—

*Mrs. Dale.* And denies that the article was ever damaged?

*Ventnor.* Eh? Well, the great thing, you see, is to keep one's self out of reach of the housemaid's brush. *(A pause.)* If you're married you can't—always. *(Smiling.)* Don't you hate to be taken down and dusted?

*Mrs. Dale (with intention).* You forget how long ago my husband died. It's fifteen years since I've been an object of interest to anybody but the public.

*Ventnor (smiling).* The only one of your admirers to whom you've ever given the least encouragement!

*Mrs. Dale.* Say rather the most easily pleased!

*Ventnor.* Or the only one you cared to please?

*Mrs. Dale.* Ah, you *haven't* kept my letters!

*Ventnor (gravely).* Is that a challenge? Look here, then! *(He draws a packet from his pocket and holds it out to her.)*

*Mrs. Dale (taking the packet and looking at him earnestly).* Why have you brought me these?

*Ventnor.* I didn't bring them; they came because I came—that's all. *(Tentatively.)* Are we unwelcome?

*Mrs. Dale (who has undone the packet and does not appear to hear him).* The very first I ever wrote you—the day after we met at the concert. How on earth did you happen to keep it? *(She glances over it.)* How

## "COPY"

perfectly absurd! Well, it's not a compromising document.

*Ventnor.* I'm afraid none of them are.

*Mrs. Dale (quickly).* Is it to that they owe their immunity? Because one could leave them about like safety matches?—Ah, here's another I remember—I wrote that the day after we went skating together for the first time. *(She reads it slowly.)* How odd! How *very* odd!

*Ventnor.* What?

*Mrs. Dale.* Why, it's the most curious thing—I had a letter of this kind to do the other day, in the novel I'm at work on now—the letter of a woman who is just—just beginning—

*Ventnor.* Yes—just beginning—?

*Mrs. Dale.* And, do you know, I find the best phrase in it, the phrase I somehow regarded as the fruit of—well, of all my subsequent discoveries—is simply plagiarized, word for word, from this!

*Ventnor (eagerly).* I told you so! You were all there!

*Mrs. Dale (critically).* But the rest of it's poorly done—very poorly. *(Reads the letter over.)* H'm—I didn't know how to leave off. It takes me forever to get out of the door.

*Ventnor (gayly).* Perhaps I was there to prevent you! *(After a pause.)* I wonder what I said in return?

*Mrs. Dale (interested).* Shall we look? *(She rises.)*

## "COPY"

Shall we—really? I have them all here, you know. *(She goes toward the cabinet.)*

*Ventnor (following her with repressed eagerness).* Oh—all!

*Mrs. Dale (throws open the door of the cabinet, revealing a number of packets).* Don't you believe me now?

*Ventnor.* Good heavens! How I must have repeated myself! But then you were so very deaf.

*Mrs. Dale (takes out a packet and returns to her seat. Ventnor extends an impatient hand for the letters).* No—no; wait! I want to find your answer to the one I was just reading. *(After a pause.)* Here it is—yes, I thought so!

*Ventnor.* What did you think?

*Mrs. Dale (triumphantly).* I thought it was the one in which you quoted *Epipsychidion*—

*Ventnor.* Mercy! Did I *quote* things? I don't wonder you were cruel.

*Mrs. Dale.* Ah, and here's the other—the one I—the one I didn't answer—for a long time. Do you remember?

*Ventnor (with emotion).* Do I remember? I wrote it the morning after we heard *Isolde*—

*Mrs. Dale (disappointed).* No—no. *That* wasn't the one I didn't answer! Here—this is the one I mean.

*Ventnor (takes it curiously).* Ah—h'm—this is very like unrolling a mummy—*(he glances at her)*—with a live grain of wheat in it, perhaps?— Oh, by Jove!

## "COPY"

*Mrs. Dale.* What?

*Ventnor.* Why, this is the one I made a sonnet out of afterward! By Jove, I'd forgotten where that idea came from. You may know the lines perhaps? They're in the fourth volume of my *Complete Edition*—It's the thing beginning

*Love came to me with unrelenting eyes—*

one of my best, I rather fancy. Of course, here it's very crudely put—the values aren't brought out—ah! this touch is good though—very good. H'm, I daresay there might be other material. *(He glances toward the cabinet.)*

*Mrs. Dale (drily).* The live grain of wheat, as you said!

*Ventnor.* Ah, well—my first harvest was sown on rocky ground—*now* I plant for the fowls of the air. *(Rising and walking toward the cabinet.)* When can I come and carry off all this rubbish?

*Mrs. Dale.* Carry it off?

*Ventnor (embarrassed).* My dear lady, surely between you and me explicitness is a burden. You must see that these letters of ours can't be left to take their chance like an ordinary correspondence—you said yourself we were public property.

*Mrs. Dale.* To take their chance? Do you suppose that, in my keeping, your letters take any chances? *(Suddenly.)* Do mine—in yours?

[ 111 ]

## "COPY"

*Ventnor (still more embarrassed).* Helen—! *(He takes a turn through the room.)* You force me to remind you that you and I are differently situated—that in a moment of madness I sacrificed the only right you ever gave me—the right to love you better than any other woman in the world. *(A pause. She says nothing and he continues, with increasing difficulty—)* You asked me just now why I carried your letters about with me—kept them, literally, in my own hands. Well, suppose it's to be sure of their not falling into some one else's?

*Mrs. Dale.* Oh!

*Ventnor (throws himself into a chair).* For God's sake don't pity me!

*Mrs. Dale (after a long pause).* Am I dull—or are you trying to say that you want to give me back my letters?

*Ventnor (starting up).* I? Give you back—? God forbid! Your letters? Not for the world! The only thing I have left! But you can't dream that in *my* hands—

*Mrs. Dale (suddenly).* You want yours, then?

*Ventnor (repressing his eagerness).* My dear friend, if I'd ever dreamed that you'd kept them—?

*Mrs. Dale (accusingly).* You *do* want them. *(A pause. He makes a deprecatory gesture.)* Why should they be less safe with me than mine with you? *I* never forfeited the right to keep them.

*Ventnor (after another pause).* It's compensation

## "COPY"

enough, almost, to have you reproach me! *(He moves nearer to her, but she makes no response.)* You forget that I've forfeited *all* my rights—even that of letting you keep my letters.

*Mrs. Dale.* You *do* want them! *(She rises, throws all the letters into the cabinet, locks the door and puts the key in her pocket.)* There's my answer.

*Ventnor.* Helen—!

*Mrs. Dale.* Ah, I paid dearly enough for the right to keep them, and I mean to! *(She turns to him passionately.)* Have you ever asked yourself how I paid for it? With what months and years of solitude, what indifference to flattery, what resistance to affection?—Oh, don't smile because I said affection, and not love. Affection's a warm cloak in cold weather; and I *have* been cold; and I shall keep on growing colder! Don't talk to me about living in the hearts of my readers! We both know what kind of a domicile that is. Why, before long I shall become a classic! Bound in sets and kept on the top book-shelf—brr, doesn't that sound freezing? I foresee the day when I shall be as lonely as an Etruscan museum! *(She breaks into a laugh.)* That's what I've paid for the right to keep your letters. *(She holds out her hand.)* And now give me mine.

*Ventnor.* Yours?

*Mrs. Dale (haughtily).* Yes; I claim them.

*Ventnor (in the same tone).* On what ground?

## "COPY"

*Mrs. Dale.* Hear the man!—Because I wrote them, of course.

*Ventnor.* But it seems to me that—under your inspiration, I admit—I also wrote mine.

*Mrs. Dale.* Oh, I don't dispute their authenticity— it's yours I deny!

*Ventnor.* Mine?

*Mrs. Dale.* You voluntarily ceased to be the man who wrote me those letters—you've admitted as much. You traded paper for flesh and blood. I don't dispute your wisdom—only you must hold to your bargain! The letters are *all* mine.

*Ventnor (groping between two tones).* Your arguments are as convincing as ever. *(He hazards a faint laugh.)* You're a marvellous dialectician—but, if we're going to settle the matter in the spirit of an arbitration treaty, why, there are accepted conventions in such cases. It's an odious way to put it, but since you won't help me, one of them is—

*Mrs. Dale.* One of them is—?

*Ventnor.* That it is usual—that technically, I mean, the letter—belongs to its writer—

*Mrs. Dale (after a pause).* Such letters as *these?*

*Ventnor.* Such letters especially—

*Mrs. Dale.* But you could n't have written them if I had n't—been willing to read them. Surely there's more of myself in them than of you.

## "COPY"

*Ventnor.* Surely there's nothing in which a man puts more of himself than in his love-letters!

*Mrs. Dale (with emotion).* But a woman's love-letters are like her child. They belong to her more than to anybody else —

*Ventnor.* And a man's?

*Mrs. Dale (with sudden violence).* Are all he risks! — There, take them. *(She flings the key of the cabinet at his feet and sinks into a chair.)*

*Ventnor (starts as though to pick up the key; then approaches and bends over her).* Helen — oh, Helen!

*Mrs. Dale (she yields her hands to him, murmuring:)* Paul! *(Suddenly she straightens herself and draws back illuminated.)* What a fool I am! I see it all now. You want them for your memoirs!

*Ventnor (disconcerted).* Helen —

*Mrs. Dale (agitated).* Come, come — the rule is to unmask when the signal's given! You want them for your memoirs.

*Ventnor (with a forced laugh).* What makes you think so?

*Mrs. Dale (triumphantly).* Because *I* want them for mine!

*Ventnor (in a changed tone).* Ah —. *(He moves away from her and leans against the mantelpiece. She remains seated, with her eyes fixed on him.)*

*Mrs. Dale.* I wonder I didn't see it sooner. Your reasons were lame enough.

## "COPY"

*Ventnor (ironically).* Yours were masterly. You're the more accomplished actor of the two. I was completely deceived.

*Mrs. Dale.* Oh, I'm a novelist. I can keep up that sort of thing for five hundred pages!

*Ventnor.* I congratulate you. *(A pause.)*

*Mrs. Dale (moving to her seat behind the tea-table).* I've never offered you any tea. *(She bends over the kettle.)* Why don't you take your letters?

*Ventnor.* Because you've been clever enough to make it impossible for me. *(He picks up the key and hands it to her. Then abruptly)*—*Was* it all acting—just now?

*Mrs. Dale.* By what right do you ask?

*Ventnor.* By right of renouncing my claim to my letters. Keep them—and tell me.

*Mrs. Dale.* I give you back your claim—and I refuse to tell you.

*Ventnor (sadly).* Ah, Helen, if you deceived me, you deceived yourself also.

*Mrs. Dale.* What does it matter, now that we're both undeceived? I played a losing game, that's all.

*Ventnor.* Why losing—since all the letters are yours?

*Mrs. Dale.* The letters? *(Slowly.)* I'd forgotten the letters—

*Ventnor (exultant).* Ah, I knew you'd end by telling me the truth!

*Mrs. Dale.* The truth? Where *is* the truth? *(Half to*

## "COPY"

*herself.)* I thought I was lying when I began—but the lies turned into truth as I uttered them! *(She looks at Ventnor.)* I *did* want your letters for my memoirs—I *did* think I'd kept them for that purpose—and I wanted to get mine back for the same reason—but now *(she puts out her hand and picks up some of her letters, which are lying scattered on the table near her)*—how fresh they seem, and how they take me back to the time when we lived instead of writing about life!

*Ventnor (smiling).* The time when we didn't prepare our impromptu effects beforehand and copyright our remarks about the weather!

*Mrs. Dale.* Or keep our epigrams in cold storage and our adjectives under lock and key!

*Ventnor.* When our emotions weren't worth ten cents a word, and a signature wasn't an autograph. Ah, Helen, after all, there's nothing like the exhilaration of spending one's capital!

*Mrs. Dale.* Of wasting it, you mean. *(She points to the letters.)* Do you suppose we could have written a word of these if we'd known we were putting our dreams out at interest? *(She sits musing, with her eyes on the fire, and he watches her in silence.)* Paul, do you remember the deserted garden we sometimes used to walk in?

*Ventnor.* The old garden with the high wall at the end of the village street? The garden with the ruined

## "COPY"

box-borders and the broken-down arbor? Why, I remember every weed in the paths and every patch of moss on the walls!

*Mrs. Dale.* Well—I went back there the other day. The village is immensely improved. There's a new hotel with gas-fires, and a trolley in the main street; and the garden has been turned into a public park, where excursionists sit on cast-iron benches admiring the statue of an Abolitionist.

*Ventnor.* An Abolitionist—how appropriate!

*Mrs. Dale.* And the man who sold the garden has made a fortune that he does n't know how to spend—

*Ventnor (rising impulsively).* Helen, *(he approaches and lays his hand on her letters),* let's sacrifice our fortune and keep the excursionists out!

*Mrs. Dale (with a responsive movement).* Paul, do you really mean it?

*Ventnor (gayly).* Mean it? Why, I feel like a landed proprietor already! It's more than a garden—it's a park.

*Mrs. Dale.* It's more than a park, it's a world—as long as we keep it to ourselves!

*Ventnor* Ah, yes—even the pyramids look small when one sees a Cook's tourist on top of them! *(He takes the key from the table, unlocks the cabinet and brings out his letters, which he lays beside hers.)* Shall we burn the key to our garden?

## "COPY"

*Mrs. Dale.* Ah, then it will indeed be boundless! *(Watching him while he throws the letters into the fire.)*

*Ventnor (turning back to her with a half-sad smile).* But not too big for us to find each other in?

*Mrs. Dale.* Since we shall be the only people there! *(He takes both her hands and they look at each other a moment in silence. Then he goes out by the door to the right. As he reaches the door she takes a step toward him, impulsively; then turning back she leans against the chimney-piece, quietly watching the letters burn.)*

# THE REMBRANDT

# THE REMBRANDT

"YOU'RE *so* artistic," my cousin Eleanor Copt began.

Of all Eleanor's exordiums it is the one I most dread. When she tells me I'm so clever I know this is merely the preamble to inviting me to meet the last literary obscurity of the moment: a trial to be evaded or endured, as circumstances dictate; whereas her calling me artistic fatally connotes the request to visit, in her company, some distressed gentlewoman whose future hangs on my valuation of her old Saxe or of her grandfather's Marc Antonios. Time was when I attempted to resist these compulsions of Eleanor's; but I soon learned that, short of actual flight, there was no refuge from her beneficent despotism. It is not always easy for the curator of a museum to abandon his post on the plea of escaping a pretty cousin's importunities; and Eleanor, aware of my predicament, is none too magnanimous to take advantage of it. Magnanimity is, in fact, not in Eleanor's line. The virtues, she once explained to me, are like bonnets: the very ones that look best on other people may not happen to suit one's own particular style; and she added, with a slight deflection of metaphor, that none of the ready-made virtues ever *had* fitted her: they all pinched some-

[ 123 ]

# THE REMBRANDT

where, and she'd given up trying to wear them.

Therefore when she said to me, "You're *so* artistic," emphasizing the conjunction with a tap of her dripping umbrella (Eleanor is out in all weathers: the elements are as powerless against her as man), I merely stipulated, "It's not old Saxe again?"

She shook her head reassuringly. "A picture—a Rembrandt!"

"Good Lord! Why not a Leonardo?"

"Well"—she smiled—"that, of course, depends on *you*."

"On me?"

"On your attribution. I dare say Mrs. Fontage would consent to the change—though she's very conservative."

A gleam of hope came to me and I pronounced: "One can't judge of a picture in this weather."

"Of course not. I'm coming for you to-morrow."

"I've an engagement to-morrow."

"I'll come before or after your engagement."

The afternoon paper lay at my elbow and I contrived a furtive consultation of the weather-report. It said "Rain to-morrow," and I answered briskly: "All right, then; come at ten"—rapidly calculating that the clouds on which I counted might lift by noon.

My ingenuity failed of its due reward; for the heavens, as if in league with my cousin, emptied themselves

# THE REMBRANDT

before morning, and punctually at ten Eleanor and the sun appeared together in my office.

I hardly listened, as we descended the Museum steps and got into Eleanor's hansom, to her vivid summing-up of the case. I guessed beforehand that the lady we were about to visit had lapsed by the most distressful degrees from opulence to a "hall-bedroom"; that her grandfather, if he had not been Minister to France, had signed the Declaration of Independence; that the Rembrandt was an heirloom, sole remnant of disbanded treasures; that for years its possessor had been unwilling to part with it, and that even now the question of its disposal must be approached with the most diplomatic obliquity.

Previous experience had taught me that all Eleanor's "cases" presented a harrowing similarity of detail. No circumstance tending to excite the spectator's sympathy and involve his action was omitted from the history of her beneficiaries; the lights and shades were indeed so skilfully adjusted that any impartial expression of opinion took on the hue of cruelty. I could have produced closetfuls of "heirlooms" in attestation of this fact; for it is one more mark of Eleanor's competence that her friends usually pay the interest on her philanthropy. My one hope was that in this case the object, being a picture, might reasonably be rated beyond my means; and as our cab drew up before a blistered brown-stone door-step I formed the self-defensive resolve to place

# THE REMBRANDT

an extreme valuation on Mrs. Fontage's Rembrandt. It is Eleanor's fault if she is sometimes fought with her own weapons.

The house stood in one of those shabby provisional-looking New York streets that seem resignedly awaiting demolition. It was the kind of house that, in its high days, must have had a bow-window with a bronze in it. The bow-window had been replaced by a plumber's *devanture,* and one might conceive the bronze to have gravitated to the limbo where Mexican onyx tables and bric-à-brac in buffalo-horn await the first signs of our next æsthetic reaction.

Eleanor swept me through a hall that smelled of poverty, up unlit stairs to a bare slit of a room. "And she must leave this in a month!" she whispered across her knock.

I had prepared myself for the limp widow's weed of a woman that one figures in such a setting; and confronted abruptly with Mrs. Fontage's white-haired erectness I had the disconcerting sense that I was somehow in her presence at my own solicitation. I instinctively charged Eleanor with this reversal of the situation; but a moment later I saw it must be ascribed to a something about Mrs. Fontage that precluded the possibility of her asking any one a favor. It was not that she was of forbidding, or even majestic, demeanor; but that one guessed, under her aquiline prettiness, a

# THE REMBRANDT

dignity nervously on guard against the petty betrayal of her surroundings. The room was unconcealably poor: the little faded "relics," the high-stocked ancestral silhouettes, the steel-engravings after Raphael and Correggio, grouped in a vain attempt to hide the most obvious stains on the wall-paper, served only to accentuate the contrast of a past evidently diversified by foreign travel and the enjoyment of the arts. Even Mrs. Fontage's dress had the air of being a last expedient, the ultimate outcome of a much-taxed ingenuity in darning and turning. One felt that all the poor lady's barriers were falling save that of her impregnable manner.

To this manner I found myself conveying my appreciation of being admitted to a view of the Rembrandt.

Mrs. Fontage's smile took my homage for granted. "It is always," she conceded, "a privilege to be in the presence of the great masters." Her slim wrinkled hand waved me to a dusky canvas near the window.

"It's *so* interesting, dear Mrs. Fontage," I heard Eleanor exclaiming, "and my cousin will be able to tell you exactly—" Eleanor, in my presence, always admits that she knows nothing about art; but she gives the impression that this is merely because she hasn't had time to look into the matter—and has had me to do it for her.

Mrs. Fontage seated herself without speaking, as

## THE REMBRANDT

though fearful that a breath might disturb my communion with the masterpiece. I felt that she thought Eleanor's reassuring ejaculations ill-timed; and in this I was of one mind with her; for the impossibility of telling her exactly what I thought of her Rembrandt had become clear to me at a glance.

My cousin's vivacities began to languish and the silence seemed to shape itself into a receptacle for my verdict. I stepped back, affecting a more distant scrutiny; and as I did so my eye caught Mrs. Fontage's profile. Her lids trembled slightly. I took refuge in the familiar expedient of asking the history of the picture, and she waved me brightly to a seat.

This was indeed a topic on which she could dilate. The Rembrandt, it appeared, had come into Mr. Fontage's possession many years ago, while the young couple were on their wedding-tour, and under circumstances so romantic that she made no excuse for relating them in all their parenthetic fulness. The picture belonged to an old Belgian Countess of redundant quarterings, whom the extravagances of an ungovernable nephew had compelled to part with her possessions (in the most private manner) about the time of the Fontages' arrival. By a really remarkable coincidence, it happened that their courier (an exceptionally intelligent and superior man) was an old servant of the Countess's, and had thus been able to put them in

# THE REMBRANDT

the way of securing the Rembrandt under the very nose of an English Duke, whose agent had been sent to Brussels to negotiate for its purchase. Mrs. Fontage could not recall the Duke's name, but he was a great collector and had a famous Highland castle, where somebody had been murdered, and which she herself had visited (by moonlight) when she had travelled in Scotland as a girl. The episode had in short been one of the most interesting "experiences" of a tour almost chromo-lithographic in vivacity of impression; and they had always meant to go back to Brussels for the sake of reliving so picturesque a moment. Circumstances (of which the narrator's surroundings declared the nature) had persistently interfered with the projected return to Europe, and the picture had grown doubly valuable as representing the high-water mark of their artistic emotions. Mrs. Fontage's moist eye caressed the canvas. "There is only," she added with a perceptible effort, "one slight drawback: the picture is not signed. But for that the Countess, of course, would have sold it to a museum. All the connoisseurs who have seen it pronounce it an undoubted Rembrandt, in the artist's best manner; but the museums"—she arched her brows in smiling recognition of a well-known weakness—"give the preference to signed examples—"

Mrs. Fontage's words evoked so touching a vision of the young tourists of fifty years ago, entrusting to an

# THE REMBRANDT

accomplished and versatile courier the direction of their helpless zeal for art, that I lost sight for a moment of the point at issue. The old Belgian Countess, the wealthy Duke with a feudal castle in Scotland, Mrs. Fontage's own maiden pilgrimage to Arthur's Seat and Holyrood, all the accessories of the naïf transaction, seemed a part of that vanished Europe to which our young race carried its indiscriminate ardors, its tender romantic credulity: the legendary castellated Europe of keepsakes, brigands and old masters, that compensated, by one such "experience" as Mrs. Fontage's, for an after-life of æsthetic privation.

I was restored to the present by Eleanor's looking at her watch. The action mutely conveyed that something was expected of me. I risked the temporizing statement that the picture was very interesting; but Mrs. Fontage's polite assent revealed the poverty of the expedient. Eleanor's impatience overflowed.

"You would like my cousin to give you an idea of its value?" she suggested.

Mrs. Fontage grew more erect. "No one," she corrected with great gentleness, "can know its value quite as well as I, who live with it—"

We murmured our hasty concurrence.

"But it might be interesting to hear"—she addressed herself to me—"as a mere matter of curiosity—what estimate would be put on it from the purely

# THE REMBRANDT

commercial point of view—if such a term may be used in speaking of a work of art."

I sounded a note of deprecation.

"Oh, I understand, of course," she delicately anticipated me, "that that could never be *your* view, your personal view; but since occasions *may* arise—do arise —when it becomes necessary to—to put a price on the priceless, as it were—I have thought—Miss Copt has suggested—"

"Some day," Eleanor encouraged her, "you might feel that the picture ought to belong to some one who has more—more opportunity of showing it—letting it be seen by the public—for educational reasons—"

"I have tried," Mrs. Fontage admitted, "to see it in that light."

The crucial moment was upon me. To escape the challenge of Mrs. Fontage's brilliant composure I turned once more to the picture. If my courage needed reinforcement, the picture amply furnished it. Looking at that lamentable canvas seemed the surest way of gathering strength to denounce it; but behind me, all the while, I felt Mrs. Fontage's shuddering pride drawn up in a final effort of self-defense. I hated myself for my sentimental perversion of the situation. Reason argued that it was more cruel to deceive Mrs. Fontage than to tell her the truth; but that merely proved the inferiority of reason to instinct in situations

## THE REMBRANDT

involving any concession to the emotions. Along with her faith in the Rembrandt I must destroy not only the whole fabric of Mrs. Fontage's past, but even that lifelong habit of acquiescence in untested formulas that makes the best part of the average feminine strength. I guessed the episode of the picture to be inextricably interwoven with the traditions and convictions which served to veil Mrs. Fontage's destitution not only from others but from herself. Viewed in that light the Rembrandt had perhaps been worth its purchase-money; and I regretted that works of art do not commonly sell on the merit of the moral support they may have rendered.

From this unavailing flight I was recalled by the sense that something must be done. To place a fictitious value on the picture was at best a provisional measure; while the brutal alternative of advising Mrs. Fontage to sell it for a hundred dollars at least afforded an opening to the charitably disposed purchaser. I intended, if other resources failed, to put myself forward in that light; but delicacy of course forbade my coupling my unflattering estimate of the Rembrandt with an immediate offer to buy it. All I could do was to inflict the wound: the healing unguent must be withheld for later application.

I turned to Mrs. Fontage, who sat motionless, her finely-lined cheeks touched with an expectant color,

# THE REMBRANDT

her eyes averted from the picture which was so evidently the one object they beheld.

"My dear madam—" I began. Her vivid smile was like a light held up to dazzle me. It shrouded every alternative in darkness and I had the flurried sense of having lost my way among the intricacies of my contention. Of a sudden I felt the hopelessness of finding a crack in her impenetrable conviction. My words slipped from me like broken weapons. "The picture," I faltered, "would of course be worth more if it were signed. As it is, I—I hardly think—on a conservative estimate—it can be valued at—at more—than—a thousand dollars, say—"

My deflected argument ran on somewhat aimlessly till it found itself plunging full tilt against the barrier of Mrs. Fontage's silence. She sat as impassive as though I had not spoken. Eleanor loosed a few fluttering words of congratulation and encouragement, but their flight was suddenly cut short. Mrs. Fontage had risen with a certain solemnity.

"I could never," she said gently—her gentleness was adamantine—"under any circumstances whatever, consider, for a moment even, the possibility of parting with the picture at such a price."

# THE REMBRANDT

## II

WITHIN three weeks a tremulous note from Mrs. Fontage requested the favor of another visit. If the writing was tremulous, however, the writer's tone was firm. She named her own day and hour, without the conventional reference to her visitor's convenience.

My first impulse was to turn the note over to Eleanor. I had acquitted myself of my share in the ungrateful business of coming to Mrs. Fontage's aid, and if, as her letter denoted, she had now yielded to the closer pressure of need, the business of finding a purchaser for the Rembrandt might well be left to my cousin's ingenuity. But here conscience put in the uncomfortable reminder that it was I who, in putting a price on the picture, had raised the real obstacle in the way of Mrs. Fontage's rescue. No one would give a thousand dollars for the Rembrandt; but to tell Mrs. Fontage so had become as unthinkable as murder. I had, in fact, on returning from my first inspection of the picture, refrained from imparting to Eleanor my opinion of its value. Eleanor is porous, and I knew that sooner or later the unnecessary truth would exude through the loose texture of her dissimulation. Not infrequently she thus creates the misery she alleviates; and I have sometimes suspected her of paining people in order

## THE REMBRANDT

that she might be sorry for them. I had, at all events, cut off retreat in Eleanor's direction; and the remaining alternative carried me straight to Mrs. Fontage.

She received me with the same commanding sweetness. The room was even barer than before—I believe the carpet was gone—but her manner built up about her a palace to which I was welcomed with high state; and it was as a mere incident of the ceremony that I was presently made aware of her decision to sell the Rembrandt. My previous unsuccess in planning how to deal with Mrs. Fontage had warned me to leave my farther course to chance; and I listened to her explanation with complete detachment. She had resolved to travel for her health; her doctor advised it, and as her absence might be indefinitely prolonged she had reluctantly decided to part with the picture in order to avoid the expense of storage and insurance. Her voice drooped at the admission, and she hurried on, detailing the vague itinerary of a journey that was to combine long-promised visits to impatient friends with various "interesting opportunities" less definitely specified. The poor lady's skill in rearing a screen of verbiage about her enforced avowal had distracted me from my own share in the situation, and it was with dismay that I suddenly caught the drift of her assumptions. She expected me to buy the Rembrandt for the Museum; she had taken my previous valuation as a tentative bid,

# THE REMBRANDT

and when I came to my senses she was in the act of accepting my offer.

Had I had a thousand dollars of my own to dispose of, the bargain would have been concluded on the spot; but I was in the impossible position of being materially unable to buy the picture and morally unable to tell her that it was not worth acquiring for the Museum.

I dashed into the first evasion in sight. I had no authority, I explained, to purchase pictures for the Museum without the consent of the committee.

Mrs. Fontage coped for a moment in silence with the incredible fact that I had rejected her offer; then she ventured, with a kind of pale precipitation: "But I understood—Miss Copt tells me that you practically decide such matters for the committee." I could guess what the effort had cost her.

"My cousin is given to generalizations. My opinion may have some weight with the committee—"

"Well, then—" she timidly prompted.

"For that very reason I can't buy the picture."

She said, with a drooping note, "I don't understand."

"Yet you told me," I reminded her, "that you knew museums didn't buy unsigned pictures."

"Not for what they are worth! Every one knows that. But I—I understood—the price you named—" Her pride shuddered back from the abasement. "It's a misunderstanding then," she faltered.

# THE REMBRANDT

To avoid looking at her, I glanced desperately at the Rembrandt. Could I—? But reason rejected the possibility. Even if the committee had been blind—and they all *were* but Crozier—I simply shouldn't have dared to do it. I stood up, feeling that to cut the matter short was the only alleviation within reach.

Mrs. Fontage had summoned her indomitable smile; but its brilliancy dropped, as I opened the door, like a candle blown out by a draught.

"If there's any one else—if you knew any one who would care to see the picture, I should be most happy—" She kept her eyes on me, and I saw that, in her case, it hurt less than to look at the Rembrandt. "I shall have to leave here, you know," she panted, "if nobody cares to have it—"

## III

THAT evening at my club I had just succeeded in losing sight of Mrs. Fontage in the fumes of an excellent cigar, when a voice at my elbow evoked her harassing image.

"I want to talk to you," the speaker said, "about Mrs. Fontage's Rembrandt."

"There isn't any," I was about to growl; but looking up I recognized the confiding countenance of Mr. Jefferson Rose.

Mr. Rose was known to me chiefly as a young man

## THE REMBRANDT

suffused with a vague enthusiasm for Virtue and my cousin Eleanor.

One glance at his glossy exterior conveyed the assurance that his morals were as immaculate as his complexion and his linen. Goodness exuded from his moist eye, his liquid voice, the warm damp pressure of his trustful hand. He had always struck me as one of the most uncomplicated organisms I had ever met. His ideas were as simple and inconsecutive as the propositions in a primer, and he spoke slowly, with a kind of uniformity of emphasis that made his words stand out like the raised type for the blind. An obvious incapacity for abstract conceptions made him peculiarly susceptible to the magic of generalization, and one felt he would have been at the mercy of any Cause that spelled itself with a capital letter. It was hard to explain how, with such a superabundance of merit, he managed to be a good fellow: I can only say that he performed the astonishing feat as naturally as he supported an invalid mother and two sisters on the slender salary of a banker's clerk. He sat down beside me with an air of bright expectancy.

"It's a remarkable picture, isn't it?" he said.

"You've seen it?"

"I've been so fortunate. Miss Copt was kind enough to get Mrs. Fontage's permission; we went this afternoon."

# THE REMBRANDT

I inwardly wished that Eleanor had selected another victim; unless indeed the visit were part of a plan whereby some third person, better equipped for the cultivation of delusions, was to be made to think the Rembrandt remarkable. Knowing the limitations of Mr. Rose's resources I began to wonder if he had any rich aunts.

"And her buying it in that way, too," he went on with his limpid smile, "from that old Countess in Brussels, makes it all the more interesting, does n't it? Miss Copt tells me it's very seldom old pictures can be traced back for more than a generation. I suppose the fact of Mrs. Fontage's knowing its history must add a good deal to its value?"

Uncertain as to his drift, I said: "In her eyes it certainly appears to."

Implications are lost on Mr. Rose, who glowingly continued: "That's the reason why I wanted to talk to you about it—to consult you. Miss Copt tells me you value it at a thousand dollars."

There was no denying this, and I grunted a reluctant assent.

"Of course," he went on earnestly, "your valuation is based on the fact that the picture is n't signed— Mrs. Fontage explained that; and it *does* make a difference, certainly. But the thing is—if the picture's really good—ought one to take advantage—? I mean

# THE REMBRANDT

—one can see that Mrs. Fontage is in a tight place, and I wouldn't for the world—"

My astonished stare arrested him.

"*You* wouldn't—?"

"I mean—you see, it's just this way"; he coughed and blushed: "I can't give more than a thousand dollars myself—it's as big a sum as I can manage to scrape together—but before I make the offer I want to be sure I'm not standing in the way of her getting more money."

My astonishment lapsed to dismay. "You're going to buy the picture for a thousand dollars?"

His blush deepened. "Why, yes. It sounds rather absurd, I suppose. It isn't much in my line, of course. I can see the picture's very beautiful, but I'm no judge—it isn't the kind of thing, naturally, that I could afford to go in for; but in this case I'm very glad to do what I can; the circumstances are so distressing; and knowing what you think of the picture I feel it's a pretty safe investment—"

"I don't think!" I blurted out.

"You—?"

"I don't think the picture's worth a thousand dollars; I don't think it's worth ten cents; I simply lied about it, that's all."

Mr. Rose looked as frightened as though I had charged him with the offense.

# THE REMBRANDT

"Hang it, man, can't you see how it happened? I saw the poor woman's pride and happiness hung on her faith in that picture. I tried to make her understand that it was worthless—but she would n't; I tried to tell her so—but I could n't. I behaved like a maudlin ass, but you shan't pay for my infernal bungling—you must n't buy the picture!"

Mr. Rose sat silent, tapping one glossy boot-tip with another. Suddenly he turned on me a glance of stored intelligence. "But you know," he said good-humoredly, "I rather think I must."

"You have n't—already?"

"Oh, no; the offer's not made."

"Well, then—"

His look gathered a brighter significance.

"But if the picture's worth nothing, nobody will buy it—"

I groaned.

"Except," he continued, "some fellow like me, who does n't know anything. *I* think it's lovely, you know; I mean to hang it in my mother's sitting-room." He rose and clasped my hand in his adhesive pressure. "I'm awfully obliged to you for telling me this; but perhaps you won't mind my asking you not to mention our talk to Miss Copt? It might bother her, you know, to think the picture is n't exactly up to the mark; and it won't make a rap of difference to me."

[ 141 ]

# THE REMBRANDT

## IV

MR. ROSE left me to a sleepless night. The next morning my resolve was formed, and it carried me straight to Mrs. Fontage's. She answered my knock by stepping out on the landing, and as she shut the door behind her I caught a glimpse of her devastated interior. She mentioned, with a careful avoidance of the note of pathos on which our last conversation had closed, that she was preparing to leave that afternoon; and the trunks obstructing the threshold showed that her preparations were nearly complete. They were, I felt certain, the same trunks that, strapped behind a rattling vettura, had accompanied the bride and groom on that memorable voyage of discovery of which the booty had till recently adorned her walls; and there was a dim consolation in the thought that those early "finds" in coral and Swiss wood-carving, in lava and alabaster, still lay behind the worn locks, in the security of worthlessness.

Mrs. Fontage, on the landing, among her strapped and corded treasures, maintained the same air of stability that made it impossible, even under such conditions, to regard her flight as anything less dignified than a departure. It was the moral support of what she tacitly assumed that enabled me to set forth with proper deliberation the object of my visit; and she re-

## THE REMBRANDT

ceived my announcement with an absence of surprise that struck me as the very flower of tact. Under cover of these mutual assumptions the transaction was rapidly concluded; and it was not till the canvas passed into my hands that, as though the physical contact had unnerved her, Mrs. Fontage suddenly faltered. "It's the giving it up—" she stammered, disguising herself to the last; and I hastened away from the collapse of her splendid effrontery.

I need hardly point out that I had acted impulsively, and that reaction from the most honorable impulses is sometimes attended by moral perturbation. My motives had indeed been mixed enough to justify some uneasiness, but this was allayed by the instinctive feeling that it is more venial to defraud an institution than a man. Since Mrs. Fontage had to be kept from starving by means not wholly defensible, it was better that the obligation should be borne by a rich institution than an impecunious youth. I doubt, in fact, if my scruples would have survived a night's sleep, had they not been complicated by some uncertainty as to my own future. It was true that, subject to the purely formal assent of the committee, I had full power to buy for the Museum, and that the one member of the committee likely to dispute my decision was opportunely travelling in Europe; but the picture once in place I must face the risk of any expert criticism to which chance

## THE REMBRANDT

might expose it. I dismissed this contingency for future study, stored the Rembrandt in the cellar of the Museum, and thanked heaven that Crozier was abroad.

Six months later he strolled into my office. I had just concluded, under conditions of exceptional difficulty, and on terms unexpectedly benign, the purchase of the great Bartley Reynolds; and this circumstance, by relegating the matter of the Rembrandt to a lower stratum of consciousness, enabled me to welcome Crozier with unmixed pleasure. My security was enhanced by his appearance. His smile was charged with amiable reminiscences, and I inferred that his trip had put him in the humor to approve of everything, or at least to ignore what fell short of his approval. I had therefore no uneasiness in accepting his invitation to dine that evening. It is always pleasant to dine with Crozier and never more so than when he is just back from Europe. His conversation gives even the food a flavor of the Café Anglais.

The repast was delightful, and it was not till we had finished a Camembert which he must have brought over with him, that my host said, in a tone of after-dinner perfunctoriness: "I see you've picked up a picture or two since I left."

I assented. "The Bartley Reynolds seemed too good an opportunity to miss, especially as the French government was after it. I think we got it cheap—"

# THE REMBRANDT

"*Connu, connu,*" said Crozier pleasantly. "I know all about the Reynolds. It was the biggest kind of a haul and I congratulate you. Best stroke of business we've done yet. But tell me about the other picture—the Rembrandt."

"I never said it was a Rembrandt." I could hardly have said why, but I felt distinctly annoyed with Crozier.

"Of course not. There's 'Rembrandt' on the frame, but I saw you'd modified it to 'Dutch School'; I apologize." He paused, but I offered no explanation. "What about it?" he went on. "Where did you pick it up?" As he leaned to the flame of the cigar-lighter his face seemed ruddy with enjoyment.

"I got it for a song," I said.

"A thousand, I think?"

"Have you seen it?" I asked abruptly.

"Went over the place this afternoon and found it in the cellar. Why hasn't it been hung, by the way?"

I paused a moment. "I'm waiting—"

"To—?"

"To have it varnished."

"Ah!" He leaned back and poured himself a second glass of Chartreuse. The smile he confided to its golden depths provoked me to challenge him with—

"What do you think of it?"

"The Rembrandt?" He lifted his eyes from the glass. "Just what you do."

# THE REMBRANDT

"It is n't a Rembrandt."

"I apologize again. You call it, I believe, a picture of the same period?"

"I 'm uncertain of the period."

"H'm." He glanced appreciatively along his cigar. "What are you certain of?"

"That it 's a damned bad picture," I said savagely.

He nodded. "Just so. That 's all we wanted to know."

"*We?*"

"We—I—the committee, in short. You see, my dear fellow, if you had n't been certain it was a damned bad picture our position would have been a little awkward. As it is, my remaining duty—I ought to explain that in this matter I 'm acting for the committee—is as simple as it 's agreeable."

"I 'll be hanged," I burst out, "if I understand one word you 're saying!"

He fixed me with a kind of cruel joyousness. "You will—you will," he assured me; "at least you 'll begin to, when you hear that I 've seen Miss Copt."

"Miss Copt?"

"And that she has told me under what conditions the picture was bought."

"She does n't know anything about the conditions! That is," I added, hastening to restrict the assertion, "she does n't know my opinion of the picture." I thirsted for five minutes with Eleanor.

[ 146 ]

# THE REMBRANDT

"Are you quite sure?" Crozier took me up. "Mr. Jefferson Rose does."

"Ah—I see."

"I thought you would," he reminded me. "As soon as I'd laid eyes on the Rembrandt—I beg your pardon!—I saw that it—well, required some explanation."

"You might have come to me."

"I meant to; but I happened to meet Miss Copt, whose encyclopædic information has often before been of service to me. I always go to Miss Copt when I want to look up anything; and I found she knew all about the Rembrandt."

"*All?*"

"Precisely. The knowledge was in fact causing her sleepless nights. Mr. Rose, who was suffering from the same form of insomnia, had taken her into his confidence, and she—ultimately—took me into hers."

"Of course!"

"I must ask you to do your cousin justice. She didn't speak till it became evident to her uncommonly quick perceptions that your buying the picture on its merits would have been infinitely worse for—for everybody—than your diverting a small portion of the Museum's funds to philanthropic uses. Then she told me the moving incident of Mr. Rose. Good fellow, Rose. And the old lady's case was desperate. Somebody had to buy that picture." I moved uneasily in my seat.

# THE REMBRANDT

"Wait a moment, will you? I haven't finished my cigar. There's a little head of Il Fiammingo's that you haven't seen, by the way; I picked it up the other day in Parma. We'll go in and have a look at it presently. But meanwhile what I want to say is that I've been charged—in the most informal way—to express to you the committee's appreciation of your admirable promptness and energy in capturing the Bartley Reynolds. We shouldn't have got it at all if you hadn't been uncommonly wide-awake, and to get it at such a price is a double triumph. We'd have thought nothing of a few more thousands—"

"I don't see," I impatiently interposed, "that, as far as I'm concerned, that alters the case."

"The case—?"

"Of Mrs. Fontage's Rembrandt. I bought the picture because, as you say, the situation was desperate, and I couldn't raise a thousand myself. What I did was of course indefensible; but the money shall be refunded to-morrow—"

Crozier raised a protesting hand. "Don't interrupt me when I'm talking ex cathedrâ. The money's been refunded already. The fact is, the Museum has sold the Rembrandt."

I stared at him wildly. "Sold it? To whom?"

"Why—to the committee.—Hold on a bit, please. —Won't you take another cigar? Then perhaps I can

## THE REMBRANDT

finish what I've got to say.—Why, my dear fellow, the committee's under an obligation to you—that's the way we look at it. I've investigated Mrs. Fontage's case, and—well, the picture had to be bought. She's eating meat now, I believe, for the first time in a year. And they'd have turned her out into the street that very day, your cousin tells me. Something had to be done at once, and you've simply given a number of well-to-do and self-indulgent gentlemen the opportunity of performing, at very small individual expense, a meritorious action in the nick of time. That's the first thing I've got to thank you for. And then—you'll remember, please, that I have the floor—that I'm still speaking for the committee—and secondly, as a slight recognition of your services in securing the Bartley Reynolds at a very much lower figure than we were prepared to pay, we beg you—the committee begs you—to accept the gift of Mrs. Fontage's Rembrandt. Now we'll go in and look at that little head. . . ."

# THE MOVING FINGER

# THE MOVING FINGER

THE news of Mrs. Grancy's death came to me with the shock of an immense blunder — one of fate's most irretrievable acts of vandalism. It was as though all sorts of renovating forces had been checked by the clogging of that one wheel. Not that Mrs. Grancy contributed any perceptible momentum to the social machine: her unique distinction was that of filling to perfection her special place in the world. So many people are like badly-composed statues, over-lapping their niches at one point and leaving them vacant at another. Mrs. Grancy's niche was her husband's life; and if it be argued that the space was not large enough for its vacancy to leave a very big gap, I can only say that, at the last resort, such dimensions must be determined by finer instruments than any ready-made standard of utility. Ralph Grancy's was in short a kind of disembodied usefulness: one of those constructive influences that, instead of crystallizing into definite forms, remain as it were a medium for the development of clear thinking and fine feeling. He faithfully irrigated his own dusty patch of life, and the fruitful moisture stole far beyond his boundaries. If, to carry on the metaphor, Grancy's life was a sedulously-cultivated enclosure, his wife was the flower he had planted in

# THE MOVING FINGER

its midst—the embowering tree, rather, which gave him rest and shade at its foot and the wind of dreams in its upper branches.

We had all—his small but devoted band of followers—known a moment when it seemed likely that Grancy would fail us. We had watched him pitted against one stupid obstacle after another—ill-health, poverty, misunderstanding and, worst of all for a man of his texture, his first wife's soft insidious egotism. We had seen him sinking under the leaden embrace of her affection like a swimmer in a drowning clutch; but just as we despaired he had always come to the surface again, blinded, panting, but striking out fiercely for the shore. When at last her death released him it became a question as to how much of the man she had carried with her. Left alone, he revealed numb withered patches, like a tree from which a parasite has been stripped. But gradually he began to put out new leaves; and when he met the lady who was to become his second wife—his one *real* wife, as his friends reckoned—the whole man burst into flower.

The second Mrs. Grancy was past thirty when he married her, and it was clear that she had harvested that crop of middle joy which is rooted in young despair. But if she had lost the surface of eighteen she had kept its inner light; if her cheek lacked the gloss of immaturity her eyes were young with the stored

# THE MOVING FINGER

youth of half a life-time. Grancy had first known her somewhere in the East—I believe she was the sister of one of our consuls out there—and when he brought her home to New York she came among us as a stranger. The idea of Grancy's remarriage had been a shock to us all. After one such calcining most men would have kept out of the fire; but we agreed that he was predestined to sentimental blunders, and we awaited with resignation the embodiment of his latest mistake. Then Mrs. Grancy came—and we understood. She was the most beautiful and the most complete of explanations. We shuffled our defeated omniscience out of sight and gave it hasty burial under a prodigality of welcome. For the first time in years we had Grancy off our minds. "He'll do something great now!" the least sanguine of us prophesied; and our sentimentalist emended: "He *has* done it—in marrying her!"

It was Claydon, the portrait-painter, who risked this hyperbole; and who soon afterward, at the happy husband's request, prepared to defend it in a portrait of Mrs. Grancy. We were all—even Claydon—ready to concede that Mrs. Grancy's unwontedness was in some degree a matter of environment. Her graces were complementary and it needed the mate's call to reveal the flash of color beneath her neutral-tinted wings. But if she needed Grancy to interpret her, how much greater was the service she rendered him! Claydon professionally described her as the right frame for him; but if she defined she also enlarged, if she threw the whole into perspective she also cleared new ground, opened fresh vistas, reclaimed whole areas of activity that had run to waste under the harsh husbandry of privation. This interaction of sympathies was not without its visible expression. Claydon was not alone in maintaining that Grancy's presence—or indeed the mere mention of his name—had a perceptible effect on his wife's appearance. It was as though a light were shifted, a curtain drawn back, as though, to borrow another of Claydon's metaphors, Love the indefatigable artist were perpetually seeking a happier "pose" for his model. In this interpretative light Mrs. Grancy acquired the charm which makes some women's faces like a book of which the last page is never turned. There was always something new to read in her eyes. What Claydon read there—or at least such scattered hints of the ritual as reached him through the sanctuary doors—his portrait in due course declared to us. When the picture was exhibited it was at once acclaimed as his masterpiece; but the people who knew Mrs. Grancy smiled and said it was flattered. Claydon, however, had not set out to paint *their* Mrs. Grancy—or ours even—but Ralph's; and Ralph knew his own at a glance. At the first confrontation he saw that Claydon had understood. As for Mrs. Grancy, when the finished picture was shown to

# THE MOVING FINGER

her she turned to the painter and said simply: "Ah, you've done me facing the east!"

The picture, then, for all its value, seemed a mere incident in the unfolding of their double destiny, a foot-note to the illuminated text of their lives. It was not till afterward that it acquired the significance of last words spoken on a threshold never to be recrossed. Grancy, a year after his marriage, had given up his town house and carried his bliss an hour's journey away, to a little place among the hills. His various duties and interests brought him frequently to New York but we necessarily saw him less often than when his house had served as the rallying-point of kindred enthusiasms. It seemed a pity that such an influence should be withdrawn, but we all felt that his long arrears of happiness should be paid in whatever coin he chose. The distance from which the fortunate couple radiated warmth on us was not too great for friendship to traverse; and our conception of a glorified leisure took the form of Sundays spent in the Grancys' library, with its sedative rural outlook, and the portrait of Mrs. Grancy illuminating its studious walls. The picture was at its best in that setting; and we used to accuse Claydon of visiting Mrs. Grancy in order to see her portrait. He met this by declaring that the portrait *was* Mrs. Grancy; and there were moments when the statement seemed unanswerable.

# THE MOVING FINGER

*faires* he acquitted himself, under trying conditions, with conspicuous zeal and discretion. A political redistribution of matter removed him from office just as he had proved his usefulness to the government; and the following summer I heard that he had come home and was down at his place in the country.

On my return to town I wrote him and his reply came by the next post. He answered as it were in his natural voice, urging me to spend the following Sunday with him, and suggesting that I should bring down any of the old set who could be persuaded to join me. I thought this a good sign, and yet—shall I own it?—I was vaguely disappointed. Perhaps we are apt to feel that our friends' sorrows should be kept like those historic monuments from which the encroaching ivy is periodically removed.

That very evening at the club I ran across Claydon. I told him of Grancy's invitation and proposed that we should go down together; but he pleaded an engagement. I was sorry, for I had always felt that he and I stood nearer Ralph than the others, and if the old Sundays were to be renewed I should have preferred that we two should spend the first alone with him. I said as much to Claydon and offered to fit my time to his; but he met this by a general refusal.

"I don't want to go to Grancy's," he said bluntly. I waited a moment, but he appended no qualifying clause.

# THE MOVING FINGER

"You've seen him since he came back?" I finally ventured.

Claydon nodded.

"And is he so awfully bad?"

"Bad? No: he's all right."

"All right? How can he be, unless he's changed beyond all recognition?"

"Oh, you'll recognize *him*," said Claydon, with a puzzling deflection of emphasis.

His ambiguity was beginning to exasperate me, and I felt myself shut out from some knowledge to which I had as good a right as he.

"You've been down there already, I suppose?"

"Yes; I've been down there."

"And you've done with each other—the partnership is dissolved?"

"Done with each other? I wish to God we had!" He rose nervously and tossed aside the review from which my approach had diverted him. "Look here," he said, standing before me, "Ralph's the best fellow going and there's nothing under heaven I wouldn't do for him—short of going down there again." And with that he walked out of the room.

Claydon was incalculable enough for me to read a dozen different meanings into his words; but none of my interpretations satisfied me. I determined, at any rate, to seek no farther for a companion; and the next

# THE MOVING FINGER

Sunday I travelled down to Grancy's alone. He met me at the station and I saw at once that he had changed since our last meeting. Then he had been in fighting array, but now if he and grief still housed together it was no longer as enemies. Physically the transformation was as marked but less reassuring. If the spirit triumphed the body showed its scars. At five-and-forty he was gray and stooping, with the tired gait of an old man. His serenity, however, was not the resignation of age. I saw that he did not mean to drop out of the game. Almost immediately he began to speak of our old interests; not with an effort, as at our former meeting, but simply and naturally, in the tone of a man whose life has flowed back into its normal channels. I remembered, with a touch of self-reproach, how I had distrusted his reconstructive powers; but my admiration for his reserved force was now tinged by the sense that, after all, such happiness as his ought to have been paid with his last coin. The feeling grew as we neared the house and I found how inextricably his wife was interwoven with my remembrance of the place: how the whole scene was but an extension of that vivid presence.

Within doors nothing was changed, and my hand would have dropped without surprise into her welcoming clasp. It was luncheon-time, and Grancy led me at once to the dining-room, where the walls, the

# THE MOVING FINGER

furniture, the very plate and porcelain, seemed a mirror in which a moment since her face had been reflected. I wondered whether Grancy, under the recovered tranquillity of his smile, concealed the same sense of her nearness, saw perpetually between himself and the actual her bright unappeasable ghost. He spoke of her once or twice, in an easy incidental way, and her name seemed to hang in the air after he had uttered it, like a chord that continues to vibrate. If he felt her presence it was evidently as an enveloping medium, the moral atmosphere in which he breathed. I had never before known how completely the dead may survive.

After luncheon we went for a long walk through the autumnal fields and woods, and dusk was falling when we re-entered the house. Grancy led the way to the library, where, at this hour, his wife had always welcomed us back to a bright fire and a cup of tea. The room faced the west, and held a clear light of its own after the rest of the house had grown dark. I remembered how young she had looked in this pale gold light, which irradiated her eyes and hair, or silhouetted her girlish outline as she passed before the windows. Of all the rooms the library was most peculiarly hers; and here I felt that her nearness might take visible shape. Then, all in a moment, as Grancy opened the door, the feeling vanished and a kind of resistance

# THE MOVING FINGER

met me on the threshold. I looked about me. Was the room changed? Had some desecrating hand effaced the traces of her presence? No; here too the setting was undisturbed. My feet sank into the same deep-piled Daghestan; the book-shelves took the firelight on the same rows of rich subdued bindings; her arm-chair stood in its old place near the tea-table; and from the opposite wall her face confronted me.

Her face — but *was* it hers? I moved nearer and stood looking up at the portrait. Grancy's glance had followed mine and I heard him move to my side.

"You see a change in it?" he said.

"What does it mean?" I asked.

"It means — that five years have passed."

"Over *her?*"

"Why not? — Look at me!" He pointed to his gray hair and furrowed temples. "What do you think kept *her* so young? It was happiness! But now—" he looked up at her with infinite tenderness. "I like her better so," he said. "It's what she would have wished."

"Have wished?"

"That we should grow old together. Do you think she would have wanted to be left behind?"

I stood speechless, my gaze travelling from his worn grief-beaten features to the painted face above. It was not furrowed like his; but a veil of years seemed to

[ 164 ]

have descended on it. The bright hair had lost its elasticity, the cheek its clearness, the brow its light: the whole woman had waned.

Grancy laid his hand on my arm. "You don't like it?" he said sadly.

"Like it? I—I've lost her!" I burst out.

"And I've found her," he answered.

"In *that*?" I cried with a reproachful gesture.

"Yes; in that." He swung round on me almost defiantly. "The other had become a sham, a lie! This is the way she would have looked—does look, I mean. Claydon ought to know, oughtn't he?"

I turned suddenly. "Did Claydon do this for you?" Grancy nodded.

"Since your return?"

"Yes. I sent for him after I'd been back a week—." He turned away and gave a thrust to the smouldering fire. I followed, glad to leave the picture behind me. Grancy threw himself into a chair near the hearth, so that the light fell on his sensitive variable face. He leaned his head back, shading his eyes with his hand, and began to speak.

### III

"YOU fellows knew enough of my early history to guess what my second marriage meant to me. I say guess, because no one could understand—really.

## THE MOVING FINGER

as I opened the library door. It was in the afternoon and the room was full of light. It fell on her picture— the picture of a young and radiant woman. She smiled at me coldly across the distance that divided us. I had the feeling that she didn't even recognize me. And then I caught sight of myself in the mirror over there —a gray-haired broken man whom she had never known!

"For a week we two lived together—the strange woman and the strange man. I used to sit night after night and question her smiling face; but no answer ever came. What did she know of me, after all? We were irrevocably separated by the five years of life that lay between us. At times, as I sat here, I almost grew to hate her; for her presence had driven away my gentle ghost, the real wife who had wept, aged, struggled with me during those awful years. . . It was the worst loneliness I've ever known. Then, gradually, I began to notice a look of sadness in the picture's eyes; a look that seemed to say: 'Don't you see that *I* am lonely too?' And all at once it came over me how she would have hated to be left behind! I remembered her comparing life to a heavy book that could not be read with ease unless two people held it together; and I thought how impatiently her hand would have turned the pages that divided us!—So the idea came to me: 'It's the picture that stands between us; the picture

## THE MOVING FINGER

that is dead, and not my wife. To sit in this room is to keep watch beside a corpse.' As this feeling grew on me the portrait became like a beautiful mausoleum in which she had been buried alive: I could hear her beating against the painted walls and crying to me faintly for help. . .

"One day I found I couldn't stand it any longer and I sent for Claydon. He came down and I told him what I'd been through and what I wanted him to do. At first he refused point-blank to touch the picture. The next morning I went off for a long tramp, and when I came home I found him sitting here alone. He looked at me sharply for a moment and then he said: 'I've changed my mind; I'll do it.' I arranged one of the north rooms as a studio and he shut himself up there for a day; then he sent for me. The picture stood there as you see it now—it was as though she'd met me on the threshold and taken me in her arms! I tried to thank him, to tell him what it meant to me, but he cut me short.

"'There's an up train at five, isn't there?' he asked. 'I'm booked for a dinner to-night. I shall just have time to make a bolt for the station and you can send my traps after me.' I haven't seen him since.

"I can guess what it cost him to lay hands on his masterpiece; but, after all, to him it was only a picture lost, to me it was my wife regained!"

# THE MOVING FINGER

## IV

AFTER that, for ten years or more, I watched the strange spectacle of a life of hopeful and productive effort based on the structure of a dream. There could be no doubt to those who saw Grancy during this period that he drew his strength and courage from the sense of his wife's mystic participation in his task. When I went back to see him a few months later I found the portrait had been removed from the library and placed in a small study up-stairs, to which he had transferred his desk and a few books. He told me he always sat there when he was alone, keeping the library for his Sunday visitors. Those who missed the portrait of course made no comment on its absence, and the few who were in his secret respected it. Gradually all his old friends had gathered about him and our Sunday afternoons regained something of their former character; but Claydon never reappeared among us.

As I look back now I see that Grancy must have been failing from the time of his return home. His invincible spirit belied and disguised the signs of weakness that afterward asserted themselves in my remembrance of him. He seemed to have an inexhaustible fund of life to draw on, and more than one of us was a pensioner on his superfluity.

# THE MOVING FINGER

Nevertheless, when I came back one summer from my European holiday and heard that he had been at the point of death, I understood at once that we had believed him well only because he wished us to.

I hastened down to the country and found him midway in a slow convalescence. I felt then that he was lost to us and he read my thought at a glance.

"Ah," he said, "I'm an old man now and no mistake. I suppose we shall have to go half-speed after this; but we shan't need towing just yet!"

The plural pronoun struck me, and involuntarily I looked up at Mrs. Grancy's portrait. Line by line I saw my fear reflected in it. It was the face of a woman *who knows that her husband is dying*. My heart stood still at the thought of what Claydon had done.

Grancy had followed my glance. "Yes, it's changed her," he said quietly. "For months, you know, it was touch and go with me — we had a long fight of it, and it was worse for her than for me." After a pause he added: "Claydon has been very kind; he's so busy nowadays that I seldom see him, but when I sent for him the other day he came down at once."

I was silent and we spoke no more of Grancy's illness; but when I took leave it seemed like shutting him in alone with his death-warrant.

The next time I went down to see him he looked much better. It was a Sunday and he received me in

# THE MOVING FINGER

the library, so that I did not see the portrait again. He continued to improve and toward spring we began to feel that, as he had said, he might yet travel a long way without being towed.

One evening, on returning to town after a visit which had confirmed my sense of reassurance, I found Claydon dining alone at the club. He asked me to join him and over the coffee our talk turned to his work.

"If you're not too busy," I said at length, "you ought to make time to go down to Grancy's again."

He looked up quickly. "Why?" he asked.

"Because he's quite well again," I returned with a touch of cruelty. "His wife's prognostications were mistaken."

Claydon stared at me a moment. "Oh, *she* knows," he affirmed with a smile that chilled me.

"You mean to leave the portrait as it is then?" I persisted.

He shrugged his shoulders. "He hasn't sent for me yet!"

A waiter came up with the cigars and Claydon rose and joined another group.

It was just a fortnight later that Grancy's housekeeper telegraphed for me. She met me at the station with the news that he had been "taken bad" and that the doctors were with him. I had to wait for some

# THE MOVING FINGER

time in the deserted library before the medical men appeared. They had the baffled manner of empirics who have been superseded by the great Healer; and I lingered only long enough to hear that Grancy was not suffering and that my presence could do him no harm.

I found him seated in his arm-chair in the little study. He held out his hand with a smile.

"You see she was right after all," he said.

"She?" I repeated, perplexed for the moment.

"My wife." He indicated the picture. "Of course I knew she had no hope from the first. I saw that"—he lowered his voice—"after Claydon had been here. But I wouldn't believe it at first!"

I caught his hands in mine. "For God's sake don't believe it now!" I adjured him.

He shook his head gently. "It's too late," he said. "I might have known that she knew."

"But, Grancy, listen to me," I began; and then I stopped. What could I say that would convince him? There was no common ground of argument on which we could meet; and after all it would be easier for him to die feeling that she *had* known. Strangely enough, I saw that Claydon had missed his mark. . .

# THE MOVING FINGER

V

GRANCY'S will named me as one of his executors; and my associate, having other duties on his hands, begged me to assume the task of carrying out our friend's wishes. This placed me under the necessity of informing Claydon that the portrait of Mrs. Grancy had been bequeathed to him; and he replied by the next post that he would send for the picture at once. I was staying in the deserted house when the portrait was taken away; and as the door closed on it I felt that Grancy's presence had vanished too. Was it his turn to follow her now, and could one ghost haunt another?

After that, for a year or two, I heard nothing more of the picture, and though I met Claydon from time to time we had little to say to each other. I had no definable grievance against the man and I tried to remember that he had done a fine thing in sacrificing his best picture to a friend; but my resentment had all the tenacity of unreason.

One day, however, a lady whose portrait he had just finished begged me to go with her to see it. To refuse was impossible, and I went with the less reluctance that I knew I was not the only friend she had invited. The others were all grouped around the easel when I entered, and after contributing my share to the chorus

# THE MOVING FINGER

of approval I turned away and began to stroll about the studio. Claydon was something of a collector and his things were generally worth looking at. The studio was a long tapestried room with a curtained archway at one end. The curtains were looped back, showing a smaller apartment, with books and flowers and a few fine bits of bronze and porcelain. The tea-table standing in this inner room proclaimed that it was open to inspection, and I wandered in. A *bleu poudré* vase first attracted me; then I turned to examine a slender bronze Ganymede, and in so doing found myself face to face with Mrs. Grancy's portrait. I stared up at her blankly and she smiled back at me in all the recovered radiance of youth. The artist had effaced every trace of his later touches and the original picture had reappeared. It throned alone on the panelled wall, asserting a brilliant supremacy over its carefully-chosen surroundings. I felt in an instant that the whole room was tributary to it: that Claydon had heaped his treasures at the feet of the woman he loved. Yes—it was the woman he had loved and not the picture; and my instinctive resentment was explained.

Suddenly I felt a hand on my shoulder.

"Ah, how could you?" I cried, turning on him.

"How could I?" he retorted. "How could I *not?* Doesn't she belong to me now?"

I moved away impatiently.

"Wait a moment," he said with a detaining gesture. "The others have gone and I want to say a word to you.—Oh, I know what you've thought of me—I can guess! You think I killed Grancy, I suppose?"

I was startled by his sudden vehemence. "I think you tried to do a cruel thing," I said.

"Ah—what a little way you others see into life!" he murmured. "Sit down a moment—here, where we can look at her—and I'll tell you."

He threw himself on the ottoman beside me and sat gazing up at the picture, with his hands clasped about his knee.

"Pygmalion," he began slowly, "turned his statue into a real woman; *I* turned my real woman into a picture. Small compensation, you think—but you don't know how much of a woman belongs to you after you've painted her!—Well, I made the best of it, at any rate—I gave her the best I had in me; and she gave me in return what such a woman gives by merely being. And after all she rewarded me enough by making me paint as I shall never paint again! There was one side of her, though, that was mine alone, and that was her beauty; for no one else understood it. To Grancy even it was the mere expression of herself—what language is to thought. Even when he saw the picture he didn't guess my secret—he was so sure she was all his! As though a man should think he owned

[ 176 ]

the moon because it was reflected in the pool at his door—

"Well—when he came home and sent for me to change the picture it was like asking me to commit murder. He wanted me to make an old woman of her—of her who had been so divinely, unchangeably young! As if any man who really loved a woman would ask her to sacrifice her youth and beauty for his sake! At first I told him I couldn't do it—but afterward, when he left me alone with the picture, something queer happened. I suppose it was because I was always so confoundedly fond of Grancy that it went against me to refuse what he asked. Anyhow, as I sat looking up at her, she seemed to say, 'I'm not yours but his, and I want you to make me what he wishes.' And so I did it. I could have cut my hand off when the work was done—I daresay he told you I never would go back and look at it. He thought I was too busy—he never understood. . .

"Well—and then last year he sent for me again— you remember. It was after his illness, and he told me he'd grown twenty years older and that he wanted her to grow older too—he didn't want her to be left behind. The doctors all thought he was going to get well at that time, and he thought so too; and so did I when I first looked at him. But when I turned to the picture—ah, now I don't ask you to believe me;

# THE MOVING FINGER

but I swear it was *her* face that told me he was dying, and that she wanted him to know it! She had a message for him and she made me deliver it."

He rose abruptly and walked toward the portrait; then he sat down beside me again.

"Cruel? Yes, it seemed so to me at first; and this time, if I resisted, it was for *his* sake and not for mine. But all the while I felt her eyes drawing me, and gradually she made me understand. If she'd been there in the flesh (she seemed to say) wouldn't she have seen before any of us that he was dying? Wouldn't he have read the news first in her face? And wouldn't it be horrible if now he should discover it instead in strange eyes?—Well—that was what she wanted of me and I did it—I kept them together to the last!" He looked up at the picture again. "But now she belongs to me," he repeated. . .

# THE CONFESSIONAL

# THE CONFESSIONAL

WHEN I was a young man I thought a great deal of local color. At that time it was still a pigment of recent discovery, and supposed to have a peculiarly stimulating effect on the mental eye. As an aid to the imagination its value was perhaps overrated; but as an object of pursuit to that vagrant faculty, it had all the merits claimed for it. I certainly never hunted any game better worth my powder; and to a young man with rare holidays and long working hours, its value was enhanced by the fact that one might bring it down at any turn, if only one kept one's eye alert and one's hand on the trigger.

Even the large manufacturing city where, for some years, my young enthusiasms were chained to an accountant's desk, was not without its romantic opportunities. Many of the mill-hands at Dunstable were Italians, and a foreign settlement had formed itself in that unsavory and unsanitary portion of the town known as the Point. The Point, like more aristocratic communities, had its residential and commercial districts, its church, its theatre and its restaurant. When the craving for local color was on me it was my habit to resort to the restaurant, a low-browed wooden build-

# THE CONFESSIONAL

ing with the appetizing announcement:

"*Aristiù di montone*"

pasted in one of its fly-blown window-panes. Here the consumption of tough macaroni or of an ambiguous *frittura* sufficed to transport me to the Cappello d' Oro in Venice, while my cup of coffee and a wasp-waisted cigar with a straw in it turned my greasy table-cloth into the marble top of one of the little round tables under the arcade of the Caffè Pedrotti at Padua. This feat of the imagination was materially aided by Agostino, the hollow-eyed and low-collared waiter, whose slimy napkin never lost its Latin flourish and whose zeal for my comfort was not infrequently displayed by his testing the warmth of my soup with his finger. Through Agostino I became acquainted with the inner history of the colony, heard the details of its feuds and vendettas, and learned to know by sight the leading characters in these domestic dramas.

The restaurant was frequented by the chief personages of the community: the overseer of the Italian hands at the Meriton Mills, the doctor, his wife the *levatrice* (a plump Neapolitan with greasy ringlets, a plush picture-hat, and a charm against the evil-eye hanging in a crease of her neck) and lastly by Don Egidio, the *parocco* of the little church across the street. The doctor and his wife came only on feast days, but the overseer and Don Egidio were regular

# THE CONFESSIONAL

patrons. The former was a quiet saturnine-looking man, of accomplished manners but reluctant speech, and I depended for my diversion chiefly on Don Egidio, whose large loosely-hung lips were always ajar for conversation. The remarks issuing from them were richly tinged by the gutturals of the Bergamasque dialect, and it needed but a slight acquaintance with Italian types to detect the Lombard peasant under the priest's rusty cassock. This inference was confirmed by Don Egidio's telling me that he came from a village of Val Camonica, the radiant valley which extends northward from the lake of Iseo to the Adamello glaciers. His step-father had been a laborer on one of the fruit-farms of a Milanese count who owned large estates in the Val Camonica; and that gentleman, taking a fancy to the lad, whom he had seen at work in his orchards, had removed him to his villa on the lake of Iseo and had subsequently educated him for the Church.

It was doubtless to this picturesque accident that Don Egidio owed the mingling of ease and simplicity that gave an inimitable charm to his stout shabby presence. It was as though some wild mountain-fruit had been transplanted to the Count's orchards and had mellowed under cultivation without losing its sylvan flavor. I have never seen the social art carried farther without suggestion of artifice. The fact that Don Egidio's amenities were mainly exercised on the mill-hands

## THE CONFESSIONAL

composing his parish proved the genuineness of his gift. It is easier to simulate gentility among gentlemen than among navvies; and the plain man is a touchstone who draws out all the alloy in the gold.

Among his parishioners Don Egidio ruled with the cheerful despotism of the good priest. On cardinal points he was inflexible, but in minor matters he had that elasticity of judgment which enables the Catholic discipline to fit itself to every inequality of the human conscience. There was no appeal from his verdict; but his judgment-seat was a revolving chair from which he could view the same act at various angles. His influence was acknowledged not only by his flock, but by the policeman at the corner, the "bar-keep'" in the dive, the ward politician in the corner grocery. The general verdict of Dunstable was that the Point would have been hell without the priest. It was perhaps not precisely heaven with him; but such light of the upper sky as pierced its murky atmosphere was reflected from Don Egidio's countenance. It is hardly possible for any one to exercise such influence without taking pleasure in it; and on the whole the priest was probably a contented man; though it does not follow that he was a happy one. On this point the first stages of our acquaintance yielded much food for conjecture. At first sight Don Egidio was the image of cheerfulness. He had all the physical indications of a mind at ease:

# THE CONFESSIONAL

the leisurely rolling gait, the ready laugh, the hospitable eye of the man whose sympathies are always on the latch. It took me some time to discover under his surface garrulity the impenetrable reticence of his profession, and under his enjoyment of trifles a levelling melancholy which made all enjoyment trifling. Don Egidio's aspect and conversation were so unsuggestive of psychological complexities that I set down this trait to poverty or home-sickness. There are few classes of men more frugal in tastes and habit than the village priest in Italy; but Don Egidio, by his own account, had been introduced, at an impressionable age, to a way of living that must have surpassed his wildest dreams of self-indulgence. To whatever privations his parochial work had since accustomed him, the influences of that earlier life were too perceptible in his talk not to have made a profound impression on his tastes; and he remained, for all his apostolic simplicity, the image of the family priest who has his seat at the rich man's table.

It chanced that I had used one of my short European holidays to explore afoot the romantic passes connecting the Valtelline with the lake of Iseo; and my remembrance of that enchanting region made it seem impossible that Don Egidio should ever look without a reminiscent pang on the grimy perspective of his parochial streets. The transition was too complete, too

## THE CONFESSIONAL

ironical, from those rich glades and Titianesque acclivities to the brick hovels and fissured sidewalks of the Point.

This impression was confirmed when Don Egidio, in response to my urgent invitation, paid his first visit to my modest lodgings. He called one winter evening, when a wood-fire in its happiest humor was giving a factitious lustre to my book-shelves and bringing out the values of the one or two old prints and Chinese porcelains that accounted for the perennial shabbiness of my wardrobe.

"Ah," said he with a murmur of satisfaction, as he laid aside his shiny hat and bulging umbrella, "it is a long time since I have been in a *casa signorile*."

My remembrance of his own room (he lodged with the doctor and the *levatrice*) saved this epithet from the suggestion of irony and kept me silent while he sank into my arm-chair with the deliberation of a tired traveller lowering himself gently into a warm bath.

"Good! good!" he repeated, looking about him. "Books, porcelains, objects of *virtù*—I am glad to see that there are still such things in the world!" And he turned a genial eye on the glass of Marsala that I had poured out for him.

Don Egidio was the most temperate of men and never exceeded his one glass; but he liked to sit by the hour puffing at my Cabañas, which I suspected him

# THE CONFESSIONAL

of preferring to the black weed of his native country. Under the influence of my tobacco he became even more blandly garrulous, and I sometimes fancied that of all the obligations of his calling none could have placed such a strain on him as that of preserving the secrets of the confessional. He often talked of his early life at the Count's villa, where he had been educated with his patron's two sons till he was of age to be sent to the seminary; and I could see that the years spent in simple and familiar intercourse with his benefactors had been the most vivid chapter in his experience. The Italian peasant's inarticulate tenderness for the beauty of his birthplace had been specialized in him by contact with cultivated tastes, and he could tell me not only that the Count had a "stupendous" collection of pictures, but that the chapel of the villa contained a sepulchral monument by Bambaja, and that the art-critics were divided as to the authenticity of the Leonardo in the family palace at Milan.

On all these subjects he was inexhaustibly voluble; but there was one point which he always avoided, and that was his reason for coming to America. I remember the round turn with which he brought me up when I questioned him.

"A priest," said he, "is a soldier and must obey orders like a soldier." He set down his glass of Marsala and strolled across the room. "I had not observed," he

## THE CONFESSIONAL

went on, "that you have here a photograph of the Sposalizio of the Brera. What a picture! *È stupendo!*" and he turned back to his seat and smilingly lit a fresh cigar.

I saw at once that I had hit on a point where his native garrulity was protected by the chain-mail of religious discipline that every Catholic priest wears beneath his cassock. I had too much respect for my friend to wish to penetrate his armor, and now and then I almost fancied he was grateful to me for not putting his reticence to the test.

Don Egidio must have been past sixty when I made his acquaintance; but it was not till the close of an exceptionally harsh winter, some five or six years after our first meeting, that I began to think of him as an old man. It was as though the long-continued cold had cracked and shrivelled him. He had grown bent and hollow-chested and his lower lip shook like an unhinged door. The summer heat did little to revive him, and in September, when I came home from my vacation, I found him just recovering from an attack of pneumonia. That autumn he did not care to venture often into the night air, and now and then I used to go and sit with him in his little room, to which I had contributed the unheard-of luxuries of an easy-chair and a gas-stove.

My engagements, however, made these visits infre-

# THE CONFESSIONAL

quent, and several weeks had elapsed without my seeing the *parocco* when, one snowy November morning, I ran across him in the railway-station. I was on my way to New York for the day and had just time to wave a greeting to him as I jumped into the railway-carriage; but a moment later, to my surprise, I saw him stiffly clambering into the same train. I found him seated in the common car, with his umbrella between his knees and a bundle done up in a red cotton handkerchief on the seat at his side. The caution with which, at my approach, he transferred this bundle to his arms caused me to glance at it in surprise; and he answered my look by saying with a smile:

"They are flowers for the dead—the most exquisite flowers—from the greenhouses of Mr. Meriton—*si figuri!*" And he waved a descriptive hand. "One of my lads, Gianpietro, is employed by the gardener there, and every year on this day he brings me a beautiful bunch of flowers—for such a purpose it is no sin," he added, with the charming Italian pliancy of judgment.

"And why are you travelling in this snowy weather, *signor parocco?*" I asked, as he ended with a cough.

He fixed me gravely with his simple shallow eye. "Because it is the day of the dead, my son," he said, "and I go to place these on the grave of the noblest man that ever lived."

"You are going to New York?"

# THE CONFESSIONAL

"To Brooklyn—"

I hesitated a moment, wishing to question him, yet uncertain whether his replies were curtailed by the persistency of his cough or by the desire to avoid interrogation.

"This is no weather to be travelling with such a cough," I said at length.

He made a deprecating gesture.

"I have never missed the day—not once in eighteen years. But for me he would have no one!" He folded his hands on his umbrella and looked away from me to hide the trembling of his lip.

I resolved on a last attempt to storm his confidence. "Your friend is buried in Calvary cemetery?"

He signed an assent.

"That is a long way for you to go alone, *signor parocco*. The streets are sure to be slippery and there is an icy wind blowing. Give me your flowers and let me send them to the cemetery by a messenger. I give you my word they shall reach their destination safely."

He turned a quiet look on me. "My son, you are young," he said, "and you don't know how the dead need us." He drew his breviary from his pocket and opened it with a smile. "*Mi scusi?*" he murmured.

The business which had called me to town obliged me to part from him as soon as the train entered the station, and in my dash for the street I left his un-

# THE CONFESSIONAL

wieldy figure laboring far behind me through the crowd on the platform. Before we separated, however, I had learned that he was returning to Dunstable by the four o'clock train, and had resolved to despatch my business in time to travel home with him. When I reached Wall Street I was received with the news that the man I had appointed to meet was ill and detained in the country. My business was "off" and I found myself with the rest of the day at my disposal. I had no difficulty in deciding how to employ my time. I was at an age when, in such contingencies, there is always a feminine alternative; and even now I don't know how it was that, on my way to a certain hospitable luncheon-table, I suddenly found myself in a cab which was carrying me at full-speed to the Twenty-third Street ferry. It was not till I had bought my ticket and seated myself in the varnished tunnel of the ferry-boat that I was aware of having been diverted from my purpose by an overmastering anxiety for Don Egidio. I rapidly calculated that he had not more than an hour's advance on me, and that, allowing for my greater agility and for the fact that I had a cab at my call, I was likely to reach the cemetery in time to see him under shelter before the gusts of sleet that were already sweeping across the river had thickened to a snow-storm.

At the gates of the cemetery I began to take a less sanguine view of my attempt. The commemorative anniversary had filled the silent avenues with visitors, and I felt the futility of my quest as I tried to fix the gate-keeper's attention on my delineation of a stout Italian priest with a bad cough and a bunch of flowers tied up in a red cotton handkerchief. The gate-keeper showed that delusive desire to oblige that is certain to send its victims in the wrong direction; but I had the presence of mind to go exactly contrary to his indication, and thanks to this precaution I came, after half an hour's search, on the figure of my poor *parocco*, kneeling on the wet ground in one of the humblest by-ways of the great necropolis. The mound before which he knelt was strewn with the spoils of Mr. Meriton's conservatories, and on the weather-worn tablet at its head I read the inscription:

IL CONTE SIVIANO
DA MILANO.

*Super flumina Babylonis, illic sedimus et flevimus.*

So engrossed was Don Egidio that for some moments I stood behind him unobserved; and when he rose and faced me, grief had left so little room for any minor emotion that he looked at me almost without surprise.

"Don Egidio," I said, "I have a carriage waiting for you at the gate. You must come home with me."

He nodded quietly and I drew his hand through my arm.

# THE CONFESSIONAL

He turned back to the grave. "One moment, my son," he said. "It may be for the last time." He stood motionless, his eyes on the heaped-up flowers which were already bruised and blackened by the cold. "To leave him alone—after sixty years! But God is everywhere—" he murmured as I led him away.

On the journey home he did not care to talk, and my chief concern was to keep him wrapped in my greatcoat and to see that his bed was made ready as soon as I had restored him to his lodgings. The *levatrice* brought a quilted coverlet from her own room and hovered over him as gently as though he had been of the sex to require her services; while Agostino, at my summons, appeared with a bowl of hot soup that was heralded down the street by a reviving waft of garlic. To these ministrations I left the *parocco*, intending to call for news of him the next evening; but an unexpected pressure of work kept me late at my desk, and the following day some fresh obstacle delayed me.

On the third afternoon, as I was leaving the office, an agate-eyed infant from the Point hailed me with a message from the doctor. The *parocco* was worse and had asked for me. I jumped into the nearest car and ten minutes later was running up the doctor's greasy stairs.

To my dismay I found Don Egidio's room cold and untenanted; but I was reassured a moment later by

## THE CONFESSIONAL

the appearance of the *levatrice*, who announced that she had transferred the blessed man to her own apartment, where he could have the sunlight and a good bed to lie in. There in fact he lay, weak but smiling, in a setting which contrasted oddly enough with his own monastic surroundings: a cheerful grimy room, hung with anecdotic chromos, photographs of lady-patients proudly presenting their offspring to the camera, and innumerable Neapolitan *santolini* decked out with shrivelled palm-leaves.

The *levatrice* whispered that the good man had the pleurisy, and that, as she phrased it, he was nearing his last mile-stone. I saw that he was in fact in a bad way, but his condition did not indicate any pressing danger, and I had the presentiment that he would still, as the saying is, put up a good fight. It was clear, however, that he knew what turn the conflict must take, and the solemnity with which he welcomed me showed that my summons was a part of that spiritual strategy with which the Catholic opposes the surprise of death.

"My son," he said, when the *levatrice* had left us, "I have a favor to ask you. You found me yesterday bidding good-bye to my best friend." His cough interrupted him. "I have never told you," he went on, "the name of the family in which I was brought up. It was Siviano, and that was the grave of the Count's eldest son, with whom I grew up as a brother. For eighteen

# THE CONFESSIONAL

years he has lain in that strange ground—*in terra aliena*—and when I die, there will be no one to care for his grave."

I saw what he waited for. "I will care for it, *signor parocco*."

"I knew I should have your promise, my child; and what you promise you keep. But my friend is a stranger to you—you are young and at your age life is a mistress who kisses away sad memories. Why should you remember the grave of a stranger? I cannot lay such a claim on you. But I will tell you his story—and then I think that neither joy nor grief will let you forget him; for when you rejoice you will remember how he sorrowed; and when you sorrow the thought of him will be like a friend's hand in yours."

## II

YOU tell me (Don Egidio began) that you know our little lake; and if you have seen it you will understand why it always used to remind me of the "garden enclosed" of the Canticles.

*Hortus inclusus; columba mea in foraminibus petræ:* the words used to come back to me whenever I returned from a day's journey across the mountains, and looking down saw the blue lake far below, hidden in its hills like a happy secret in a stern heart. We were never envious of the glory of the great lakes. They are

# THE CONFESSIONAL

like the show pictures that some nobleman hangs in his public gallery; but our Iseo is the treasure that he hides in his inner chamber.

You tell me you saw it in summer, when it looks up like a saint's eye, reflecting the whole of heaven. It was then too that I first saw it. My future friend, the old Count, had found me at work on one of his fruit-farms up the valley, and hearing that I was ill-treated by my step-father—a drunken pedlar from the Val Mastellone, whom my poor mother a year or two earlier had come across at the fair of Lovere—he had taken me home with him to Iseo. I used to serve mass in our hill-village of Cerveno, and the village children called me "the little priest" because when my work was done I often crept back to the church to get away from my step-father's blows and curses. "I will make a real priest of him," the Count declared; and that afternoon, perched on the box of his travelling-carriage, I was whirled away from the dark scenes of my childhood into a world where, as it seemed to me, every one was as happy as an angel on a *presepio*.

I wonder if you remember the Count's villa? It lies on the shore of the lake, facing the green knoll of Monte Isola, and overlooked by the village of Siviano and by the old parish-church where I said mass for fifteen happy years. The village hangs on a ledge of the mountain; but the villa dips its foot in the lake,

# THE CONFESSIONAL

smiling at its reflection like a bather lingering on the brink. What Paradise it seemed to me that day! In our church up the valley there hung an old brown picture, with a Saint Sabastian in the foreground; and behind him the most wonderful palace, with terraced gardens adorned with statues and fountains, where fine folk in resplendent dresses walked up and down without heeding the blessed martyr's pangs. The Count's villa, with its terraces, its roses, its marble steps descending to the lake, reminded me of that palace; only instead of being inhabited by wicked people engrossed in their selfish pleasures it was the home of the kindest friends that ever took a poor lad by the hand.

The old Count was a widower when I first knew him. He had been twice married, and his first wife had left him two children, a son and a daughter. The eldest, Donna Marianna, was then a girl of twenty, who kept her father's house and was a mother to the two lads. She was not handsome or learned, and had no taste for the world; but she was like the lavender-plant in a poor man's window—just a little gray flower, but a sweetness that fills the whole house. Her brother, Count Roberto, had been ailing from his birth, and was a studious lad with a melancholy musing face such as you may see in some of Titian's portraits of young men. He looked like an exiled prince dressed in mourning.

# THE CONFESSIONAL

There was one child by the second marriage, Count Andrea, a boy of my own age, handsome as a Saint George, but not as kind as the others. No doubt, being younger, he was less able to understand why an uncouth peasant lad should have been brought to his father's table; and the others were so fearful of hurting my feelings that, but for his teasing, I might never have mended my clumsy manners or learned how to behave in the presence of my betters. Count Andrea was not sparing in such lessons, and Count Roberto, in spite of his weak arms, chastised his brother roundly when he thought the discipline had been too severe; but for my part it seemed to me natural enough that such a godlike being should lord it over a poor clodhopper like myself.

Well—I will not linger over the beginning of my new life for my story has to do with its close. Only I should like to make you understand what the change meant to me—an ignorant peasant lad, coming from hard words and blows and a smoke-blackened hut in the hills to that great house full of rare and beautiful things, and of beings who seemed to me even more rare and beautiful. Do you wonder I was ready to kiss the ground they trod, and would have given the last drop of my blood to serve them?

In due course I was sent to the seminary at Lodi; and on holidays I used to visit the family in Milan.

# THE CONFESSIONAL

Count Andrea was growing up to be one of the handsomest young men imaginable, but a trifle wild; and the old Count married him in haste to the daughter of a Venetian noble, who brought as her dower a great estate in Istria. The Countess Gemma, as this lady was called, was as light as thistledown and had an eye like a baby's; but while she was cooing for the moon her pretty white hands were always stealing toward something within reach that she had not been meant to have. The old Count was not alert enough to follow these manœuvres; and the Countess hid her designs under a torrent of guileless chatter, as pick-pockets wear long sleeves to conceal their movements. Her only fault, he used to say, was that one of her aunts had married an Austrian; and this event having taken place before she was born he laughingly acquitted her of any direct share in it. She confirmed his good opinion of her by giving her husband two sons; and Roberto showing no inclination to marry, these boys naturally came to be looked on as the heirs of the house.

Meanwhile I had finished my course of studies, and the old Count, on my twenty-first birthday, had appointed me priest of the parish of Siviano. It was the year of Count Andrea's marriage and there were great festivities at the villa. Three years later the old Count died, to the sorrow of his two eldest children. Donna

# THE CONFESSIONAL

Marianna and Count Roberto closed their apartments in the palace at Milan and withdrew for a year to Siviano. It was then that I first began to know my friend. Before that I had loved him without understanding him; now I learned of what metal he was made. His bookish tastes inclined him to a secluded way of living; and his younger brother perhaps fancied that he would not care to assume the charge of the estate. But if Andrea thought this he was disappointed. Roberto resolutely took up the tradition of his father's rule, and, as if conscious of lacking the old Count's easy way with the peasants, made up for it by a redoubled zeal for their welfare. I have seen him toil for days to adjust some trifling difficulty that his father would have set right with a ready word; like the sainted bishop who, when a beggar asked him for a penny, cried out: "Alas, my brother, I have not a penny in my purse; but here are two gold pieces, if they can be made to serve you instead!" We had many conferences over the condition of his people, and he often sent me up the valley to look into the needs of the peasantry on the fruit-farms. No grievance was too trifling for him to consider it, no abuse too deep-seated for him to root it out; and many an hour that other men of his rank would have given to books or pleasure was devoted to adjusting a quarrel about boundary-lines or to weighing the merits of a complaint against the tax-collector. I often said that

# THE CONFESSIONAL

he was as much his people's priest as I; and he smiled and answered that every landowner was a king and that in old days the king was always a priest.

Donna Marianna was urgent with him to marry, but he always declared that he had a family in his tenantry, and that, as for a wife, she had never let him feel the want of one. He had that musing temper which gives a man a name for coldness; though in fact he may all the while be storing fuel for a great conflagration. But to me he whispered another reason for not marrying. A man, he said, does not take wife and rejoice while his mother is on her death-bed; and Italy, his mother, lay dying, with the foreign vultures waiting to tear her apart.

You are too young to know anything of those days, my son; and how can any one understand them who did not live through them? Italy lay dying indeed; but Lombardy was her heart, and the heart still beat, and sent the faint blood creeping to her cold extremities. Her torturers, weary of their work, had allowed her to fall into a painless stupor; but just as she was sinking from sleep to death, heaven sent Radetsky to scourge her back to consciousness; and at the first sting of his lash she sprang maimed and bleeding to her feet.

Ah, those days, those days, my son! Italy—Italy— was the word on our lips; but the thought in our hearts was just *Austria*. We clamored for liberty, unity, the

## THE CONFESSIONAL

franchise; but under our breath we prayed only to smite the white-coats. Remove the beam from our eye, we cried, and we shall see our salvation clearly enough! We priests in the north were all liberals and worked with the nobles and the men of letters. Gioberti was our breviary and his Holiness the new Pope was soon to be the Tancred of our crusade. But meanwhile, mind you, all this went on in silence, underground as it were, while on the surface Lombardy still danced, feasted, married, and took office under the Austrian. In the iron-mines up our valley there used to be certain miners who stayed below ground for months at a time; and, like one of these, Roberto remained buried in his purpose, while life went its way overhead. Though I was not in his confidence I knew well enough where his thoughts were, for he went among us with the eye of a lover, the visionary look of one who hears a Voice. We all heard that Voice, to be sure, mingling faintly with the other noises of life; but to Roberto it was already as the roar of mighty waters, drowning every other sound with its thunder.

On the surface, as I have said, things looked smooth enough. An Austrian cardinal throned in Milan and an Austrian-hearted Pope ruled in Rome. In Lombardy, Austria couched like a beast of prey, ready to spring at our throats if we stirred or struggled. The Moderates, to whose party Count Roberto belonged, talked

## THE CONFESSIONAL

of prudence, compromise, the education of the masses; but if their words were a velvet sheath their thought was a dagger. For many years, as you know, the Milanese had maintained an outward show of friendliness with their rulers. The nobles had accepted office under the vice-roy, and in the past there had been frequent intermarriage between the two aristocracies. But now, one by one, the great houses had closed their doors against official society. Though some of the younger and more careless, those who must dance and dine at any cost, still went to the palace and sat beside the enemy at the opera, fashion was gradually taking sides against them, and those who had once been laughed at as old fogeys were now applauded as patriots. Among these, of course, was Count Roberto, who for several years had refused to associate with the Austrians, and had silently resented his easy-going brother's disregard of political distinctions. Andrea and Gemma belonged to the moth tribe, who flock to the brightest light; and Gemma's Istrian possessions, and her family's connection with the Austrian nobility, gave them a pretext for fluttering about the vice-regal candle. Roberto let them go their way, but his own course was a tacit protest against their conduct. They were always welcome at the palazzo Siviano; but he and Donna Marianna withdrew from society in order to have an excuse for not showing themselves at

## THE CONFESSIONAL

the Countess Gemma's entertainments. If Andrea and Gemma were aware of his disapproval they were clever enough to ignore it; for the rich elder brother who paid their debts and never meant to marry was too important a person to be quarrelled with on political grounds. They seemed to think that if he married it would be only to spite them; and they were persuaded that their future depended on their giving him no cause to take such reprisals. I shall never be more than a plain peasant at heart and I have little natural skill in discerning hidden motives; but the experience of the confessional gives every priest a certain insight into the secret springs of action, and I often wondered that the worldly wisdom of Andrea and Gemma did not help them to a clearer reading of their brother's character. For my part I knew that, in Roberto's heart, no great passion could spring from a mean motive; and I had always thought that if he ever loved any woman as he loved Italy, it must be from his country's hand that he received his bride. And so it came about.

Have you ever noticed, on one of those still autumn days before a storm, how here and there a yellow leaf will suddenly detach itself from the bough and whirl through the air as though some warning of the gale had reached it? So it was then in Lombardy. All round was the silence of decay; but now and then a word, a look, a trivial incident, fluttered ominously through the

# THE CONFESSIONAL

stillness. It was in '45. Only a year earlier the glorious death of the Bandiera brothers had sent a long shudder through Italy. In the Romagna, Renzi and his comrades had tried to uphold by action the protest set forth in the "Manifesto of Rimini"; and their failure had sowed the seed which d'Azeglio and Cavour were to harvest. Everywhere the forces were silently gathering; and nowhere was the hush more profound, the least reverberation more audible, than in the streets of Milan.

It was Count Roberto's habit to attend early mass in the Cathedral; and one morning, as he was standing in the aisle, a young girl passed him with her father. Roberto knew the father, a beggarly Milanese of the noble family of Intelvi, who had cut himself off from his class by accepting an appointment in one of the government offices. As the two went by he saw a group of Austrian officers looking after the girl, and heard one of them say: "Such a choice morsel as that is too good for slaves;" and another answer with a laugh: "Yes, it's a dish for the master's table!"

The girl heard too. She was as white as a windflower and he saw the words come out on her cheek like the red mark from a blow. She whispered to her father, but he shook his head and drew her away without so much as a glance at the Austrians. Roberto heard mass and then hastened out and placed himself

[ 205 ]

## THE CONFESSIONAL

in the porch of the Cathedral. A moment later the officers appeared, and they too stationed themselves near the doorway. Presently the girl came out on her father's arm. Her admirers stepped forward to greet Intelvi; and the cringing wretch stood there exchanging compliments with them, while their insolent stare devoured his daughter's beauty. She, poor thing, shook like a leaf, and her eyes, in avoiding theirs, suddenly encountered Roberto's. Her look was a wounded bird that flew to him for shelter. He carried it away in his breast and its live warmth beat against his heart. He thought that Italy had looked at him through those eyes; for love is the wiliest of masqueraders and has a thousand disguises at his command.

Within a month Faustina Intelvi was his wife. Donna Marianna and I rejoiced; for we knew he had chosen her because he loved her, and she seemed to us almost worthy of such a choice. As for Count Andrea and his wife, I leave you to guess what ingredients were mingled in the kiss with which they welcomed the bride. They were all smiles at Roberto's marriage, and had only words of praise for his wife. Donna Marianna, who had sometimes taxed me with suspecting their motives, rejoiced in this fresh proof of their magnanimity; but for my part I could have wished to see them a little less kind. All such twilight fears, however, vanished in the flush of my friend's happiness. Over some na-

# THE CONFESSIONAL

tures love steals gradually, as the morning light widens across a valley; but it had flashed on Roberto like the leap of dawn to a snow-peak. He walked the world with the wondering step of a blind man suddenly restored to sight; and once he said to me with a laugh: "Love makes a Columbus of every one of us!"

And the Countess—? The Countess, my son, was eighteen, and her husband was forty. Count Roberto had the heart of a poet, but he walked with a limp and his skin was sallow. Youth plucks the fruit for its color rather than its flavor; and first love does not serenade its mistress on a church-organ. In Italy girls are married as land is sold; if two estates adjoin two lives are united. As for the portionless girl, she is a knick-knack that goes to the highest bidder. Faustina was handed over to her purchaser as if she had been a picture for his gallery; and the transaction doubtless seemed as natural to her as to her parents. She walked to the altar like an Iphigenia; but pallor becomes a bride, and it looks well for a daughter to weep on leaving her mother. Perhaps it would have been different if she had guessed that the threshold of her new home was carpeted with love and its four corners hung with tender thoughts of her; but her husband was a silent man, who never called attention to his treasures.

The great palace in Milan was a gloomy house for a girl to enter. Roberto and his sister lived in it as if

# THE CONFESSIONAL

it had been a monastery, going nowhere and receiving only those who labored for the Cause. To Faustina, accustomed to the easy Austrian society, the Sunday evening receptions at the palazzo Siviano must have seemed as dreary as a scientific congress. It pleased Roberto to regard her as a victim of barbarian insolence, an embodiment of his country desecrated by the desire of the enemy; but though, like any handsome penniless girl, Faustina had now and then been exposed to a free look or a familiar word, I doubt if she connected such incidents with the political condition of Italy. She knew, of course, that in marrying Siviano she was entering a house closed against the Austrian. One of Siviano's first cares had been to pension his father-in-law, with the stipulation that Intelvi should resign his appointment and give up all relations with the government; and the old hypocrite, only too glad to purchase idleness on such terms, embraced the liberal cause with a zeal which left his daughter no excuse for half-heartedness. But he found it less easy than he had expected to recover a footing among his own people. In spite of his patriotic bluster the Milanese held aloof from him; and being the kind of man who must always take his glass in company he gradually drifted back to his old associates. It was impossible to forbid Faustina to visit her parents; and in their house she breathed an air that was at least tolerant of Austria.

# THE CONFESSIONAL

But I must not let you think that the young Countess appeared ungrateful or unhappy. She was silent and shy, and it needed a more enterprising temper than Roberto's to break down the barrier between them. They seemed to talk to one another through a convent-grating, rather than across a hearth; but if Roberto had asked more of her than she could give, outwardly she was a model wife. She chose me at once as her confessor and I watched over the first steps of her new life. Never was younger sister tenderer to her elder than she to Donna Marianna; never was young wife more mindful of her religious duties, kinder to her dependents, more charitable to the poor; yet to be with her was like living in a room with shuttered windows. She was always the caged bird, the transplanted flower: for all Roberto's care she never bloomed or sang.

Donna Marianna was the first to speak of it. "The child needs more light and air," she said.

"Light? Air?" Roberto repeated. "Does she not go to mass every morning? Does she not drive on the Corso every evening?"

Donna Marianna was not called clever, but her heart was wiser than most women's heads.

"At our age, brother," said she, "the windows of the mind face north and look out on a landscape full of lengthening shadows. Faustina needs another outlook. She is as pale as a hyacinth grown in a cellar."

## THE CONFESSIONAL

Roberto himself turned pale and I saw that she had uttered his own thought.

"You want me to let her go to Gemma's!" he exclaimed.

"Let her go wherever there is a little careless laughter."

"Laughter—now!" he cried, with a gesture toward the sombre line of portraits above his head.

"Let her laugh while she can, my brother."

That evening after dinner he called Faustina to him.

"My child," he said, "go and put on your jewels. Your sister Gemma gives a ball to-night and the carriage waits to take you there. I am too much of a recluse to be at ease in such scenes, but I have sent word to your father to go with you."

Andrea and Gemma welcomed their young sister-in-law with effusion, and from that time she was often in their company. Gemma forbade any mention of politics in her drawing-room, and it was natural that Faustina should be glad to escape from the solemn conclaves of the palazzo Siviano to a house where life went as gaily as in that villa above Florence where Boccaccio's careless story-tellers took refuge from the plague. But meanwhile the political distemper was rapidly spreading, and in spite of Gemma's Austrian affiliations it was no longer possible for her to receive the enemy openly. It was whispered that her door was still ajar to her old friends; but the rumor may have risen from the fact that one of the Austrian cavalry officers stationed at Milan was her own cousin, the son of the aunt on whose misalliance the old Count had so often bantered her. No one could blame the Countess Gemma for not turning her own flesh and blood out of doors; and the social famine to which the officers of the garrison were reduced made it natural that young Welkenstern should press the claims of consanguinity.

All this must have reached Roberto's ears; but he made no sign and his wife came and went as she pleased. When they returned the following year to the old dusky villa at Siviano she was like the voice of a brook in a twilight wood: one could not look at her without ransacking the spring for new similes to paint her freshness. With Roberto it was different. I found him older, more preoccupied and silent; but I guessed that his preoccupations were political, for when his eye rested on his wife it cleared like the lake when a cloud-shadow lifts from it.

Count Andrea and his wife occupied an adjoining villa; and during the *villeggiatura* the two households lived almost as one family. Roberto, however, was often absent in Milan, called thither on business of which the nature was not hard to guess. Sometimes he brought back guests to the villa; and on these occasions Faustina and Donna Marianna went to Count Andrea's for

# THE CONFESSIONAL

the day. I have said that I was not in his confidence; but he knew my sympathies were with the liberals and now and then he let fall a word of the work going on underground. Meanwhile the new Pope had been elected, and from Piedmont to Calabria we hailed in him the Banner that was to lead our hosts to war.

So time passed and we reached the last months of '47. The villa on Iseo had been closed since the end of August. Roberto had no great liking for his gloomy palace in Milan, and it had been his habit to spend nine months of the year at Siviano; but he was now too much engrossed in his work to remain away from Milan, and his wife and sister had joined him there as soon as the midsummer heat was over. During the autumn he had called me once or twice to the city to consult me on business connected with his fruit-farms; and in the course of our talks he had sometimes let fall a hint of graver matters. It was in July of that year that a troop of Croats had marched into Ferrara, with muskets and cannon loaded. The lighted matches of their cannon had fired the sleeping hate of Austria, and the whole country now echoed the Lombard cry: "Out with the barbarian!" All talk of adjustment, compromise, reorganization, shrivelled on lips that the live coal of patriotism had touched. Italy for the Italians, and then — monarchy, federation, republic, it mattered not what!

# THE CONFESSIONAL

The oppressor's grip had tightened on our throats and the clear-sighted saw well enough that Metternich's policy was to provoke a rebellion and then crush it under the Croat heel. But it was too late to cry prudence in Lombardy. With the first days of the new year the tobacco riots had drawn blood in Milan. Soon afterward the Lions' Club was closed, and edicts were issued forbidding the singing of Pio Nono's hymn, the wearing of white and blue, the collecting of subscriptions for the victims of the riots. To each prohibition Milan returned a fresh defiance. The ladies of the nobility put on mourning for the rioters who had been shot down by the soldiery. Half the members of the Guardia Nobile resigned and Count Borromeo sent back his Golden Fleece to the Emperor. Fresh regiments were continually pouring into Milan and it was no secret that Radetsky was strengthening the fortifications. Late in January several leading liberals were arrested and sent into exile, and two weeks later martial law was proclaimed in Milan. At the first arrests several members of the liberal party had hastily left Milan, and I was not surprised to hear, a few days later, that orders had been given to reopen the villa at Siviano. The Count and Countess arrived there early in February.

It was seven months since I had seen the Countess, and I was struck with the change in her appearance.

## THE CONFESSIONAL

She was paler than ever, and her step had lost its lightness. Yet she did not seem to share her husband's political anxieties; one would have said that she was hardly aware of them. She seemed wrapped in a veil of lassitude, like Iseo on a still gray morning, when dawn is blood-red on the mountains but a mist blurs its reflection in the lake. I felt as though her soul were slipping away from me, and longed to win her back to my care; but she made her ill-health a pretext for not coming to confession, and for the present I could only wait and carry the thought of her to the altar. She had not been long at Siviano before I discovered that this drooping mood was only one phase of her humor. Now and then she flung back the cowl of melancholy and laughed life in the eye; but next moment she was in shadow again, and her muffled thoughts had given us the slip. She was like the lake on one of those days when the wind blows twenty ways and every promontory holds a gust in ambush.

Meanwhile there was a continual coming and going of messengers between Siviano and the city. They came mostly at night, when the household slept, and were away again with the last shadows; but the news they brought stayed and widened, shining through every cranny of the old house. The whole of Lombardy was up. From Pavia to Mantua, from Como to Brescia, the streets ran blood like the arteries of one

# THE CONFESSIONAL

great body. At Pavia and Padua the universities were closed. The frightened vice-roy was preparing to withdraw from Milan to Verona, and Radetsky continued to pour his men across the Alps, till a hundred thousand were massed between the Piave and the Ticino. And now every eye was turned to Turin. Ah, how we watched for the blue banner of Piedmont on the mountains! Charles Albert was pledged to our cause; his whole people had armed to rescue us, the streets echoed with *avanti, Savoia!* and yet Savoy was silent and hung back. Each day was a life-time strained to the cracking-point with hopes and disappointments. We reckoned the hours by rumors, the very minutes by hearsay. Then suddenly—ah, it was worth living through!—word came to us that Vienna was in revolt. The points of the compass had shifted and our sun had risen in the north. I shall never forget that day at the villa. Roberto sent for me early, and I found him smiling and resolute, as becomes a soldier on the eve of action. He had made all his preparations to leave for Milan and was awaiting a summons from his party. The whole household felt that great events impended, and Donna Marianna, awed and tearful, had pleaded with her brother that they should all receive the sacrament together the next morning. Roberto and his sister had been to confession the previous day, but the Countess Faustina had again excused herself. I

# THE CONFESSIONAL

did not see her while I was with the Count, but as I left the house she met me in the laurel-walk. The morning was damp and cold, and she had drawn a black scarf over her hair, and walked with a listless dragging step; but at my approach she lifted her head quickly and signed to me to follow her into one of the recesses of clipped laurel that bordered the path.

"Don Egidio," she said, "you have heard the news?"

I assented.

"The Count goes to Milan to-morrow?"

"It seems probable, your excellency."

"There will be fighting—we are on the eve of war, I mean?"

"We are in God's hands, your excellency."

"In God's hands!" she murmured. Her eyes wandered and for a moment we stood silent; then she drew a purse from her pocket. "I was forgetting," she exclaimed. "This is for that poor girl you spoke to me about the other day—what was her name? The girl who met the Austrian soldier at the fair at Peschiera—"

"Ah, Vannina," I said; "but she is dead, your excellency."

"Dead!" She turned white and the purse dropped from her hand. I picked it up and held it out to her, but she put back my hand. "That is for masses, then,"

[ 216 ]

# THE CONFESSIONAL

she said; and with that she moved away toward the house.

I walked on to the gate; but before I had reached it I heard her step behind me.

"Don Egidio!" she called; and I turned back.

"You are coming to say mass in the chapel to-morrow morning?"

"That is the Count's wish."

She wavered a moment. "I am not well enough to walk up to the village this afternoon," she said at length. "Will you come back later and hear my confession here?"

"Willingly, your excellency."

"Come at sunset then." She looked at me gravely. "It is a long time since I have been to confession," she added.

"My child, the door of heaven is always unlatched."

She made no answer and I went my way.

I returned to the villa a little before sunset, hoping for a few words with Roberto. I felt with Faustina that we were on the eve of war, and the uncertainty of the outlook made me treasure every moment of my friend's company. I knew he had been busy all day, but hoped to find that his preparations were ended and that he could spare me a half hour. I was not disappointed; for the servant who met me asked me

# THE CONFESSIONAL

to follow him to the Count's apartment. Roberto was sitting alone, with his back to the door, at a table spread with maps and papers. He stood up and turned an ashen face on me.

"Roberto!" I cried, as if we had been boys together.

He signed to me to be seated.

"Egidio," he said suddenly, "my wife has sent for you to confess her?"

"The Countess met me on my way home this morning and expressed a wish to receive the sacrament to-morrow morning with you and Donna Marianna, and I promised to return this afternoon to hear her confession."

Roberto sat silent, staring before him as though he hardly heard. At length he raised his head and began to speak.

"You have noticed lately that my wife has been ailing?" he asked.

"Every one must have seen that the Countess is not in her usual health. She has seemed nervous, out of spirits—I have fancied that she might be anxious about your excellency."

He leaned across the table and laid his wasted hand on mine. "Call me Roberto," he said.

There was another pause before he went on. "Since I saw you this morning," he said slowly, "something horrible has happened. After you left I sent for An-

# THE CONFESSIONAL

drea and Gemma to tell them the news from Vienna and the probability of my being summoned to Milan before night. You know as well as I that we have reached a crisis. There will be fighting within twenty-four hours, if I know my people; and war may follow sooner than we think. I felt it my duty to leave my affairs in Andrea's hands, and to entrust my wife to his care. Don't look startled," he added with a faint smile. "No reasonable man goes on a journey without setting his house in order; and if things take the turn I expect it may be some months before you see me back at Siviano.—But it was not to hear this that I sent for you." He pushed his chair aside and walked up and down the room with his short limping step. "My God!" he broke out wildly, "how can I say it?—When Andrea had heard me, I saw him exchange a glance with his wife, and she said with that infernal sweet voice of hers, 'Yes, Andrea, it is our duty.'

"'Your duty?' I asked. 'What is your duty?'

"Andrea wetted his lips with his tongue and looked at her again; and her look was like a blade in his hand.

"'Your wife has a lover,' he said.

"She caught my arm as I flung myself on him. He is ten times stronger than I, but you remember how I made him howl for mercy in the old days when he used to bully you.

# THE CONFESSIONAL

"'Let me go,' I said to his wife. 'He must live to unsay it.'

"Andrea began to whimper. 'Oh, my poor brother, I would give my heart's blood to unsay it!'

"'The secret has been killing us,' she chimed in.

"'The secret? Whose secret? How dare you—?'

"Gemma fell on her knees like a tragedy actress. 'Strike me—kill me—it is I who am the offender! It was at my house that she met him—'

"'Him?'

"'Franz Welkenstern—my cousin,' she wailed.

"I suppose I stood before them like a stunned ox, for they repeated the name again and again, as if they were not sure of my having heard it.—Not hear it!" he cried suddenly, dropping into a chair and hiding his face in his hands. "Shall I ever on earth hear anything else again?"

He sat a long time with his face hidden and I waited. My head was like a great bronze bell with one thought for the clapper.

After a while he went on in a low deliberate voice, as though his words were balancing themselves on the brink of madness. With strange composure he repeated each detail of his brother's charges: the meetings in the Countess Gemma's drawing-room, the innocent friendliness of the two young people, the talk of mysterious visits to a villa outside the Porta Tici-

# THE CONFESSIONAL

nese, the ever-widening circle of scandal that had spread about their names. At first, Andrea said, he and his wife had refused to listen to the reports which reached them. Then, when the talk became too loud, they had sent for Welkenstern, remonstrated with him, implored him to exchange into another regiment; but in vain. The young officer indignantly denied the reports and declared that to leave his post at such a moment would be desertion.

With a laborious accuracy Roberto went on, detailing one by one each incident of the hateful story, till suddenly he cried out, springing from his chair—"And now to leave her with this lie unburied!"

His cry was like the lifting of a grave-stone from my breast. "You must not leave her!" I exclaimed.

He shook his head. "I am pledged."

"This is your first duty."

"It would be any other man's; not an Italian's."

I was silent: in those days the argument seemed unanswerable.

At length I said: "No harm can come to her while you are away. Donna Marianna and I are here to watch over her. And when you come back—"

He looked at me gravely. "*If* I come back—"

"Roberto!"

"We are men, Egidio; we both know what is coming. Milan is up already; and there is a rumor that

# THE CONFESSIONAL

Charles Albert is moving. This year the spring rains will be red in Italy."

"In your absence not a breath shall touch her!"

"And if I never come back to defend her? They hate her as hell hates, Egidio!—They kept repeating, 'He is of her own age and youth draws youth—.' She is in their way, Egidio!"

"Consider, my son. They do not love her, perhaps; but why should they hate her at such cost? She has given you no child."

"No child!" He paused. "But what if—? She has ailed lately!" he cried, and broke off to grapple with the stabbing thought.

"Roberto! Roberto!" I adjured him.

He jumped up and gripped my arm.

"Egidio! You believe in her?"

"She's as pure as a lily on the altar!"

"Those eyes are wells of truth—and she has been like a daughter to Marianna.—Egidio! do I look like an old man?"

"Quiet yourself, Roberto," I entreated.

"Quiet myself? With this sting in my blood? A lover—and an Austrian lover! Oh, Italy, Italy, my bride!"

"I stake my life on her truth," I cried, "and who knows better than I? Has her soul not lain before me like the bed of a clear stream?"

# THE CONFESSIONAL

"And if what you saw there was only the reflection of your faith in her?"

"My son, I am a priest, and the priest penetrates to the soul as the angel passed through the walls of Peter's prison. I see the truth in her heart as I see Christ in the host!"

"No, no, she is false!" he cried.

I sprang up terrified. "Roberto, be silent!"

He looked at me with a wild incredulous smile. "Poor simple man of God!" he said.

"I would not exchange my simplicity for yours — the dupe of envy's first malicious whisper!"

"Envy — you think that?"

"Is it questionable?"

"You would stake your life on it?"

"My life!"

"Your faith?"

"My faith!"

"Your vows as a priest?"

"My vows — " I stopped and stared at him. He had risen and laid his hand on my shoulder.

"You see now what I would be at," he said quietly. "I must take your place presently — "

"My place — ?"

"When my wife comes down. You understand me."

"Ah, now you are quite mad!" I cried breaking away from him.

# THE CONFESSIONAL

"Am I?" he returned, maintaining his strange composure. "Consider a moment. She has not confessed to you before since our return from Milan—"

"Her ill-health—"

He cut me short with a gesture. "Yet to-day she sends for you—"

"In order that she may receive the sacrament with you on the eve of your first separation."

"If that is her only reason her first words will clear her. I must hear those words, Egidio!"

"You are quite mad," I repeated.

"Strange," he said slowly. "You stake your life on my wife's innocence, yet you refuse me the only means of vindicating it!"

"I would give my life for any one of you—but what you ask is not mine to give."

"The priest first—the man afterward?" he sneered.

"Long afterward!"

He measured me with a contemptuous eye. "We laymen are ready to give the last shred of flesh from our bones, but you priests intend to keep your cassocks whole."

"I tell you my cassock is not mine," I repeated.

"And, by God," he cried, "you are right; for it's mine! Who put it on your back but my father? What kept it there but my charity? Peasant! beggar! Hear his holiness pontificate!"

[ 224 ]

# THE CONFESSIONAL

"Yes," I said, "I was a peasant and a beggar when your father found me; and if he had left me one I might have been excused for putting my hand to any ugly job that my betters required of me; but he made me a priest, and so set me above all of you, and laid on me the charge of your souls as well as mine."

He sat down shaken with dreadful tears. "Ah," he broke out, "would you have answered me thus when we were boys together, and I stood between you and Andrea?"

"If God had given me the strength."

"You call it strength to make a woman's soul your stepping-stone to heaven?"

"Her soul is in my care, not yours, my son. She is safe with me."

"She? But I? I go out to meet death, and leave a worse death behind me!" He leaned over and clutched my arm. "It is not for myself I plead but for her—for her, Egidio! Don't you see to what a hell you condemn her if I don't come back? What chance has she against that slow unsleeping hate? Their lies will fasten themselves to her and suck out her life. You and Marianna are powerless against such enemies."

"You leave her in God's hands, my son."

"Easily said—but, ah, priest, if you were a man! What if their poison works in me and I go to battle thinking that every Austrian bullet may be sent by

# THE CONFESSIONAL

her lover's hand? What if I die not only to free Italy but to free my wife as well?"

I laid my hand on his shoulder. "My son, I answer for her. Leave your faith in her in my hands and I will keep it whole."

He stared at me strangely. "And what if your own fail you?"

"In her? Never. I call every saint to witness!"

"And yet—and yet—ah, this is a blind," he shouted; "you know all and perjure yourself to spare me!"

At that, my son, I felt a knife in my breast. I looked at him in anguish and his gaze was a wall of metal. Mine seemed to slip away from it, like a clawless thing struggling up the sheer side of a precipice.

"You know all," he repeated, "and you dare not let me hear her!"

"I dare not betray my trust."

He waved the answer aside.

"Is this a time to quibble over church discipline? If you believed in her you would save her at any cost!"

I said to myself, "Eternity can hold nothing worse than this for me—" and clutched my resolve again like a cross to my bosom.

Just then there was a hand on the door and we heard Donna Marianna.

"Faustina has sent to know if the *signor parocco* is here."

# THE CONFESSIONAL

"He is here. Bid her come down to the chapel." Roberto spoke quietly, and closed the door on her so that she should not see his face. We heard her patter away across the brick floor of the *salone*.

Roberto turned to me. "Egidio!" he said; and all at once I was no more than a straw on the torrent of his will.

The chapel adjoined the room in which we sat. He opened the door, and in the twilight I saw the light glimmering before the Virgin's shrine and the old carved confessional standing like a cowled watcher in its corner. But I saw it all in a dream; for nothing in heaven or earth was real to me but the iron grip on my shoulder.

"Quick!" he said and drove me forward. I heard him shoot back the bolt of the outer door and a moment later I stood alone in the garden. The sun had set and the cold spring dusk was falling. Lights shone here and there in the long front of the villa; the statues glimmered gray among the thickets. Through the window-pane of the chapel I caught the faint red gleam of the Virgin's lamp; but I turned my back on it and walked away.

· · · · · · · ·

All night I lay like a heretic on the fire. Before dawn there came a call from the villa. The Count had received a second summons from Milan and was to set

## THE CONFESSIONAL

out in an hour. I hurried down the cold dewy path to the lake. All was new and hushed and strange as on the day of resurrection; and in the dark twilight of the garden alleys the statues stared at me like the shrouded dead.

In the *salone*, where the old Count's portrait hung, I found the family assembled. Andrea and Gemma sat together, a little pinched, I thought, but decent and self-contained, like mourners who expect to inherit. Donna Marianna drooped near them, with something black over her head and her face dim with weeping. Roberto received me calmly and then turned to his sister.

"Go fetch my wife," he said.

While she was gone there was silence. We could hear the cold drip of the garden-fountain and the patter of rats in the wall. Andrea and his wife stared out of window and Roberto sat in his father's carved seat at the head of the long table. Then the door opened and Faustina entered.

When I saw her I stopped breathing. She seemed no more than the shell of herself, a hollow thing that grief has voided. Her eyes returned our images like polished agate, but conveyed to her no sense of our presence. Marianna led her to a seat, and she crossed her hands and nailed her dull gaze on Roberto. I looked from one to another, and in that spectral light it seemed

## THE CONFESSIONAL

to me that we were all souls come to judgment and naked to each other as to God. As to my own wrongdoing, it weighed on me no more than dust. The only feeling I had room for was fear—a fear that seemed to fill my throat and lungs and bubble coldly over my drowning head.

Suddenly Roberto began to speak. His voice was clear and steady, and I clutched at his words to drag myself above the surface of my terror. He touched on the charge that had been made against his wife—he did not say by whom—the foul rumor that had made itself heard on the eve of their first parting. Duty, he said, had sent him a double summons; to fight for his country and for his wife. He must clear his wife's name before he was worthy to draw sword for Italy. There was no time to tame the slander before throttling it; he had to take the shortest way to its throat. At this point he looked at me and my soul shook. Then he turned to Andrea and Gemma.

"When you came to me with this rumor," he said quietly, "you agreed to consider the family honor satisfied if I could induce Don Egidio to let me take his place and overhear my wife's confession, and if that confession convinced me of her innocence. Was this the understanding?"

Andrea muttered something and Gemma tapped a sullen foot.

# THE CONFESSIONAL

"After you had left," Roberto continued, "I laid the case before Don Egidio and threw myself on his mercy." He looked at me fixedly. "So strong was his faith in my wife's innocence that for her sake he agreed to violate the sanctity of the confessional. I took his place."

Marianna sobbed and crossed herself and a strange look flitted over Faustina's face.

There was a moment's pause; then Roberto, rising, walked across the room to his wife and took her by the hand.

"Your seat is beside me, Countess Siviano," he said, and led her to the empty chair by his own.

Gemma started to her feet, but her husband pulled her down again.

"Jesus! Mary!" We heard Donna Marianna moan.

Roberto raised his wife's hand to his lips. "You forgive me," he said, "the means I took to defend you?" And turning to Andrea he added slowly: "I declare my wife innocent and my honor satisfied. You swear to stand by my decision?"

What Andrea stammered out, what hissing serpents of speech Gemma's clinched teeth bit back, I never knew—for my eyes were on Faustina, and her face was a wonder to behold.

She had let herself be led across the room like a blind woman, and had listened without change of fea-

# THE CONFESSIONAL

ture to her husband's first words; but as he ceased her frozen gaze broke and her whole body seemed to melt against his breast. He put his arm out, but she slipped to his feet and Marianna hastened forward to raise her up. At that moment we heard the stroke of oars across the quiet water and saw the Count's boat touch the landing-steps. Four strong oarsmen from Monte Isola were to row him down to Iseo, to take horse for Milan, and his servant, knapsack on shoulder, knocked warningly at the terrace window.

"No time to lose, excellency!" he cried.

Roberto turned and gripped my hand. "Pray for me," he said low; and with a brief gesture to the others ran down the terrace to the boat.

Marianna was bathing Faustina with happy tears.

"Look up, dear! Think how soon he will come back! And there is the sunrise—see!"

Andrea and Gemma had slunk away like ghosts at cock-crow, and a red dawn stood over Milan.

· · · · · · · ·

If that sun rose red it set scarlet. It was the first of the Five Days in Milan—the Five Glorious Days, as they are called. Roberto reached the city just before the gates closed. So much we knew—little more. We heard of him in the Broletto (whence he must have escaped when the Austrians blew in the door) and in the Casa Vidiserti, with Casati, Cattaneo and the rest;

## THE CONFESSIONAL

but after the barricading began we could trace him only as having been seen here and there in the thick of the fighting, or tending the wounded under Bertani's orders. His place, one would have said, was in the council-chamber, with the soberer heads; but that was an hour when every man gave his blood where it was most needed, and Cernuschi, Dandolo, Anfossi, della Porta fought shoulder to shoulder with students, artisans and peasants. Certain it is that he was seen on the fifth day; for among the volunteers who swarmed after Manara in his assault on the Porta Tosa was a servant of palazzo Siviano; and this fellow swore he had seen his master charge with Manara in the last assault—had watched him, sword in hand, press close to the gates, and then, as they swung open before the victorious dash of our men, had seen him drop and disappear in the inrushing tide of peasants that almost swept the little company off its feet. After that we heard nothing. There was savage work in Milan in those days, and more than one well-known figure lay lost among the heaps of dead hacked and disfeatured by Croat blades.

At the villa we waited breathless. News came to us hour by hour: the very wind seemed to carry it, and it was swept to us on the incessant rush of the rain. On the twenty-third Radetsky had fled from Milan, to face Venice rising in his path. On the

# THE CONFESSIONAL

twenty-fourth the first Piedmontese had crossed the Ticino, and Charles Albert himself was in Pavia on the twenty-ninth. The bells of Milan had carried the word from Turin to Naples, from Genoa to Ancona, and the whole country was pouring like a flood-tide into Lombardy. Heroes sprang up from the bloody soil as thick as wheat after rain, and every day carried some new name to us; but never the one for which we prayed and waited. Weeks passed. We heard of Pastrengo, Goito, Rivoli; of Radetsky hemmed into the Quadrilateral, and our troops closing in on him from Rome, Tuscany and Venetia. Months passed—and we heard of Custozza. We saw Charles Albert's broken forces flung back from the Mincio to the Oglio, from the Oglio to the Adda. We followed the dreadful retreat from Milan, and saw our rescuers dispersed like dust before the wind. But all the while no word came to us of Roberto.

These were dark days in Lombardy; and nowhere darker than in the old villa on Iseo. In September Donna Marianna and the young Countess put on black, and Count Andrea and his wife followed their example. In October the Countess gave birth to a daughter. Count Andrea then took possession of the palazzo Siviano, and the two women remained at the villa. I have no heart to tell you of the days that followed. Donna Marianna wept and prayed incessantly, and it

# THE CONFESSIONAL

was long before the baby could snatch a smile from her. As for the Countess Faustina, she went among us like one of the statues in the garden. The child had a wet-nurse from the village, and it was small wonder there was no milk for it in that marble breast. I spent much of my time at the villa, comforting Donna Marianna as best I could; but sometimes, in the long winter evenings, when we three sat in the dimly-lit *salone*, with the old Count's portrait overhead, and I looked up and saw the Countess Faustina in the tall carved seat beside her husband's empty chair, my spine grew chill and I felt a cold wind in my hair.

The end of it was that in the spring I went to see my bishop and laid my sin before him. He was a saintly and merciful old man, and gave me a patient hearing.

"You believed the lady innocent?" he asked when I had ended.

"Monsignore, on my soul!"

"You thought to avert a great calamity from the house to which you owed more than your life?"

"It was my only thought."

He laid his hand on my shoulder.

"Go home, my son. You shall learn my decision."

Three months later I was ordered to resign my living and go to America, where a priest was needed for the Italian mission church in New York. I packed

## THE CONFESSIONAL

my possessions and set sail from Genoa. I knew no more of America than any peasant up in the hills. I fully expected to be speared by naked savages on landing; and for the first few months after my arrival I wished at least once a day that such a blessed fate had befallen me. But it is no part of my story to tell you what I suffered in those early days. The Church had dealt with me mercifully, as is her wont, and her punishment fell far below my deserts. . .

I had been some four years in New York, and no longer thought of looking back from the plough, when one day word was brought me that an Italian professor lay ill and had asked for a priest. There were many Italian refugees in New York at that time, and the greater number, being well-educated men, earned a living by teaching their language, which was then included among the accomplishments of fashionable New York. The messenger led me to a poor boarding-house and up to a small bare room on the top floor. On the visiting-card nailed to the door I read the name "De Roberti, Professor of Italian." Inside, a gray-haired haggard man tossed on the narrow bed. He turned a glazed eye on me as I entered, and I recognized Roberto Siviano.

I steadied myself against the door-post and stood staring at him without a word.

# THE CONFESSIONAL

"What's the matter?" asked the doctor who was bending over the bed. I stammered that the sick man was an old friend.

"He wouldn't know his oldest friend just now," said the doctor. "The fever's on him; but it will go down toward sunset."

I sat down at the head of the bed and took Roberto's hand in mine.

"Is he going to die?" I asked.

"I don't believe so; but he wants nursing."

"I will nurse him."

The doctor nodded and went out. I sat in the little room, with Roberto's burning hand in mine. Gradually his skin cooled, the fingers grew quiet, and the flush faded from his sallow cheek-bones. Toward dusk he looked up at me and smiled.

"Egidio," he said quietly.

I administered the sacrament, which he received with the most fervent devotion; then he fell into a deep sleep.

During the weeks that followed I had no time to ask myself the meaning of it all. My one business was to keep him alive if I could. I fought the fever day and night, and at length it yielded. For the most part he raved or lay unconscious; but now and then he knew me for a moment, and whispered "Egidio" with a look of peace.

# THE CONFESSIONAL

I had stolen many hours from my duties to nurse him; and as soon as the danger was past I had to go back to my parish work. Then it was that I began to ask myself what had brought him to America; but I dared not face the answer.

On the fourth day I snatched a moment from my work and climbed to his room. I found him sitting propped against his pillows, weak as a child but clear-eyed and quiet. I ran forward, but his look stopped me.

"*Signor parocco,*" he said, "the doctor tells me that I owe my life to your nursing, and I have to thank you for the kindness you have shown to a friendless stranger."

"A stranger?" I gasped.

He looked at me steadily. "I am not aware that we have met before," he said.

For a moment I thought the fever was on him; but a second glance convinced me that he was master of himself.

"Roberto!" I cried, trembling.

"You have the advantage of me," he said civilly. "But my name is Roberti, not Roberto."

The floor swam under me and I had to lean against the wall.

"You are not Count Roberto Siviano of Milan?"

"I am Tommaso de Roberti, professor of Italian, from Modena."

# THE CONFESSIONAL

"And you have never seen me before?"

"Never that I know of."

"Were you never at Siviano, on the lake of Iseo?" I faltered.

He said calmly: "I am unacquainted with that part of Italy."

My heart grew cold and I was silent.

"You mistook me for a friend, I suppose?" he added.

"Yes," I cried, "I mistook you for a friend;" and with that I fell on my knees by his bed and cried like a child.

Suddenly I felt a touch on my shoulder. "Egidio," said he in a broken voice, "look up."

I raised my eyes, and there was his old smile above me, and we clung to each other without a word. Presently, however, he drew back, and put me quietly aside.

"Sit over there, Egidio. My bones are like water and I am not good for much talking yet."

"Let us wait, Roberto. Sleep now—we can talk to-morrow."

"No. What I have to say must be said at once." He examined me thoughtfully. "You have a parish here in New York?"

I assented.

"And my work keeps me here. I have pupils. It is too late to make a change."

# THE CONFESSIONAL

"A change?"

He continued to look at me calmly. "It would be difficult for me," he explained, "to find employment in a new place."

"But why should you leave here?"

"I shall have to," he returned deliberately, "if you persist in recognizing in me your former friend Count Siviano."

"Roberto!"

He lifted his hand. "Egidio," he said, "I am alone here, and without friends. The companionship, the sympathy of my parish priest would be a consolation in this strange city; but it must not be the companionship of the *parocco* of Siviano. You understand?"

"Roberto," I cried, "it is too dreadful to understand!"

"Be a man, Egidio," said he with a touch of impatience. "The choice lies with you, and you must make it now. If you are willing to ask no questions, to name no names, to make no allusions to the past, let us live as friends together, in God's name! If not, as soon as my legs can carry me I must be off again. The world is wide, luckily—but why should we be parted?"

I was on my knees at his side in an instant. "We must never be parted!" I cried. "Do as you will with me. Give me your orders and I obey—have I not always obeyed you?"

# THE CONFESSIONAL

I felt his hand close sharply on mine. "Egidio!" he admonished me.

"No—no—I shall remember. I shall say nothing—"

"Think nothing?"

"Think nothing," I said with a last effort.

"God bless you!" he answered.

My son, for eight years I kept my word to him. We met daily almost, we ate and walked and talked together, we lived like David and Jonathan—but without so much as a glance at the past. How he had escaped from Milan—how he had reached New York—I never knew. We talked often of Italy's liberation—as what Italians would not?—but never touched on his share in the work. Once only a word slipped from him; and that was when one day he asked me how it was that I had been sent to America. The blood rushed to my face, and before I could answer he had raised a silencing hand.

"I see," he said; "it was *your* penance too."

During the first years he had plenty of work to do, but he lived so frugally that I guessed he had some secret use for his earnings. It was easy to conjecture what it was. All over the world Italian exiles were toiling and saving to further the great cause. He had political friends in New York, and sometimes he went to other cities to attend meetings and make addresses.

# THE CONFESSIONAL

His zeal never slackened; and but for me he would often have gone hungry that some shivering patriot might dine. I was with him heart and soul, but I had the parish on my shoulders, and perhaps my long experience of men had made me a little less credulous than Christian charity requires; for I could have sworn that some of the heroes who hung on him had never had a whiff of Austrian blood, and would have fed out of the same trough with the white-coats if there had been polenta enough to go round. Happily my friend had no such doubts. He believed in the patriots as devoutly as in the cause; and if some of his hard-earned dollars travelled no farther than the nearest wine-cellar or cigar-shop, he never suspected the course they took.

His health was never the same after the fever; and by and by he began to lose his pupils, and the patriots cooled off as his pockets fell in. Toward the end I took him to live in my shabby attic. He had grown weak and had a troublesome cough, and he spent the greater part of his days indoors. Cruel days they must have been to him, but he made no sign, and always welcomed me with a cheerful word. When his pupils dropped off, and his health made it difficult for him to pick up work outside, he set up a letter-writer's sign, and used to earn a few pennies by serving as amanuensis to my poor parishioners; but it went against him

# THE CONFESSIONAL

to take their money, and half the time he did the work for nothing. I knew it was hard for him to live on charity, as he called it, and I used to find what jobs I could for him among my friends the *negozianti*, who would send him letters to copy, accounts to make up and what not; but we were all poor together, and the master had licked the platter before the dog got it.

So lived that just man, my son; and so, after eight years of exile, he died one day in my arms. God had let him live long enough to see Solferino and Villafranca; and was perhaps never more merciful than in sparing him Monte Rotondo and Mentana. But these are things of which it does not become me to speak. The new Italy does not wear the face of our visions; but it is written that God shall know His own, and it cannot be that He shall misread the hearts of those who dreamed of fashioning her in His image.

As for my friend, he is at peace, I doubt not; and his just life and holy death intercede for me, who sinned for his sake alone.

SANCTUARY

# PART I

## I

IT is not often that youth allows itself to feel undividedly happy: the sensation is too much the result of selection and elimination to be within reach of the awakening clutch on life. But Kate Orme, for once, had yielded herself to happiness, letting it permeate every faculty as a spring rain soaks into a germinating meadow. There was nothing to account for this sudden sense of beatitude; but was it not this precisely which made it so irresistible, so overwhelming? There had been, within the last two months—since her engagement to Denis Peyton—no distinct addition to the sum of her happiness, and no possibility, she would have affirmed, of adding perceptibly to a total already incalculable. Inwardly and outwardly the conditions of her life were unchanged; but whereas, before, the air had been full of flitting wings, now they seemed to pause over her and she could trust herself to their shelter.

Many influences had combined to build up the centre of brooding peace in which she found herself. Her nature answered to the finest vibrations, and at first her joy in loving had been too great not to bring with it a certain confusion, a readjusting of the whole scenery of life. She found herself in a new country, wherein he who had led her there was least able to be her guide. There were moments when she felt that the first stranger in the street could have interpreted her happiness for her more easily than Denis. Then, as her eye adapted itself, as the lines flowed into each other, opening deep vistas upon new horizons, she began to enter into possession of her kingdom, to entertain the actual sense of its belonging to her. But she had never before felt that she also belonged to it; and this was the feeling which now came to complete her happiness, to give it the hallowing sense of permanence.

She rose from the writing-table where, list in hand, she had been going over the wedding-invitations, and walked toward the drawing-room window. Everything about her seemed to contribute to that rare harmony of feeling which levied a tax on every sense. The large coolness of the room, its fine traditional air of spacious living, its outlook over field and woodland toward the lake lying under the silver bloom of September; the very scent of the late violets in a glass on the writing-table; the rosy-mauve masses of hydrangea in tubs along the terrace; the fall, now and then, of a leaf through the still air—all, somehow, were mingled in the suffusion of well-being that yet made them seem but so much dross upon its current.

The girl's smile prolonged itself at the sight of a figure approaching from the lower slopes above the lake. The path was a short cut from the Peyton place, and she had known that Denis would appear in it at about that hour.

# SANCTUARY

Her smile, however, was prolonged not so much by his approach as by her sense of the impossibility of communicating her mood to him. The feeling did not disturb her. She could not imagine sharing her deepest moods with any one, and the world in which she lived with Denis was too bright and spacious to admit of any sense of constraint. Her smile was in truth a tribute to that clear-eyed directness of his which was so often a refuge from her own complexities.

Denis Peyton was used to being met with a smile. He might have been pardoned for thinking smiles the habitual wear of the human countenance; and his estimate of life and of himself was necessarily tinged by the cordial terms on which they had always met each other. He had in fact found life, from the start, an uncommonly agreeable business, culminating fitly enough in his engagement to the only girl he had ever wished to marry, and the inheritance, from his unhappy step-brother, of a fortune which agreeably widened his horizon. Such a combination of circumstances might well justify a young man in thinking himself of some account in the universe; and it seemed the final touch of fitness that the mourning which Denis still wore for poor Arthur should lend a new distinction to his somewhat florid good looks.

Kate Orme was not without an amused perception of her future husband's point of view; but she could enter into it with the tolerance which allows for the inconscient element in all our judgments. There was, for instance, no one more sentimentally humane than Denis's mother, the second Mrs. Peyton, a scented silvery person whose lavender silks and neutral-tinted manner expressed a mind with its blinds drawn down toward all the unpleasantness of life; yet it was clear that Mrs. Peyton saw a "dispensation" in the fact that her step-son had never married, and that his death had enabled Denis, at the right moment, to step gracefully into affluence. Was it not, after all, a sign of healthy-mindedness to take the gifts of the gods in this religious spirit, discovering fresh evidence of "design" in what had once seemed the sad fact of Arthur's inaccessibility to correction? Mrs. Peyton, beautifully conscious of having done her "best" for Arthur, would have thought it unchristian to repine at the providential failure of her efforts. Denis's deductions were, of course, a little less direct than his mother's. He had, besides, been fond of Arthur, and his efforts to keep the poor fellow straight had been less didactic and more spontaneous. Their result read itself, if not in any change in Arthur's character, at least in the revised wording of his will; and Denis's moral sense was pleasantly fortified by the discovery that it very substantially paid to be a good fellow.

The sense of general providentialness on which Mrs. Peyton reposed had in fact been confirmed by events which reduced Denis's mourning to a mere tribute of respect—since it would have been a mockery to deplore the

## SANCTUARY

disappearance of any one who had left behind him such an unsavory wake as poor Arthur. Kate did not quite know what had happened: her father was as firmly convinced as Mrs. Peyton that young girls should not be admitted to any open discussion of life. She could only gather, from the silences and evasions amid which she moved, that a woman had turned up—a woman who was of course "dreadful," and whose dreadfulness appeared to include a sort of shadowy claim upon Arthur. But the claim, whatever it was, had been promptly discredited. The whole question had vanished and the woman with it. The blinds were drawn again on the ugly side of things, and life was resumed on the usual assumption that no such side existed. Kate knew only that a darkness had crossed her sky and left it as unclouded as before.

Was it, perhaps, she now asked herself, the very lifting of the cloud—remote, unthreatening as it had been—which gave such new serenity to her heaven? It was horrible to think that one's deepest security was a mere sense of escape—that happiness was no more than a reprieve. The perversity of such ideas was emphasized by Peyton's approach. He had the gift of restoring things to their normal relations, of carrying one over the chasms of life through the closed tunnel of an incurious cheerfulness. All that was restless and questioning in the girl subsided in his presence, and she was content to take her love as a gift of grace, which began just where the office of reason ended.

# SANCTUARY

She was more than ever, to-day, in this mood of charmed surrender. More than ever he seemed the keynote of the accord between herself and life, the centre of a delightful complicity in every surrounding circumstance. One could not look at him without seeing that there was always a fair wind in his sails.

It was carrying him toward her, as usual, at a quick confident pace, which nevertheless lagged a little, she noticed, as he emerged from the beech-grove and struck across the lawn. He walked as though he were tired. She had meant to wait for him on the terrace, held in check by her usual inclination to linger on the threshold of her pleasures; but now something drew her toward him, and she went quickly down the steps and across the lawn.

"Denis, you look tired. I was afraid something had happened."

She had slipped her hand through his arm, and as they moved forward she glanced up at him, struck not so much by any new look in his face as by the fact that her approach had made no change in it.

"I am rather tired.—Is your father in?"

"Papa?" She looked up in surprise. "He went to town yesterday. Don't you remember?"

"Of course—I'd forgotten. You're alone, then?" She dropped his arm and stood before him. He was very pale now, with the furrowed look of extreme physical weariness.

"Denis—are you ill? *Has* anything happened?"

# SANCTUARY

He forced a smile. "Yes—but you need n't look so frightened."

She drew a deep breath of reassurance. *He* was safe, after all! And all else, for a moment, seemed to swing below the rim of her world.

"Your mother—?" she then said, with a fresh start of fear.

"It 's not my mother." They had reached the terrace, and he moved toward the house. "Let us go indoors. There 's such a beastly glare out here."

He seemed to find relief in the cool obscurity of the drawing-room, where, after the brightness of the afternoon light, their faces were almost indistinguishable to each other. She sat down, and he moved a few paces away. Before the writing-table he paused to look at the neatly sorted heaps of wedding-cards.

"They are to be sent out to-morrow?"

"Yes."

He turned back and stood before her.

"It 's about the woman," he began abruptly—"the woman who pretended to be Arthur's wife."

Kate started as at the clutch of an unacknowledged fear.

"She *was* his wife, then?"

Peyton made an impatient movement of negation. "If she was, why did n't she prove it? She had n't a shred of evidence. The courts rejected her appeal."

"Well, then—?"

"Well, she's dead." He paused, and the next words came with difficulty. "She and the child."

"The child? There was a child?"

"Yes."

Kate started up and then sank down. These were not things about which young girls were told. The confused sense of horror had been nothing to this first sharp edge of fact.

"And both are dead?"

"Yes."

"How do you know? My father said she had gone away—gone back to the West—"

"So we thought. But this morning we found her."

"Found her?"

He motioned toward the window. "Out there—in the lake."

"Both?"

"Both."

She drooped before him shudderingly, her eyes hidden, as though to exclude the vision. "She had drowned herself?"

"Yes."

"Oh, poor thing—poor thing!"

They paused awhile, the minutes delving an abyss between them till he threw a few irrelevant words across the silence.

"One of the gardeners found them."

"Poor thing!"

"It was sufficiently horrible."

"Horrible—oh!" She had swung round again to her pole. "Poor Denis! *You* were not there—*you* did n't have to—?"

"I had to see her." She felt the instant relief in his voice. He could talk now, could distend his nerves in the warm air of her sympathy. "I had to identify her." He rose nervously and began to pace the room. "It 's knocked the wind out of me. I—my God! I could n't foresee it, could I?" He halted before her with outstretched hands of argument. "I did all I could—it 's not *my* fault, is it?"

"Your fault? Denis!"

"She would n't take the money—" He broke off, checked by her awakened glance.

"The money? What money?" Her face changed, hardening as his relaxed. "Had you offered her *money* to give up the case?"

He stared a moment, and then dismissed the implication with a laugh.

"No—no; after the case was decided against her. She seemed hard up, and I sent Hinton to her with a cheque."

"And she refused it?"

"Yes."

"What did she say?"

"Oh, I don't know—the usual thing. That she 'd only

# SANCTUARY

wanted to prove she was his wife—on the child's account. That she 'd never wanted his money. Hinton said she was very quiet—not in the least excited—but she sent back the cheque."

Kate sat motionless, her head bent, her hands clasped about her knees. She no longer looked at Peyton.

"Could there have been a mistake?" she asked slowly.

"A mistake?"

She raised her head now, and fixed her eyes on his, with a strange insistence of observation. "Could they have been married?"

"The courts did n't think so."

"Could the courts have been mistaken?"

He started up again, and threw himself into another chair. "Good God, Kate! We gave her every chance to prove her case—why did n't she do it? You don't know what you 're talking about—such things are kept from girls. Why, whenever a man of Arthur's kind dies, such—such women turn up. There are lawyers who live on such jobs—ask your father about it. Of course, this woman expected to be bought off—"

"But if she would n't take your money?"

"She expected a big sum, I mean, to drop the case. When she found we meant to fight it, she saw the game was up. I suppose it was her last throw, and she was desperate; we don't know how many times she may have been through the same thing before. That kind of woman is

# SANCTUARY

always trying to make money out of the heirs of any man who—who has been about with them."

Kate received this in silence. She had a sense of walking along a narrow ledge of consciousness above a sheer hallucinating depth into which she dared not look. But the depth drew her, and she plunged one terrified glance into it.

"But the child—the child was Arthur's?"

Peyton shrugged his shoulders. "There again—how can we tell? Why, I don't suppose the woman herself—I wish to heaven your father were here to explain!"

She rose and crossed over to him, laying her hands on his shoulders with a gesture almost maternal.

"Don't let us talk of it," she said. "You did all you could. Think what a comfort you were to poor Arthur."

He let her hands lie where she had placed them, without response or resistance.

"I tried—I tried hard to keep him straight!"

"We all know that—every one knows it. And we know how grateful he was—what a difference it made to him in the end. It would have been dreadful to think of his dying out there alone."

She drew him down on a sofa and seated herself by his side. A deep lassitude was upon him, and the hand she had possessed herself of lay in her hold inert.

"It was splendid of you to travel day and night as you did. And then that dreadful week before he died! But for you he would have died alone among strangers."

## SANCTUARY

He sat silent, his head dropping forward, his eyes fixed. "Among strangers," he repeated absently.

She looked up, as if struck by a sudden thought. "That poor woman—did you ever see her while you were out there?"

He drew his hand away and gathered his brows together as if in an effort of remembrance.

"I saw her—oh, yes, I saw her." He pushed the tumbled hair from his forehead and stood up. "Let us go out," he said. "My head is in a fog. I want to get away from it all."

A wave of compunction drew her to her feet.

"It was my fault! I ought not to have asked so many questions." She turned and rang the bell. "I'll order the ponies—we shall have time for a drive before sunset."

## II

WITH the sunset in their faces they swept through the keen-scented autumn air at the swiftest pace of Kate's ponies. She had given the reins to Peyton, and he had turned the horses' heads away from the lake, rising by woody upland lanes to the high pastures which still held the sunlight. The horses were fresh enough to claim his undivided attention, and he drove in silence, his smooth fair profile turned to his companion, who sat silent also.

Kate Orme was engaged in one of those rapid mental

## SANCTUARY

excursions which were forever sweeping her from the straight path of the actual into uncharted regions of conjecture. Her survey of life had always been marked by the tendency to seek out ultimate relations, to extend her researches to the limit of her imaginative experience. But hitherto she had been like some young captive brought up in a windowless palace whose painted walls she takes for the actual world. Now the palace had been shaken to its base, and through a cleft in the walls she looked out upon life. For the first moment all was indistinguishable blackness; then she began to detect vague shapes and confused gestures in the depths. There were people below there, men like Denis, girls like herself—for under the unlikeness she felt the strange affinity—all struggling in that awful coil of moral darkness, with agonized hands reaching up for rescue. Her heart shrank from the horror of it, and then, in a passion of pity, drew back to the edge of the abyss. Suddenly her eyes turned toward Denis. His face was grave, but less disturbed. And men knew about these things! They carried this abyss in their bosoms, and went about smiling, and sat at the feet of innocence. Could it be that Denis—Denis even— Ah, no! She remembered what he had been to poor Arthur; she understood, now, the vague allusions to what he had tried to do for his brother. He had seen Arthur down there, in that coiling blackness, and had leaned over and tried to drag him out. But Arthur was too deep down, and his arms were interlocked with

## SANCTUARY

other arms—they had dragged each other deeper, poor souls, like drowning people who fight together in the waves! Kate's visualizing habit gave a hateful precision and persistency to the image she had evoked—she could not rid herself of the vision of anguished shapes striving together in the darkness. The horror of it took her by the throat—she drew a choking breath, and felt the tears on her face.

Peyton turned to her. The horses were climbing a hill, and his attention had strayed from them.

"This has done me good," he began; but as he looked his voice changed. "Kate! What is it? Why are you crying? Oh, for God's sake, *don't!*" he ended, his hand closing on her wrist.

She steadied herself and raised her eyes to his.

"I—I could n't help it," she stammered, struggling in the sudden release of her pent compassion. "It seems so awful that we should stand so close to this horror—that it might have been you who—"

"I who—what on earth do you mean?" he broke in stridently.

"Oh, don't you see? I found myself exulting that you and I were so far from it—above it—safe in ourselves and each other—and then the other feeling came—the sense of selfishness, of going by on the other side; and I tried to realize that it might have been you and I who—who were down there in the night and the flood—"

# SANCTUARY

Peyton let the whip fall on the ponies' flanks. "Upon my soul," he said with a laugh, "you must have a nice opinion of both of us."

The words fell chillingly on the blaze of her self-immolation. Would she never learn to remember that Denis was incapable of mounting such hypothetical pyres? He might be as alive as herself to the direct demands of duty, but of its imaginative claims he was robustly unconscious. The thought brought a wholesome reaction of thankfulness.

"Ah, well," she said, the sunset dilating through her tears, "don't you see that I can bear to think such things only because they're impossibilities? It's easy to look over into the depths if one has a rampart to lean on. What I most pity poor Arthur for is that, instead of that woman lying there, so dreadfully dead, there might have been a girl like me, so exquisitely alive because of him; but it seems cruel, does n't it, to let what he was *not* add ever so little to the value of what you are? To let him contribute ever so little to my happiness by the difference there is between you?"

She was conscious, as she spoke, of straying again beyond his reach, through intricacies of sensation new even to her exploring susceptibilities. A happy literalness usually enabled him to strike a short cut through such labyrinths, and rejoin her smiling on the other side; but now she became wonderingly aware that he had been caught in the thick of her hypothesis.

# SANCTUARY

"It's the difference that makes you care for me, then?" he broke out, with a kind of violence which seemed to renew his clutch on her wrist.

"The difference?"

He lashed the ponies again, so sharply that a murmur escaped her, and he drew them up, quivering, with an inconsequent "Steady, boys," at which their back-laid ears protested.

"It's because I'm moral and respectable, and all that, that you're fond of me," he went on; "you're—you're simply in love with my virtues. You couldn't imagine caring if I were down there in the ditch, as you say, with Arthur?"

The question fell on a silence which seemed to deepen suddenly within herself. Every thought hung bated on the sense that something was coming: her whole consciousness became a void to receive it.

"Denis!" she cried.

He turned on her almost savagely. "I don't want your pity, you know," he burst out. "You can keep that for Arthur. I had an idea women loved men for themselves— through everything, I mean. But I wouldn't steal your love—I don't want it on false pretenses, you understand. Go and look into other men's lives, that's all I ask of you. I slipped into it—it was just a case of holding my tongue when I ought to have spoken—but I—I—for God's sake, don't sit there staring! I suppose you've seen all along that I knew he was married to the woman."

# SANCTUARY

## III

THE housekeeper's reminding her that Mr. Orme would be at home the next day for dinner, and did she think he would like the venison with claret sauce or jelly, roused Kate to the first consciousness of her surroundings. Her father would return on the morrow: he would give to the dressing of the venison such minute consideration as, in his opinion, every detail affecting his comfort or convenience quite obviously merited. And if it were not the venison it would be something else; if it were not the housekeeper it would be Mr. Orme, charged with the results of a conference with his agent, a committee-meeting at his club, or any of the other incidents which, by happening to himself, became events. Kate found herself caught in the inexorable continuity of life, found herself gazing over a scene of ruin lit up by the punctual recurrence of habit as nature's calm stare lights the morrow of a whirlwind.

Life was going on, then, and dragging her at its wheels. She could neither check its rush nor wrench loose from it and drop out—oh, how blessedly—into darkness and cessation. She must go bounding on, racked, broken, but alive in every fibre. The most she could hope was a few hours' respite, not from her own terrors, but from the pressure of outward claims: the midday halt, during which the victim is unbound while his torturers rest from their

## SANCTUARY

efforts. Till her father's return she would have the house to herself, and, the question of the venison despatched, could give herself to long lonely pacings of the empty rooms, and shuddering subsidences upon her pillow.

Her first impulse, as the mist cleared from her brain, was the habitual one of reaching out for ultimate relations. She wanted to know the worst; and for her, as she saw in a flash, the worst of it was the core of fatality in what had happened. She shrank from her own way of putting it— nor was it even figuratively true that she had ever felt, under faith in Denis, any such doubt as the perception implied. But that was merely because her imagination had never put him to the test. She was fond of exposing herself to hypothetical ordeals, but somehow she had never carried Denis with her on these adventures. What she saw now was that, in a world of strangeness, he remained the object least strange to her. She was not in the tragic case of the girl who suddenly sees her lover unmasked. No mask had dropped from Denis's face: the pink shades had simply been lifted from the lamps, and she saw him for the first time in an unmitigated glare.

Such exposure does not alter the features, but it lays an ugly emphasis on the most charming lines, pushing the smile to a grin, the curve of good-nature to the droop of slackness. And it was precisely into the flagging lines of extreme weakness that Denis's graceful contour flowed. In the terrible talk which had followed his avowal, and

[ 262 ]

wherein every word flashed a light on his moral processes, she had been less startled by what he had done than by the way in which his conscience had already become a passive surface for the channelling of consequences. He was like a child who had put a match to the curtains, and stands agape at the blaze. It was horribly naughty to put the match—but beyond that the child's responsibility did not extend. In this business of Arthur's, where all had been wrong from the beginning—where self-defence might well find a plea for its casuistries in the absence of a definite right to be measured by—it had been easy, after the first slip, to drop a little lower with each struggle. The woman —oh, the woman was—well, of the kind who prey on such men. Arthur, out there, at his lowest ebb, had drifted into living with her as a man drifts into drink or opium. He knew what she was—he knew where she had come from. But he had fallen ill, and she had nursed him—nursed him devotedly, of course. That was her chance, and she knew it. Before he was out of the fever she had the noose around him—he came to and found himself married. Such cases were common enough—if the man recovered he bought off the woman and got a divorce. It was all a part of the business—the marriage, the bribe, the divorce. Some of those women made a big income out of it—they were married and divorced once a year. If Arthur had only got well —but, instead, he had a relapse and died. And there was the woman, made his widow by mischance as it were, with her child on her arm—whose child?—and a scoundrelly black-mailing lawyer to work up her case for her. Her claim was clear enough—the right of dower, a third of his estate. But if he had never meant to marry her? If he had been trapped as patently as a rustic fleeced in a gambling-hell? Arthur, in his last hours, had confessed to the marriage, but had also acknowledged its folly. And after his death, when Denis came to look about him and make inquiries, he found that the witnesses, if there had been any, were dispersed and undiscoverable. The whole question hinged on Arthur's statement to his brother. Suppress that statement, and the claim vanished, and with it the scandal, the humiliation, the life-long burden of the woman and child dragging the name of Peyton through heaven knew what depths. He had thought of that first, Denis swore, rather than of the money. The money, of course, had made a difference,—he was too honest not to own it—but not till afterward, he declared—would have declared on his honour, but that the word tripped him up, and sent a flush to his forehead.

Thus, in broken phrases, he flung his defence at her: a defence improvised, pieced together as he went along, to mask the crude instinctiveness of his act. For with increasing clearness Kate saw, as she listened, that there had been no real struggle in his mind; that, but for the grim logic of chance, he might never have felt the need of any justification. If the woman, after the manner of such baffled huntresses, had wandered off in search of fresh prey, he might, quite sincerely, have congratulated himself on having saved a decent name and an honest fortune from her talons. It was the price she had paid to establish her claim that for the first time brought him to a startled sense of its justice. His conscience responded only to the concrete pressure of facts.

It was with the anguish of this discovery that Kate Orme locked herself in at the end of their talk. How the talk had ended, how at length she had got him from the room and the house, she recalled but confusedly. The tragedy of the woman's death, and of his own share in it, were as nothing in the disaster of his bright irreclaimableness. Once, when she had cried out, "You would have married me and said nothing," and he groaned back, "But I *have* told you," she felt like a trainer with a lash above some bewildered animal.

But she persisted savagely. "You told me because you had to; because your nerves gave way; because you knew it could n't hurt you to tell." The perplexed appeal of his gaze had almost checked her. "You told me because it was a relief; but nothing will really relieve you—nothing will really help you—till you have told some one who—who *will* hurt you."

"Who will hurt me—?"

"Till you have told the truth as—as openly as you lied."

# SANCTUARY

He started up, ghastly with fear. "I don't understand you."

"You must confess, then—publicly—openly—you must go to the judge. I don't know how it's done."

"To the judge? When they're both dead? When everything is at an end? What good could that do?" he groaned.

"Everything is not at an end for you—everything is just beginning. You must clear yourself of this guilt; and there is only one way—to confess it. And you must give back the money."

This seemed to strike him as conclusive proof of her irrelevance. "I wish I had never heard of the money! But to whom would you have me give it back? I tell you she was a waif out of the gutter. I don't believe any one knew her real name—I don't believe she had one."

"She must have had a mother and father."

"Am I to devote my life to hunting for them through the slums of California? And how shall I know when I have found them? It's impossible to make you understand. I did wrong—I did horribly wrong—but that is not the way to repair it."

"What is, then?"

He paused, a little askance at the question. "To do better—to do my best," he said, with a sudden flourish of firmness. "To take warning by this dreadful—"

"Oh, be silent," she cried out, and hid her face. He looked at her hopelessly.

# SANCTUARY

At last he said: "I don't know what good it can do to go on talking. I have only one more thing to say. Of course you know that you are free."

He spoke simply, with a sudden return to his old voice and accent, at which she weakened as under a caress. She lifted her head and gazed at him. "Am I?" she said musingly.

"Kate!" burst from him; but she raised a silencing hand.

"It seems to me," she said, "that I am imprisoned—imprisoned with you in this dreadful thing. First I must help you to get out—then it will be time enough to think of myself."

His face fell and he stammered: "I don't understand you."

"I can't say what I shall do—or how I shall feel—till I know what you are going to do and feel."

"You must see how I feel—that I'm half dead with it."

"Yes—but that is only half."

He turned this over for a perceptible space of time before asking slowly: "You mean that you'll give me up, if I don't do this crazy thing you propose?"

She paused in turn. "No," she said; "I don't want to bribe you. You must feel the need of it yourself."

"The need of proclaiming this thing publicly?"

"Yes."

# SANCTUARY

He sat staring before him. "Of course you realize what it would mean?" he began at length.

"To you?" she returned.

"I put that aside. To others—to you. I should go to prison."

"I suppose so," she said simply.

"You seem to take it very easily—I'm afraid my mother would n't."

"Your mother?" This produced the effect he had expected.

"You had n't thought of her, I suppose? It would probably kill her."

"It would have killed her to think that you could do what you have done!"

"It would have made her very unhappy; but there's a difference."

Yes: there was a difference; a difference which no rhetoric could disguise. The secret sin would have made Mrs. Peyton wretched, but it would not have killed her. And she would have taken precisely Denis's view of the elasticity of atonement: she would have accepted private regrets as the genteel equivalent of open expiation. Kate could even imagine her extracting a "lesson" from the providential fact that her son had not been found out.

"You see it's not so simple," he broke out, with a tinge of doleful triumph.

"No: it's not simple," she assented.

# SANCTUARY

"One must think of others," he continued, gathering faith in his argument as he saw her reduced to acquiescence.

She made no answer, and after a moment he rose to go. So far, in retrospect, she could follow the course of their talk; but when, in the act of parting, argument lapsed into entreaty, and renunciation into the passionate appeal to give him at least one more hearing, her memory lost itself in a tumult of pain, and she recalled only that, when the door closed on him, he took with him her promise to see him once again.

## IV

SHE had promised to see him again; but the promise did not imply that she had rejected his offer of freedom. In the first rush of misery she had not fully repossessed herself, had felt herself entangled in his fate by a hundred meshes of association and habit; but after a sleepless night spent with the thought of him—that dreadful bridal of their souls—she woke to a morrow in which he had no part. She had not sought her freedom, nor had he given it; but a chasm had opened at their feet, and they found themselves on different sides.

Now she was able to scan the disaster from the melancholy vantage of her independence. She could even draw a solace from the fact that she had ceased to love Denis. It was inconceivable that an emotion so interwoven with every fibre of consciousness should cease as suddenly as the flow of sap in an uprooted plant; but she had never allowed herself to be tricked by the current phraseology of sentiment, and there were no stock axioms to protect her from the truth.

It was probably because she had ceased to love him that she could look forward with a kind of ghastly composure to seeing him again. She had stipulated, of course, that the wedding should be put off, but she had named no other condition beyond asking for two days to herself —two days during which he was not even to write. She wished to shut herself in with her misery, to accustom herself to it as she had accustomed herself to happiness. But actual seclusion was impossible: the subtle reactions of life almost at once began to break down her defences. She could no more have her wretchedness to herself than any other emotion: all the lives about her were so many unconscious factors in her sensations. She tried to concentrate herself on the thought as to how she could best help poor Denis; for love, in ebbing, had laid bare an unsuspected depth of pity. But she found it more and more difficult to consider his situation in the abstract light of right and wrong. Open expiation still seemed to her the only possible way of healing; but she tried vainly to think of Mrs. Peyton as taking such a view. Yet Mrs. Peyton ought at least to know what had happened: was it not, in the last resort, she who should pronounce on her son's

# SANCTUARY

course? For a moment Kate was fascinated by this evasion of responsibility; she had nearly decided to tell Denis that he must begin by confessing everything to his mother. But almost at once she began to shrink from the consequences. There was nothing she so dreaded for him as that any one should take a light view of his act: should turn its irremediableness into an excuse. And this, she foresaw, was what Mrs. Peyton would do. The first burst of misery over, she would envelop the whole situation in a mist of expediency. Brought to the bar of Kate's judgment, she at once revealed herself incapable of higher action.

Kate's conception of her was still under arraignment when the actual Mrs. Peyton fluttered in. It was the afternoon of the second day, as the girl phrased it in the dismal re-creation of her universe. She had been thinking so hard of Mrs. Peyton that the lady's silvery insubstantial presence seemed hardly more than a projection of the thought; but as Kate collected herself, and regained contact with the outer world, her preoccupation yielded to surprise. It was unusual for Mrs. Peyton to pay visits. For years she had remained enthroned in a semi-invalidism which prohibited effort while it did not preclude diversion; and the girl at once divined a special purpose in her coming.

Mrs. Peyton's traditions would not have permitted any direct method of attack; and Kate had to sit through the usual prelude of ejaculation and anecdote. Presently, however, the elder lady's voice gathered significance, and laying her hand on Kate's she murmured: "I have come to talk to you of this sad affair."

Kate began to tremble. Was it possible that Denis had after all spoken? A rising hope checked her utterance, and she saw in a flash that it still lay with him to regain his hold on her. But Mrs. Peyton went on delicately: "It has been a great shock to my poor boy. To be brought in contact with Arthur's past was in itself inexpressibly painful; but this last dreadful business—that woman's wicked act—"

"Wicked?" Kate exclaimed.

Mrs. Peyton's gentle stare reproved her. "Surely religion teaches us that suicide is a sin? And to murder her child! I ought not to speak to you of such things, my dear. No one has ever mentioned anything so dreadful in my presence: my dear husband used to screen me so carefully from the painful side of life. Where there is so much that is beautiful to dwell upon, we should try to ignore the existence of such horrors. But nowadays everything is in the papers; and Denis told me he thought it better that you should hear the news first from him."

Kate nodded without speaking.

"He felt how *dreadful* it was to have to tell you. But I tell him he takes a morbid view of the case. Of course one is shocked at the woman's crime—but, if one looks a little deeper, how can one help seeing that it may have

# SANCTUARY

been designed as the means of rescuing that poor child from a life of vice and misery? That is the view I want Denis to take: I want him to see how all the difficulties of life disappear when one has learned to look for a divine purpose in human sufferings."

Mrs. Peyton rested a moment on this period, as an experienced climber pauses to be overtaken by a less agile companion; but presently she became aware that Kate was still far below her, and perhaps needed a stronger incentive to the ascent.

"My dear child," she said adroitly, "I said just now that I was sorry you had been obliged to hear of this sad affair; but after all it is only you who can avert its consequences."

Kate drew an eager breath. "Its consequences?" she faltered.

Mrs. Peyton's voice dropped solemnly. "Denis has told me everything," she said.

"Everything?"

"That you insist on putting off the marriage. Oh, my dear, I do implore you to reconsider that!"

Kate sank back with the sense of having passed again into a region of leaden shadow. "Is that all he told you?"

Mrs. Peyton gazed at her with arch raillery. "All? Is n't it everything—to him?"

"Did he give you my reason, I mean?"

"He said you felt that, after this shocking tragedy,

## SANCTUARY

there ought, in decency, to be a delay; and I quite understand the feeling. It does seem too unfortunate that the woman should have chosen this particular time! But you will find as you grow older that life is full of such sad contrasts."

Kate felt herself slowly petrifying under the warm drip of Mrs. Peyton's platitudes.

"It seems to me," the elder lady continued, "that there is only one point from which we ought to consider the question—and that is, its effect on Denis. But for that we ought to refuse to know anything about it. But it has made my boy so unhappy. The law-suit was a cruel ordeal to him—the dreadful notoriety, the revelation of poor Arthur's infirmities. Denis is as sensitive as a woman; it is his unusual refinement of feeling that makes him so worthy of being loved by you. But such sensitiveness may be carried to excess. He ought not to let this unhappy incident prey on him: it shows a lack of trust in the divine ordering of things. That is what troubles me: his faith in life has been shaken. And—you must forgive me, dear child—you *will* forgive me, I know—but I can't help blaming you a little—"

Mrs. Peyton's accent converted the accusation into a caress, which prolonged itself in a tremulous pressure of Kate's hand.

The girl gazed at her blankly. "You blame *me*——?"

"Don't be offended, my child. I only fear that your

## SANCTUARY

excessive sympathy with Denis, your own delicacy of feeling, may have led you to encourage his morbid ideas. He tells me you were very much shocked—as you naturally would be—as any girl must be—I would not have you otherwise, dear Kate! It is *beautiful* that you should both feel so; most beautiful; but you know religion teaches us not to yield too much to our grief. Let the dead bury their dead; the living owe themselves to each other. And what had this wretched woman to do with either of you? It is a misfortune for Denis to have been connected in any way with a man of Arthur Peyton's character; but after all, poor Arthur did all he could to atone for the disgrace he brought on us, by making Denis his heir—and I am sure I have no wish to question the decrees of Providence."

Mrs. Peyton paused again, and then softly absorbed both of Kate's hands. "For my part," she continued, "I see in it another instance of the beautiful ordering of events. Just after dear Denis's inheritance has removed the last obstacle to your marriage, this sad incident comes to show how desperately he needs you, how cruel it would be to ask him to defer his happiness."

She broke off, shaken out of her habitual placidity by the abrupt withdrawal of the girl's hands. Kate sat inertly staring, but no answer rose to her lips.

At length Mrs. Peyton resumed, gathering her draperies about her with a tentative hint of leave-taking: "I may go home and tell him that you will not put off the wedding?"

Kate was still silent, and her visitor looked at her with the mild surprise of an advocate unaccustomed to plead in vain.

"If your silence means refusal, my dear, I think you ought to realize the responsibility you assume." Mrs. Peyton's voice had acquired an edge of righteous asperity. "If Denis has a fault it is that he is too gentle, too yielding, too readily influenced by those he cares for. Your influence is paramount with him now—but if you turn from him just when he needs your help, who can say what the result will be?"

The argument, though impressively delivered, was hardly of a nature to carry conviction to its hearer; but it was perhaps for that very reason that she suddenly and unexpectedly replied to it by sinking back into her seat with a burst of tears. To Mrs. Peyton, however, tears were the signal of surrender, and, at Kate's side in an instant she hastened to temper her triumph with magnanimity.

"Don't think I don't feel with you; but we must both forget ourselves for our boy's sake. I told him I should come back with your promise."

The arm she had slipped about Kate's shoulder fell back with the girl's start. Kate had seen in a flash what capital would be made of her emotion.

"No, no, you misunderstand me. I can make no promise," she declared.

The older lady sat a moment irresolute; then she restored her arm to the shoulder from which it had been so abruptly displaced.

"My dear child," she said, in a tone of tender confidence, "if I have misunderstood you, ought you not to enlighten me? You asked me just now if Denis had given me your reason for this strange postponement. He gave me one reason, but it seems hardly sufficient to explain your conduct. If there is any other,—and I know you well enough to feel sure there is,—will you not trust me with it? If my boy has been unhappy enough to displease you, will you not give his mother the chance to plead his cause? Remember, no one should be condemned unheard. As Denis's mother, I have the right to ask for your reason."

"My reason? My reason?" Kate stammered, panting with the exhaustion of the struggle. Oh, if only Mrs. Peyton would release her! "If you have the right to know it, why does n't he tell you?" she cried.

Mrs. Peyton stood up, quivering. "I will go home and ask him," she said. "I will tell him he had your permission to speak."

She moved toward the door, with the nervous haste of a person unaccustomed to decisive action. But Kate sprang before her.

"No, no; don't ask him! I implore you not to ask him," she cried.

Mrs. Peyton turned on her with sudden authority of voice and gesture. "Do I understand you?" she said.

# SANCTUARY

"You admit that you have a reason for putting off your marriage, and yet you forbid me—me, Denis's mother—to ask him what it is? My poor child, I need n't ask, for I know already. If he has offended you, and you refuse him the chance to defend himself, I need n't look farther for your reason: it is simply that you have ceased to love him."

Kate fell back from the door which she had instinctively barricaded.

"Perhaps that is it," she murmured, letting Mrs. Peyton pass.

## V

MR. ORME'S returning carriage-wheels crossed Mrs. Peyton's indignant flight; and an hour later Kate, in the bland candle-light of the dinner-hour, sat listening with practised fortitude to her father's comments on the venison.

She had wondered, as she awaited him in the drawing-room, if he would notice any change in her appearance. It seemed to her that the flagellation of her thoughts must have left visible traces. But Mr. Orme was not a man of subtle perceptions, save where his personal comfort was affected: though his egoism was clothed in the finest feelers, he did not suspect a similar surface in others. His daughter, as part of himself, came within the normal range of his solicitude; but she was an outlying region, a

# SANCTUARY

subject province; and Mr. Orme's was a highly centralized polity.

News of the painful incident—he often used Mrs. Peyton's vocabulary—had reached him at his club, and to some extent disturbed the assimilation of a carefully ordered breakfast; but since then two days had passed, and it did not take Mr. Orme forty-eight hours to resign himself to the misfortunes of others. It was all very nasty, of course, and he wished to heaven it had n't happened to any one about to be connected with him; but he viewed it with the transient annoyance of a gentleman who has been splashed by the mud of a fatal runaway.

Mr. Orme affected, under such circumstances, a bluff and hearty stoicism as remote as possible from Mrs. Peyton's deprecating evasion of facts. It was a bad business; he was sorry Kate should have been mixed up with it; but she would be married soon now, and then she would see that life was n't exactly a Sunday-school story. Everybody was exposed to such disagreeable accidents: he remembered a case in their own family—oh, a distant cousin whom Kate would n't have heard of—a poor fellow who had got entangled with just such a woman, and having (most properly) been sent packing by his father, had justified the latter's course by promptly forging his name—a very nasty affair altogether; but luckily the scandal had been hushed up, the woman bought off, and the prodigal, after a season of probation, safely married to a nice girl with a good income, who was told by the family that the doctors recommended his settling in California.

*Luckily the scandal was hushed up:* the phrase blazed out against the dark background of Kate's misery. That was doubtless what most people felt—the words represented the consensus of respectable opinion. The best way of repairing a fault was to hide it: to tear up the floor and bury the victim at night. Above all, no coroner and no autopsy!

She began to feel a strange interest in her distant cousin. "And his wife—did she know what he had done?"

Mr. Orme stared. His moral pointed, he had returned to the contemplation of his own affairs.

"His wife? Oh, of course not. The secret has been most admirably kept; but her property was put in trust, so she's quite safe with him."

Her property! Kate wondered if her faith in her husband had also been put in trust, if her sensibilities had been protected from his possible inroads.

"Do you think it quite fair to have deceived her in that way?"

Mr. Orme gave her a puzzled glance: he had no taste for the by-paths of ethical conjecture.

"His people wanted to give the poor fellow another chance; they did the best they could for him."

"And—he has done nothing dishonourable since?"

"Not that I know of: the last I heard was that they

had a little boy, and that he was quite happy. At that distance he's not likely to bother *us*, at all events."

Long after Mr. Orme had left the topic, Kate remained lost in its contemplation. She had begun to perceive that the fair surface of life was honeycombed by a vast system of moral sewage. Every respectable household had its special arrangements for the private disposal of family scandals; it was only among the reckless and improvident that such hygienic precautions were neglected. Who was she to pass judgment on the merits of such a system? The social health must be preserved: the means devised were the result of long experience and the collective instinct of self-preservation. She had meant to tell her father that evening that her marriage had been put off; but she now abstained from doing so, not from any doubt of Mr. Orme's acquiescence—he could always be made to feel the force of conventional scruples—but because the whole question sank into insignificance beside the larger issue which his words had raised.

In her own room, that night, she passed through that travail of the soul of which the deeper life is born. Her first sense was of a great moral loneliness—an isolation more complete, more impenetrable, than that in which the discovery of Denis's act had plunged her. For she had vaguely leaned, then, on a collective sense of justice that should respond to her own ideas of right and wrong: she still believed in the logical correspondence of theory and practice. Now she saw that, among those nearest her, there was no one who recognized the moral need of expiation. She saw that to take her father or Mrs. Peyton into her confidence would be but to widen the circle of sterile misery in which she and Denis moved. At first the aspect of life thus revealed to her seemed simply mean and base—a world where honour was a pact of silence between adroit accomplices. The network of circumstance had tightened round her, and every effort to escape drew its meshes closer. But as her struggles subsided she felt the spiritual release which comes with acceptance: not connivance in dishonour, but recognition of evil. Out of that dark vision light was to come, the shaft of cloud turning to the pillar of fire. For here, at last, life lay before her as it was: not brave, garlanded and victorious, but naked, grovelling and diseased, dragging its maimed limbs through the mud, yet lifting piteous hands to the stars. Love itself, once throned aloft on an altar of dreams, how it stole to her now, storm-beaten and scarred, pleading for the shelter of her breast! Love, indeed, not in the old sense in which she had conceived it, but a graver, austerer presence—the charity of the mystic three. She thought she had ceased to love Denis —but what had she loved in him but her happiness and his? Their affection had been the *garden enclosed* of the Canticles, where they were to walk forever in a delicate isolation of bliss. But now love appeared to her as something more than this—something wider, deeper, more enduring

## SANCTUARY

than the selfish passion of a man and a woman. She saw it in all its far-reaching issues, till the first meeting of two pairs of young eyes kindled a light which might be a high-lifted beacon across dark waters of humanity.

All this did not come to her clearly, consecutively, but in a series of blurred and shifting images. Marriage had meant to her, as it means to girls brought up in ignorance of life, simply the exquisite prolongation of wooing. If she had looked beyond, to the vision of wider ties, it was as a traveller gazes over a land veiled in golden haze, and so far distant that the imagination delays to explore it. But now through the blur of sensations one image strangely persisted—the image of Denis's child. Had she ever before thought of their having a child? She could not remember. She was like one who wakens from a long fever: she recalled nothing of her former self or of her former feelings. She knew only that the vision persisted—the vision of the child whose mother she was not to be. It was impossible that she should marry Denis—her inmost soul rejected him . . . but it was just because she was not to be the child's mother that its image followed her so pleadingly. For she saw with perfect clearness the inevitable course of events. Denis would marry some one else—he was one of the men who are fated to marry, and she needed not his mother's reminder that her abandonment of him at an emotional crisis would fling him upon the first sympathy within reach. He would marry a girl who knew nothing of his secret—for

# SANCTUARY

Kate was intensely aware that he would never again willingly confess himself—he would marry a girl who trusted him and leaned on him, as she, Kate Orme—the earlier Kate Orme—had done but two days since! And with this deception between them their child would be born: born to an inheritance of secret weakness, a vice of the moral fibre, as it might be born with some hidden physical taint which would destroy it before the cause should be detected. . . . Well, and what of it? Was she to hold herself responsible? Were not thousands of children born with some such unsuspected taint? . . . Ah, but if here was one that she could save? What if she, who had had so exquisite a vision of wifehood, should reconstruct from its ruins this vision of protecting maternity—if her love for her lover should be, not lost, but transformed, enlarged, into this passion of charity for his race? If she might expiate and redeem his fault by becoming a refuge from its consequences? Before this strange extension of her love all the old limitations seemed to fall. Something had cleft the surface of self, and there welled up the mysterious primal influences, the sacrificial instinct of her sex, a passion of spiritual motherhood that made her long to fling herself between the unborn child and its fate. . . .

She never knew, then or after, how she reached this mystic climax of effacement; she was only conscious, through her anguish, of that lift of the heart which made one of the saints declare that joy was the inmost core of

## SANCTUARY

sorrow. For it was indeed a kind of joy she felt, if old names must serve for such new meanings; a surge of liberating faith in life, the old *credo quia absurdum* which is the secret cry of all supreme endeavour.

## PART II

### I

"DOES it look nice, mother?"

Dick Peyton met her with the question on the threshold, drawing her gaily into the little square room, and adding, with a laugh with a blush in it: "You know she's an uncommonly noticing person, and little things tell with her."

He swung round on his heel to follow his mother's smiling inspection of the apartment.

"She seems to have *all* the qualities," Mrs. Denis Peyton remarked, as her circuit finally brought her to the prettily appointed tea-table.

"*All*," he declared, taking the sting from her emphasis by his prompt adoption of it. Dick had always had a wholesome way of thus appropriating to his own use such small shafts of maternal irony as were now and then aimed at him.

Kate Peyton laughed and loosened her furs. "It looks charmingly," she pronounced, ending her survey by an approach to the window, which gave, far below, the oblique perspective of a long side-street leading to Fifth Avenue.

The high-perched room was Dick Peyton's private

office, a retreat partitioned off from the larger enclosure in which, under a north light and on a range of deal tables, three or four young draughtsmen were busily engaged in elaborating his architectural projects. The outer door of the office bore the sign: *Peyton and Gill, Architects;* but Gill was an utilitarian person, as unobtrusive as his name, who contented himself with a desk in the workroom, and left Dick to lord it alone in the small apartment to which clients were introduced, and where the social part of the business was carried on.

It was to serve, on this occasion, as the scene of a tea designed, as Kate Peyton was vividly aware, to introduce a certain young lady to the scene of her son's labours. Mrs. Peyton had been hearing a great deal lately about Clemence Verney. Dick was naturally expansive, and his close intimacy with his mother—an intimacy fostered by his father's early death—if it had suffered some natural impairment in his school and college days, had of late been revived by four years of comradeship in Paris, where Mrs. Peyton, in a tiny apartment of the Rue de Varennes, had kept house for him during his course of studies at the Beaux Arts. There were indeed not lacking critics of her own sex who accused Kate Peyton of having figured too largely in her son's life; of having failed to efface herself at a period when it is agreed that young men are best left free to try conclusions with the world. Mrs. Peyton, had she cared to defend herself, might have said that Dick, if communicative, was not impressionable, and that the closeness of texture which enabled him to throw off her sarcasms preserved him also from the infiltration of her prejudices. He was certainly no knight of the apron-string, but a seemingly resolute and self-sufficient young man, whose romantic friendship with his mother had merely served to throw a veil of suavity over the hard angles of youth.

But Mrs. Peyton's real excuse was after all one which she would never have given. It was because her intimacy with her son was the one need of her life that she had, with infinite tact and discretion, but with equal persistency, clung to every step of his growth, dissembling herself, adapting herself, rejuvenating herself in the passionate effort to be always within reach, but never in the way.

Denis Peyton had died after seven years of marriage, when his boy was barely six. During those seven years he had managed to squander the best part of the fortune he had inherited from his step-brother; so that, at his death, his widow and son were left with a scant competence. Mrs. Peyton, during her husband's life, had apparently made no effort to restrain his expenditure. She had even been accused by those judicious persons who are always ready with an estimate of their neighbours' motives, of having encouraged poor Denis's improvidence for the gratification of her own ambition. She had in fact, in the early days of their marriage, tried to launch him in politics, and

## SANCTUARY

had perhaps drawn somewhat heavily on his funds in the first heat of the contest; but the experiment ending in failure, as Denis Peyton's experiments were apt to end, she had made no farther demands on his exchequer. Her personal tastes were in fact unusually simple, but her outspoken indifference to money was not, in the opinion of her critics, designed to act as a check upon her husband; and it resulted in leaving her, at his death, in straits from which it was impossible not to deduce a moral.

Her small means, and the care of the boy's education, served the widow as a pretext for secluding herself in a socially remote suburb, where it was inferred that she was expiating, on queer food and in ready-made boots, her rash defiance of fortune. Whether or not Mrs. Peyton's penance took this form, she hoarded her substance to such good purpose that she was not only able to give Dick the best of schooling, but to propose, on his leaving Harvard, that he should prolong his studies by another four years at the Beaux Arts. It had been the joy of her life that her boy had early shown a marked bent for a special line of work. She could not have borne to see him reduced to a mere money-getter, yet she was not sorry that their small means forbade the cultivation of an ornamental leisure. In his college days Dick had troubled her by a superabundance of tastes, a restless flitting from one form of artistic expression to another. Whatever art he enjoyed he wished to practise, and he passed from music

## SANCTUARY

to painting, from painting to architecture, with an ease which seemed to his mother to indicate lack of purpose rather than excess of talent. She had observed that these changes were usually due, not to self-criticism, but to some external discouragement. Any depreciation of his work was enough to convince him of the uselessness of pursuing that special form of art, and the reaction produced the immediate conviction that he was really destined to shine in some other line of work. He had thus swung from one calling to another till, at the end of his college career, his mother took the decisive step of transplanting him to the Beaux Arts, in the hope that a definite course of study, combined with the stimulus of competition, might fix his wavering aptitudes. The result justified her expectation, and their four years in the Rue de Varennes yielded the happiest confirmation of her belief in him. Dick's ability was recognized not only by his mother, but by his professors. He was engrossed in his work, and his first successes developed his capacity for application. His mother's only fear was that praise was still too necessary to him. She was uncertain how long his ambition would sustain him in the face of failure. He gave lavishly where he was sure of a return; but it remained to be seen if he were capable of production without recognition. She had brought him up in a wholesome scorn of material rewards, and nature seemed, in this direction, to have seconded her training. He was genuinely indifferent to money, and his enjoyment

# SANCTUARY

of beauty was of that happy sort which does not generate the wish for possession. As long as the inner eye had food for contemplation, he cared very little for the deficiencies in his surroundings; or, it might rather be said, he felt, in the sum-total of beauty about him, an ownership of appreciation that left him free from the fret of personal desire. Mrs. Peyton had cultivated to excess this disregard of material conditions; but she now began to ask herself whether, in so doing, she had not laid too great a strain on a temperament naturally exalted. In guarding against other tendencies she had perhaps fostered in him too exclusively those qualities which circumstances had brought to an unusual development in herself. His enthusiasms and his disdains were alike too unqualified for that happy mean of character which is the best defence against the surprises of fortune. If she had taught him to set an exaggerated value on ideal rewards, was not that but a shifting of the danger-point on which her fears had always hung? She trembled sometimes to think how little love and a lifelong vigilance had availed in the deflecting of inherited tendencies.

Her fears were in a measure confirmed by the first two years of their life in New York, and the opening of his career as a professional architect. Close on the easy triumphs of his studentships there came the chilling reaction of public indifference. Dick, on his return from Paris, had formed a partnership with an architect who had had sev-

## SANCTUARY

eral years of practical training in a New York office; but the quiet and industrious Gill, though he attracted to the new firm a few small jobs which overflowed from the business of his former employer, was not able to infect the public with his own faith in Peyton's talents, and it was trying to a genius who felt himself capable of creating palaces to have to restrict his efforts to the building of suburban cottages or the planning of cheap alterations in private houses.

Mrs. Peyton expended all the ingenuities of tenderness in keeping up her son's courage; and she was seconded in the task by a friend whose acquaintance Dick had made at the Beaux Arts, and who, two years before the Peytons, had returned to New York to start on his own career as an architect. Paul Darrow was a young man full of crude seriousness, who, after a youth of struggling work and study in his native northwestern state, had won a scholarship which sent him abroad for a course at the Beaux Arts. His two years there coincided with the first part of Dick's residence, and Darrow's gifts had at once attracted the younger student. Dick was unstinted in his admiration of rival talent, and Mrs. Peyton, who was romantically given to the cultivation of such generosities, had seconded his enthusiasm by the kindest offers of hospitality to the young student. Darrow thus became the grateful frequenter of their little *salon;* and after their return to New York the intimacy between the young men was renewed, though Mrs. Peyton found it more difficult to coax Dick's friend to her New York drawing-room than to the informal surroundings of the Rue de Varennes. There, no doubt, secluded and absorbed in her son's work, she had seemed to Darrow almost a fellow-student; but seen among her own associates she became once more the woman of fashion, divided from him by the whole breadth of her ease and his awkwardness. Mrs. Peyton, whose tact had divined the cause of his estrangement, would not for an instant let it affect the friendship of the two young men. She encouraged Dick to frequent Darrow, in whom she divined a persistency of effort, an artistic self-confidence, in curious contrast to his social hesitancies. The example of his obstinate capacity for work was just the influence her son needed, and if Darrow would not come to them she insisted that Dick must seek him out, must never let him think that any social discrepancy could affect a friendship based on deeper things. Dick, who had all the loyalties, and who took an honest pride in his friend's growing success, needed no urging to maintain the intimacy; and his copious reports of midnight colloquies in Darrow's lodgings showed Mrs. Peyton that she had a strong ally in her invisible friend.

It had been, therefore, somewhat of a shock to learn in the course of time that Darrow's influence was being shared, if not counteracted, by that of a young lady in whose honour Dick was now giving his first professional tea. Mrs. Peyton had heard a great deal about Miss Clem-

# SANCTUARY

ence Verney, first from the usual purveyors of such information, and more recently from her son, who, probably divining that rumour had been before him, adopted his usual method of disarming his mother by taking her into his confidence. But, ample as her information was, it remained perplexing and contradictory, and even her own few meetings with the girl had not helped her to a definite opinion. Miss Verney, in conduct and ideas, was patently of the "new school": a young woman of feverish activities and broad-cast judgments, whose very versatility made her hard to define. Mrs. Peyton was shrewd enough to allow for the accidents of environment; what she wished to get at was the residuum of character beneath Miss Verney's shifting surface.

"It looks charmingly," Mrs. Peyton repeated, giving a loosening touch to the chrysanthemums in a tall vase on her son's desk.

Dick laughed, and glanced at his watch.

"They won't be here for another quarter of an hour. I think I'll tell Gill to clean out the work-room before they come."

"Are we to see the drawings for the competition?" his mother asked.

He shook his head smilingly. "Can't—I've asked one or two of the Beaux Arts fellows, you know; and besides, old Darrow's actually coming."

"Impossible!" Mrs. Peyton exclaimed.

"He swore he would last night." Dick laughed again, with a tinge of self-satisfaction. "I've an idea he wants to see Miss Verney."

"Ah," his mother murmured. There was a pause before she added: "Has Darrow really gone in for this competition?"

"Rather! I should say so! He's simply working himself to the bone."

Mrs. Peyton sat revolving her muff on a meditative hand; at length she said: " I'm not sure I think it quite nice of him."

Her son halted before her with an incredulous stare. "*Mother!*" he exclaimed.

The rebuke sent a blush to her forehead. "Well—considering your friendship—and everything."

"Everything? What do you mean by everything? The fact that he had more ability than I have and is therefore more likely to succeed? The fact that he needs the money and the success a deuced sight more than any of us? Is that the reason you think he ought n't to have entered? Mother! I never heard you say an ungenerous thing before."

The blush deepened to crimson, and she rose with a nervous laugh. "It *was* ungenerous," she conceded. "I suppose I'm jealous for you. I hate these competitions!"

Her son smiled reassuringly. "You need n't. I'm not afraid: I think I shall pull it off this time. In fact, Paul's the only man I'm afraid of—I'm always afraid of Paul—but the mere fact that he's in the thing is a tremendous stimulus."

His mother continued to study him with an anxious tenderness. "Have you worked out the whole scheme? Do you *see* it yet?"

"Oh, broadly, yes. There's a gap here and there—a hazy bit, rather—it's the hardest problem I've ever had to tackle; but then it's my biggest opportunity, and I've simply *got* to pull it off!"

Mrs. Peyton sat silent, considering his flushed face and illumined eye, which were rather those of the victor nearing the goal than of the runner just beginning the race. She remembered something that Darrow had once said of him: "Dick always sees the end too soon."

"You have n't too much time left," she murmured.

"Just a week. But I shan't go anywhere after this. I shall renounce the world." He glanced smilingly at the festal tea-table and the embowered desk. "When I next appear, it will either be with my heel on Paul's neck—poor old Paul—or else—or else—being dragged lifeless from the arena!"

His mother nervously took up the laugh with which he ended. "Oh, not lifeless," she said.

His face clouded. "Well, maimed for life, then," he muttered.

Mrs. Peyton made no answer. She knew how much

# SANCTUARY

hung on the possibility of his winning the competition which for weeks past had engrossed him. It was a design for the new museum of sculpture, for which the city had recently voted half a million. Dick's taste ran naturally to the grandiose, and the erection of public buildings had always been the object of his ambition. Here was an unmatched opportunity, and he knew that, in a competition of the kind, the newest man had as much chance of success as the firm of most established reputation, since every competitor entered on his own merits, the designs being submitted to a jury of architects who voted on them without knowing the names of the contestants. Dick, characteristically, was not afraid of the older firms; indeed, as he had told his mother, Paul Darrow was the only rival he feared. Mrs. Peyton knew that, to a certain point, self-confidence was a good sign; but somehow her son's did not strike her as being of the right substance—it seemed to have no dimension but extent. Her fears were complicated by a suspicion that, under his professional eagerness for success, lay the knowledge that Miss Verney's favour hung on the victory. It was that, perhaps, which gave a feverish touch to his ambition; and Mrs. Peyton, surveying the future from the height of her material apprehensions, divined that the situation depended mainly on the girl's view of it. She would have given a great deal to know Clemence Verney's conception of success.

SANCTUARY

II

MISS VERNEY, when she presently appeared, in the wake of the impersonal and exclamatory young married woman who served as a background to her vivid outline, seemed competent to impart at short notice any information required of her. She had never struck Mrs. Peyton as more alert and efficient. A melting grace of line and colour tempered her edges with the charming haze of youth; but it occurred to her critic that she might emerge from this morning mist as a dry and metallic old woman.

If Miss Verney suspected a personal application in Dick's hospitality, it did not call forth in her the usual tokens of self-consciousness. Her manner may have been a shade more vivid than usual, but she preserved all her bright composure of glance and speech, so that one guessed, under the rapid dispersal of words, an undisturbed steadiness of perception. She was lavishly but not indiscriminately interested in the evidences of her host's industry, and as the other guests assembled, straying with vague ejaculations through the labyrinth of scale drawings and blue prints, Mrs. Peyton noted that Miss Verney alone knew what these symbols stood for.

To his visitors' requests to be shown his plans for the competition, Peyton had opposed a laughing refusal, enforced by the presence of two fellow-architects, young men with lingering traces of the Beaux Arts in their costume and vocabulary, who stood about in Gavarni attitudes and dazzled the ladies by allusions to fenestration and entasis. The party had already drifted back to the tea-table when a hesitating knock announced Darrow's approach. He entered with his usual air of having blundered in by mistake, embarrassed by his hat and great-coat, and thrown into deeper confusion by the necessity of being introduced to the ladies grouped about the urn. To the men he threw a gruff nod of fellowship, and Dick having relieved him of his encumbrances, he retreated behind the shelter of Mrs. Peyton's welcome. The latter judiciously gave him time to recover, and when she turned to him he was engaged in a surreptitious inspection of Miss Verney, whose dusky slenderness, relieved against the bare walls of the office, made her look like a young St. John of Donatello's. The girl returned his look with one of her clear glances, and the group having presently broken up again, Mrs. Peyton saw that she had drifted to Darrow's side. The visitors at length wandered back to the work-room to see a portfolio of Dick's water-colours; but Mrs. Peyton remained seated behind the urn, listening to the interchange of talk through the open door while she tried to coördinate her impressions.

She saw that Miss Verney was sincerely interested in Dick's work: it was the nature of her interest that remained in doubt. As if to solve this doubt, the girl presently reappeared alone on the threshold, and discovering Mrs. Peyton, advanced toward her with a smile.

"Are you tired of hearing us praise Mr. Peyton's things?" she asked, dropping into a low chair beside her hostess. "Unintelligent admiration must be a bore to people who know, and Mr. Darrow tells me you are almost as learned as your son."

Mrs. Peyton returned the smile, but evaded the question. "I should be sorry to think your admiration unintelligent," she said. "I like to feel that my boy's work is appreciated by people who understand it."

"Oh, I have the usual smattering," said Miss Verney carelessly. "I *think* I know why I admire his work; but then I am sure I see more in it when some one like Mr. Darrow tells me how remarkable it is."

"Does Mr. Darrow say that?" the mother exclaimed, losing sight of her object in the rush of maternal pleasure.

"He has said nothing else: it seems to be the only subject which loosens his tongue. I believe he is more anxious to have your son win the competition than to win it himself."

"He is a very good friend," Mrs. Peyton assented. She was struck by the way in which the girl led the topic back to the special application of it which interested her. She had none of the artifices of prudery.

"He feels sure that Mr. Peyton *will* win," Miss Verney continued. "It was very interesting to hear his reasons. He

SANCTUARY

is an extraordinarily interesting man. It must be a tremendous incentive to have such a friend."

Mrs. Peyton hesitated. "The friendship is delightful; but I don't know that my son needs the incentive. He is almost too ambitious."

Miss Verney looked up brightly. "Can one be?" she said. "Ambition is so splendid! It must be so glorious to be a man and go crashing through obstacles, straight up to the thing one is after. I'm afraid I don't care for people who are superior to success. I like marriage by capture!" She rose with her wandering laugh, and stood flushed and sparkling above Mrs. Peyton, who continued to gaze at her gravely.

"What do you call success?" the latter asked. "It means so many different things."

"Oh, yes, I know—the inward approval, and all that. Well, I'm afraid I like the other kind: the drums and wreaths and acclamations. If I were Mr. Peyton, for instance, I'd much rather win the competition than—than be as disinterested as Mr. Darrow."

Mrs. Peyton smiled. "I hope you won't tell him so," she said half seriously. "He is over-stimulated already; and he is so easily influenced by any one who—whose opinion he values."

She stopped abruptly, hearing herself, with a strange inward shock, reëcho the words which another man's mother had once spoken to her. Miss Verney did not

# SANCTUARY

seem to take the allusion to herself, for she continued to fix on Mrs. Peyton a gaze of impartial sympathy.

"But we can't help being interested!" she declared.

"It's very kind of you; but I wish you would all help him to feel that his competition is after all of very little account compared with other things—his health and his peace of mind, for instance. He is looking horribly used up."

The girl glanced over her shoulder at Dick, who was just reëntering the room at Darrow's side.

"Oh, do you think so?" she said. "I should have thought it was his friend who was used up."

Mrs. Peyton followed the glance with surprise. She had been too preoccupied to notice Darrow, whose crudely modelled face was always of a dull pallour, to which his slow-moving grey eye lent no relief except in rare moments of expansion. Now the face had the fallen lines of a death-mask, in which only the smile he turned on Dick remained alive; and the sight smote her with compunction. Poor Darrow! He did look horribly fagged out: as if he needed care and petting and good food. No one knew exactly how he lived. His rooms, according to Dick's report, were fireless and ill kept, but he stuck to them because his landlady, whom he had fished out of some financial plight, had difficulty in obtaining other lodgers. He belonged to no clubs, and wandered out alone for his meals, mysteriously refusing the hospitality which his

[ 302 ]

# SANCTUARY

friends pressed on him. It was plain that he was very poor, and Dick conjectured that he sent what he earned to an aunt in his native village; but he was so silent about such matters that, outside of his profession, he seemed to have no personal life.

Miss Verney's companion having presently advised her of the lapse of time, there ensued a general leave-taking, at the close of which Dick accompanied the ladies to their carriage. Darrow was meanwhile blundering into his greatcoat, a process which always threw him into a state of perspiring embarrassment; but Mrs. Peyton, surprising him in the act, suggested that he should defer it and give her a few moments' talk.

"Let me make you some fresh tea," she said, as Darrow blushingly shed the garment, "and when Dick comes back we'll all walk home together. I've not had a chance to say two words to you this winter."

Darrow sank into a chair at her side and nervously contemplated his boots. "I've been tremendously hard at work," he said.

"I know: *too* hard at work, I'm afraid. Dick tells me you have been wearing yourself out over your competition plans."

"Oh, well, I shall have time to rest now," he returned. "I put the last stroke to them this morning."

Mrs. Peyton gave him a quick look. "You're ahead of Dick, then."

# SANCTUARY

"In point of time only," he said smiling.

"That is in itself an advantage," she answered with a tinge of asperity. In spite of an honest effort for impartiality she could not, at the moment, help regarding Darrow as an obstacle in her son's path.

"I wish the competition were over!" she exclaimed, conscious that her voice had betrayed her. "I hate to see you both looking so fagged."

Darrow smiled again, perhaps at her studied inclusion of himself.

"Oh, *Dick*'s all right," he said. "He'll pull himself together in no time."

He spoke with an emphasis which might have struck her, if her sympathies had not again been deflected by the allusion to her son.

"Not if he doesn't win," she exclaimed.

Darrow took the tea she had poured for him, knocking the spoon to the floor in his eagerness to perform the feat gracefully. In bending to recover the spoon he struck the tea-table with his shoulder, and set the cups dancing. Having regained a measure of composure, he took a swallow of the hot tea and set it down with a gasp, precariously near the edge of the tea-table. Mrs. Peyton rescued the cup, and Darrow, apparently forgetting its existence, rose and began to pace the room. It was always hard for him to sit still when he talked.

"You mean he's so tremendously set on it?" he broke out.

# SANCTUARY

Mrs. Peyton hesitated. "You know him almost as well as I do," she said. "He's capable of anything where there is a possibility of success; but I'm always afraid of the reaction."

"Oh, well, Dick's a man," said Darrow bluntly. "Besides, he's going to succeed."

"I wish he did n't feel so sure of it. You must n't think I'm afraid for him. He's a man, and I want him to take his chances with other men; but I wish he did n't care so much about what people think."

"People?"

"Miss Verney, then: I suppose you know."

Darrow paused in front of her. "Yes: he's talked a good deal about her. You think she wants him to succeed?"

"At any price!"

He drew his brows together. "What do you call any price?"

"Well—herself, in this case, I believe."

Darrow bent a puzzled stare on her. "You mean she attached that amount of importance to this competition?"

"She seems to regard it as symbolical: that's what I gather. And I'm afraid she's given him the same impression."

Darrow's sunken face was suffused by his rare smile. "Oh, well, he'll pull it off then!" he said.

Mrs. Peyton rose with a distracted sigh. "I half hope he won't, for such a motive," she exclaimed.

"The motive won't show in his work," said Darrow.

He added, after a pause probably devoted to the search for the right word: "He seems to think a great deal of her."

Mrs. Peyton fixed him thoughtfully. "I wish I knew what *you* think of her."

"Why, I never saw her before."

"No; but you talked with her to-day. You've formed an opinion: I think you came here on purpose."

He chuckled joyously at her discernment: she had always seemed to him gifted with supernatural insight. "Well, I did want to see her," he owned.

"And what do you think?"

He took a few vague steps and then halted before Mrs. Peyton. "I think," he said, smiling, "that she likes to be helped first, and to have everything on her plate at once."

III

AT dinner, with a rush of contrition, Mrs. Peyton remembered that she had after all not spoken to Darrow about his health. He had distracted her by beginning to talk of Dick; and besides, much as Darrow's opinions interested her, his personality had never fixed her attention. He always seemed to her simply a vehicle for the transmission of ideas.

It was Dick who recalled her to a sense of her omission

# SANCTUARY

by asking if she hadn't thought that old Paul looked rather more ragged than usual.

"He did look tired," Mrs. Peyton conceded. "I meant to tell him to take care of himself."

Dick laughed at the futility of the measure. "Old Paul is never tired: he can work twenty-five hours out of the twenty-four. The trouble with him is that he's ill. Something wrong with the machinery, I'm afraid."

"Oh, I'm sorry. Has he seen a doctor?"

"He wouldn't listen to me when I suggested it the other day; but he's so deuced mysterious that I don't know what he may have done since." Dick rose, putting down his coffee-cup and half-smoked cigarette. "I've half a mind to pop in on him tonight and see how he's getting on."

"But he lives at the other end of the earth; and you're tired yourself."

"I'm not tired; only a little strung-up," he returned, smiling. "And besides, I'm going to meet Gill at the office by and by and put in a night's work. It won't hurt me to take a look at Paul first."

Mrs. Peyton was silent. She knew it was useless to contend with her son about his work, and she tried to fortify herself with the remembrance of her own words to Darrow: Dick was a man and must take his chance with other men.

But Dick, glancing at his watch, uttered an exclamation

of annoyance. "Oh, by Jove, I shan't have time after all. Gill is waiting for me now; we must have dawdled over dinner." He went to give his mother a caressing tap on the cheek. "Now don't worry," he adjured her; and as she smiled back at him he added with a sudden happy blush: "She does n't, you know: she's so sure of me."

Mrs. Peyton's smile faded, and laying a detaining hand on his, she said with sudden directness: "Sure of you, or of your success?"

He hesitated. "Oh, she regards them as synonymous. She thinks I 'm bound to get on."

"But if you don't?"

He shrugged laughingly, but with a slight contraction of his confident brows. "Why, I shall have to make way for some one else, I suppose. That 's the law of life."

Mrs. Peyton sat upright, gazing at him with a kind of solemnity. "Is it the law of love?" she asked.

He looked down on her with a smile that trembled a little. "My dear romantic mother, I don't want her pity, you know!"

Dick, coming home the next morning shortly before daylight, left the house again after a hurried breakfast, and Mrs. Peyton heard nothing of him till nightfall. He had promised to be back for dinner, but a few moments before eight, as she was coming down to the drawing-room, the parlour-maid handed her a hastily pencilled note.

# SANCTUARY

"Don't wait for me," it ran. "Darrow is ill and I can't leave him. I'll send a line when the doctor has seen him."

Mrs. Peyton, who was a woman of rapid reactions, read the words with a pang. She was ashamed of the jealous thoughts she had harboured of Darrow, and of the selfishness which had made her lose sight of his troubles in the consideration of Dick's welfare. Even Clemence Verney, whom she secretly accused of a want of heart, had been struck by Darrow's ill looks, while she had had eyes only for her son. Poor Darrow! How cold and self-engrossed he must have thought her! In the first rush of penitence her impulse was to drive at once to his lodgings; but the infection of his own shyness restrained her. Dick's note gave no details; the illness was evidently grave, but might not Darrow regard her coming as an intrusion? To repair her negligence of yesterday by a sudden invasion of his privacy might be only a greater failure in tact; and after a moment of deliberation she resolved on sending to ask Dick if he wished her to go to him.

The reply, which came late, was what she had expected. "No, we have all the help we need. The doctor has sent a good nurse, and is coming again later. It's pneumonia, but of course he does n't say much yet. Let me have some beef-juice as soon as the cook can make it."

The beef-juice ordered and dispatched, she was left to a vigil in melancholy contrast to that of the previous evening. Then she had been enclosed in the narrow limits of

## SANCTUARY

her maternal interests; now the barriers of self were broken down, and her personal preoccupations swept away on the current of a wider sympathy. As she sat there in the radius of lamp-light which, for so many evenings, had held Dick and herself in a charmed circle of tenderness, she saw that her love for her boy had come to be merely a kind of extended egotism. Love had narrowed instead of widening her, had rebuilt between herself and life the very walls which, years and years before, she had laid low with bleeding fingers. It was horrible, how she had come to sacrifice everything to the one passion of ambition for her boy. . . .

At daylight she sent another messenger, one of her own servants, who returned without having seen Dick. Mr. Peyton had sent word that there was no change. He would write later; he wanted nothing. The day wore on drearily. Once Kate found herself computing the precious hours lost to Dick's unfinished task. She blushed at her ineradicable selfishness, and tried to turn her mind to poor Darrow. But she could not master her impulses; and now she caught herself indulging the thought that his illness would at least exclude him from the competition. But no—she remembered that he had said his work was finished. Come what might, he stood in the path of her boy's success. She hated herself for the thought, but it would not down.

Evening drew on, but there was no note from Dick. At

# SANCTUARY

length, in the shamed reaction from her fears, she rang for a carriage and went upstairs to dress. She could stand aloof no longer: she must go to Darrow, if only to escape from her wicked thoughts of him. As she came down again she heard Dick's key in the door. She hastened her steps, and as she reached the hall he stood before her without speaking.

She looked at him and the question died on her lips. He nodded, and walked slowly past her.

"There was no hope from the first," he said.

The next day Dick was taken up with the preparations for the funeral. The distant aunt, who appeared to be Darrow's only relation, had been duly notified of his death; but no answer having been received from her, it was left to his friend to fulfil the customary duties. He was again absent for the best part of the day; and when he returned at dusk Mrs. Peyton, looking up from the tea-table behind which she awaited him, was startled by the deep-lined misery of his face.

Her own thoughts were too painful for ready expression, and they sat for a while in a mute community of wretchedness.

"Is everything arranged?" she asked at length.

"Yes. Everything."

"And you have not heard from the aunt?"

He shook his head.

# SANCTUARY

"Can you find no trace of any other relations?"

"None. I went over all his papers. There were very few, and I found no address but the aunt's." He sat thrown back in his chair, disregarding the cup of tea she had mechanically poured for him. "I found this, though," he added, after a pause, drawing a letter from his pocket and holding it out to her.

She took it doubtfully. "Ought I to read it?"

"Yes."

She saw then that the envelope, in Darrow's hand, was addressed to her son. Within were a few pencilled words, dated on the first day of his illness, the morrow of the day on which she had last seen him.

"Dear Dick," she read, "I want you to use my plans "for the museum if you can get any good out of them. "Even if I pull out of this I want you to. I shall have "other chances, and I have an idea this one means a lot "to you."

Mrs. Peyton sat speechless, gazing at the date of the letter, which she had instantly connected with her last talk with Darrow. She saw that he had understood her, and the thought scorched her to the soul.

"Was n't it glorious of him?" Dick said.

She dropped the letter, and hid her face in her hands.

# SANCTUARY

## IV

THE funeral took place the next morning, and on the return from the cemetery Dick told his mother that he must go and look over things at Darrow's office. He had heard the day before from his friend's aunt, a helpless person to whom telegraphy was difficult and travel inconceivable, and who, in eight pages of unpunctuated eloquence, made over to Dick what she called the melancholy privilege of winding up her nephew's affairs.

Mrs. Peyton looked anxiously at her son. "Is there no one who can do this for you? He must have had a clerk or some one who knows about his work."

Dick shook his head. "Not lately. He has n't had much to do this winter, and these last months he had chucked everything to work alone over his plans."

The word brought a faint colour to Mrs. Peyton's cheek. It was the first allusion that either of them had made to Darrow's bequest.

"Oh, of course you must do all you can," she murmured, turning alone into the house.

The emotions of the morning had stirred her deeply, and she sat at home during the day, letting her mind dwell, in a kind of retrospective piety, on the thought of poor Darrow's devotion. She had given him too little time while he lived, had acquiesced too easily in his growing habits of seclusion; and she felt it as a proof of insensibility that she had not been more closely drawn to the one person who had loved Dick as she loved him. The evidence of that love, as shown in Darrow's letter, filled her with a vain compunction. The very extravagance of his offer lent it a deeper pathos. It was wonderful that, even in the urgency of affection, a man of his almost morbid rectitude should have overlooked the restrictions of professional honour, should have implied the possibility of his friend's overlooking them. It seemed to make his sacrifice the more complete that it had, unconsciously, taken the form of a subtle temptation.

The last word arrested Mrs. Peyton's thoughts. A temptation? To whom? Not, surely, to one capable, as her son was capable, of rising to the height of his friend's devotion. The offer, to Dick, would mean simply, as it meant to her, the last touching expression of an inarticulate fidelity: the utterance of a love which at last had found its formula. Mrs. Peyton dismissed as morbid any other view of the case. She was annoyed with herself for supposing that Dick could be ever so remotely affected by the possibility at which poor Darrow's renunciation hinted. The nature of the offer removed it from practical issues to the idealizing region of sentiment.

Mrs. Peyton had been sitting alone with these thoughts for the greater part of the afternoon, and dusk was falling when Dick entered the drawing-room. In the dim light, with his pallour heightened by the sombre effect of his mourning, he came upon her almost startlingly, with a revival of some long-effaced impression which, for a moment, gave her the sense of struggling among shadows. She did not, at first, know what had produced the effect; then she saw that it was his likeness to his father.

"Well—is it over?" she asked, as he threw himself into a chair without speaking.

"Yes: I 've looked through everything." He leaned back, crossing his hands behind his head, and gazing past her with a look of utter lassitude.

She paused a moment, and then said tentatively: "Tomorrow you will be able to go back to your work."

"Oh—my work," he exclaimed, as if to brush aside an ill-timed pleasantry.

"Are you too tired?"

"No." He rose and began to wander up and down the room. "I 'm not tired.—Give me some tea, will you?" He paused before her while she poured the cup, and then, without taking it, turned away to light a cigarette.

"Surely there is still time?" she suggested, with her eyes on him.

"Time? To finish my plans? Oh, yes—there 's time. But they 're not worth it."

"Not worth it?" She started up, and then dropped back into her seat, ashamed of having betrayed her anxiety. "They are worth as much as they were last week," she said with an attempt at cheerfulness.

# SANCTUARY

"Not to me," he returned. "I had n't seen Darrow's then."

There was a long silence. Mrs. Peyton sat with her eyes fixed on her clasped hands, and her son paced the room restlessly.

"Are they so wonderful?" she asked at length.

"Yes."

She paused again, and then said, lifting a tremulous glance to his face: "That makes his offer all the more beautiful."

Dick was lighting another cigarette, and his face was turned from her. "Yes—I suppose so," he said in a low tone.

"They were quite finished, he told me," she continued, unconsciously dropping her voice to the pitch of his.

"Yes."

"Then they will be entered, I suppose?"

"Of course—why not?" he answered almost sharply.

"Shall you have time to attend to all that and to finish yours too?"

"Oh, I suppose so. I 've told you it is n't a question of time. I see now that mine are not worth bothering with."

She rose and approached him, laying her hands on his shoulders. "You are tired and unstrung; how can you judge? Why not let me look at both designs to-morrow?"

Under her gaze he flushed abruptly and drew back with a half-impatient gesture.

He took her hand as if ashamed of his impatience.

# SANCTUARY

"Oh, I'm afraid that would n't help me; you 'd be sure to think mine best," he said with a laugh.

"But if I could give you good reasons?" she pressed him.

He took her hand, as if ashamed of his impatience. "Dear mother, if you had any reasons their mere existence would prove that they were bad."

His mother did not return his smile. "You won't let me see the two designs then?" she said with a faint tinge of insistence.

"Oh, of course—if you want to— if you only won't talk about it now! Can't you see that I'm pretty nearly deadbeat?" he burst out uncontrollably; and as she stood silent, he added with a weary fall in his voice, "I think I'll go upstairs and see if I can't get a nap before dinner."

Though they had separated upon the assurance that she should see the two designs if she wished it, Mrs. Peyton knew they would not be shown to her. Dick, indeed, would not again deny her request; but had he not reckoned on the improbability of her renewing it? All night she lay confronted by that question. The situation shaped itself before her with that hallucinating distinctness which belongs to the midnight vision. She knew now why Dick had suddenly reminded her of his father: had she not once before seen the same thought moving behind the same eyes? She was sure it had occurred to Dick to use Darrow's drawings. As she lay awake in the darkness she could

## SANCTUARY

hear him, long after midnight, pacing the floor overhead: she held her breath, listening to the recurring beat of his foot, which seemed that of an imprisoned spirit revolving wearily in the cage of the same thought. She felt in every fibre that a crisis in her son's life had been reached, that the act now before him would have a determining effect on his whole future. The circumstances of her past had raised to clairvoyance her natural insight into human motive, had made of her a moral barometer responding to the faintest fluctuations of atmosphere, and years of anxious meditation had familiarized her with the form which her son's temptations were likely to take. The peculiar misery of her situation was that she could not, except indirectly, put this intuition, this foresight, at his service. It was a part of her discernment to be aware that life is the only real counsellor, that wisdom unfiltered through personal experience does not become a part of the moral tissues. Love such as hers had a great office, the office of preparation and direction; but it must know how to hold its hand and keep its counsel, how to attend upon its object as an invisible influence rather than as an active interference.

All this Kate Peyton had told herself again and again, during those hours of anxious calculation in which she had tried to cast Dick's horoscope; but not in her moments of most fantastic foreboding had she figured so cruel a test of her courage. If her prayers for him had taken precise shape, she might have asked that he should be spared the spectacular, the dramatic appeal to his will-power: that his temptations should slip by him in a dull disguise. She had secured him against all ordinary forms of baseness; the vulnerable point lay higher, in that region of idealizing egotism which is the seat of life in such natures.

Years of solitary foresight gave her mind a singular alertness in dealing with such possibilities. She saw at once that the peril of the situation lay in the minimum of risk it involved. Darrow had employed no assistant in working out his plans for the competition, and his secluded life made it almost certain that he had not shown them to any one, and that she and Dick alone knew them to have been completed. Moreover, it was a part of Dick's duty to examine the contents of his friend's office, and in doing this nothing would be easier than to possess himself of the drawings and make use of any part of them that might serve his purpose. He had Darrow's authority for doing so; and though the act involved a slight breach of professional probity, might not his friend's wishes be invoked as a secret justification? Mrs. Peyton found herself almost hating poor Darrow for having been the unconscious instrument of her son's temptation. But what right had she, after all, to suspect Dick of considering, even for a moment, the act of which she was so ready to accuse him? His unwillingness to let her see the drawings might have been the accidental result of lassitude and discouragement. He was tired and troubled, and she had chosen the wrong

## SANCTUARY

moment to make the request. His want of readiness might even be due to the wish to conceal from her how far his friend had surpassed him. She knew his sensitiveness on this point, and reproached herself for not having foreseen it. But her own arguments failed to convince her. Deep beneath her love for her boy and her faith in him there lurked a nameless doubt. She could hardly now, in looking back, define the impulse upon which she had married Denis Peyton: she knew only that the deeps of her nature had been loosened, and that she had been borne forward on their current to the very fate from which her heart recoiled. But if in one sense her marriage remained a problem, there was another in which her motherhood seemed to solve it. She had never lost the sense of having snatched her child from some dim peril which still lurked and hovered; and he became more closely hers with every effort of her vigilant love. For the act of rescue had not been accomplished once and for all in the moment of immolation: it had not been by a sudden stroke of heroism, but by ever-renewed and indefatigable effort, that she had built up for him the miraculous shelter of her love. And now that it stood there, a hallowed refuge against failure, she could not even set a light in the pane, but must let him grope his way to it unaided.

# SANCTUARY

## V

MRS. PEYTON'S midnight musings summed themselves up in the conclusion that the next few hours would end her uncertainty. She felt the day to be decisive. If Dick offered to show her the drawings, her fears would be proved groundless; if he avoided the subject, they were justified.

She dressed early in order not to miss him at breakfast; but as she entered the dining-room the parlour-maid told her that Mr. Peyton had overslept himself, and had rung to have his breakfast sent upstairs. Was it a pretext to avoid her? She was vexed at her own readiness to see a portent in the simplest incident; but while she blushed at her doubts she let them govern her. She left the dining-room door open, determined not to miss him if he came downstairs while she was at breakfast; then she went back to the drawing-room and sat down at her writing-table, trying to busy herself with some accounts while she listened for his step. Here too she had left the door open; but presently even this slight departure from her daily usage seemed a deviation from the passive attitude she had adopted, and she rose and shut the door. She knew that she could still hear his step on the stairs—he had his father's quick swinging gait—but as she sat listening, and vainly trying to write, the closed door seemed to symbolize a refusal to share in his trial, a hardening of herself against his need of her. What if he should come down intending to speak, and should be turned from his purpose? Slighter obstacles have deflected the course of events in those indeterminate moments when the soul floats between two tides. She sprang up quickly, and as her hand touched the latch she heard his step on the stairs.

When he entered the drawing-room she had regained the writing-table and could lift a composed face to his. He came in hurriedly, yet with a kind of reluctance beneath his haste: again it was his father's step. She smiled, but looked away from him as he approached her; she seemed to be re-living her own past as one re-lives things in the distortion of fever.

"Are you off already?" she asked, glancing at the hat in his hand.

"Yes; I'm late as it is. I overslept myself." He paused and looked vaguely about the room. "Don't expect me till late—don't wait dinner for me."

She stirred impulsively. "Dick, you're overworking—you'll make yourself ill."

"Nonsense. I'm as fit as ever this morning. Don't be imagining things."

He dropped his habitual kiss on her forehead, and turned to go. On the threshold he paused, and she felt that something in him sought her and then drew back. "Good-bye," he called to her as the door closed on him.

## SANCTUARY

She sat down and tried to survey the situation divested of her midnight fears. He had not referred to her wish to see the drawings: but what did the omission signify? Might he not have forgotten her request? Was she not forcing the most trivial details to fit in with her apprehensions? Unfortunately for her own reassurance, she knew that her familiarity with Dick's processes was based on such minute observation, and that, to such intimacy as theirs, no indications were trivial. She was as certain as if he had spoken, that when he had left the house that morning he was weighing the possibility of using Darrow's drawings, of supplementing his own incomplete design from the fulness of his friend's invention. And with a bitter pang she divined that he was sorry he had shown her Darrow's letter.

It was impossible to remain face to face with such conjectures, and though she had given up all her engagements during the few days since Darrow's death, she now took refuge in the thought of a concert which was to take place at a friend's house that morning. The music-room, when she entered, was thronged with acquaintances, and she found transient relief in that dispersal of attention which makes society an anesthetic for some forms of wretchedness. Contact with the pressure of busy indifferent life often gives remoteness to questions which have clung as close as the flesh to the bone; and if Mrs. Peyton did not find such complete release, she at least interposed between herself

## SANCTUARY

and her anxiety the obligation to dissemble it. But the relief was only momentary, and when the first bars of the overture turned from her the smiles of recognition among which she had tried to lose herself, she felt a deeper sense of isolation. The music, which at another time would have swept her away on some rich current of emotion, now seemed to island her in her own thoughts, to create an artificial solitude in which she found herself more immitigably face to face with her fears. The silence, the *recueillement*, about her gave resonance to the inner voices, lucidity to the inner vision, till she seemed enclosed in a luminous empty horizon against which every possibility took the sharp edge of accomplished fact. With relentless precision the course of events was unrolled before her: she saw Dick yielding to his opportunity, snatching victory from dishonour, winning love, happiness and success in the act by which he lost himself. It was all so simple, so easy, so inevitable, that she felt the futility of struggling or hoping against it. He would win the competition, would marry Miss Verney, would press on to achievement through the opening which the first success had made for him.

As Mrs. Peyton reached this point in her forecast, she found her outward gaze arrested by the face of the young lady who so dominated her inner vision. Miss Verney, a few rows distant, sat intent upon the music, in that attitude of poised motion which was her nearest approach to repose. Her slender brown profile with its breezy hair, her quick eye, and the lips which seemed to listen as well as speak, all betokened to Mrs. Peyton a nature through which the obvious energies blew free, a bare open stretch of consciousness without shelter for tenderer growths. She shivered to think of Dick's frail scruples exposed to those rustling airs. And then, suddenly, a new thought struck her. What if she might turn this force to her own use, make it serve, unconsciously to Dick, as the means of his deliverance? Hitherto she had assumed that her son's worst danger lay in the chance of his confiding his difficulty to Clemence Verney; and she had, in her own past, a precedent which made her think such a confidence not unlikely. If he did carry his scruples to the girl, she argued, the latter's imperviousness, her frank inability to understand them, would have the effect of dispelling them like mist; and he was acute enough to know this and profit by it. So she had hitherto reasoned; but now the girl's presence seemed to clarify her perceptions, and she told herself that something in Dick's nature, something which she herself had put there, would resist this short cut to safety, would make him take the more tortuous way to his goal rather than gain it through the privacies of the heart he loved. For she had lifted him thus far above his father, that it would be a disenchantment to him to find that Clemence Verney did not share his scruples. On this much, his mother now exultingly felt, she could count in her passive struggle for supremacy. No, he would never,

# SANCTUARY

never tell Clemence Verney—and his one hope, his sure salvation, therefore lay in some one else's telling her.

The excitement of this discovery had nearly, in mid-concert, swept Mrs. Peyton from her seat to the girl's side. Fearing to miss the latter in the throng at the entrance, she slipped out during the last number and, lingering in the farther drawing-room, let the dispersing audience drift her in Miss Verney's direction. The girl shone sympathetically on her approach, and in a moment they had detached themselves from the crowd and taken refuge in the perfumed emptiness of the conservatory.

The girl, whose sensations were always easily set in motion, had at first a good deal to say of the music, for which she claimed, on her hearer's part, an active show of approval or dissent; but this dismissed, she turned a melting face on Mrs. Peyton and said with one of her rapid modulations of tone: "I was so sorry about poor Mr. Darrow."

Mrs. Peyton uttered an assenting sigh. "It was a great grief to us—a great loss to my son."

"Yes—I know. I can imagine what you must have felt. And then it was so unlucky that it should have happened just now."

Mrs. Peyton shot a reconnoitring glance at her profile. "His dying, you mean, on the eve of success?"

Miss Verney turned a frank smile upon her. "One ought to feel that, of course—but I'm afraid I am very selfish

# SANCTUARY

where my friends are concerned, and I was thinking of Mr. Peyton's having to give up his work at such a critical moment." She spoke without a note of deprecation: there was a pagan freshness in her opportunism.

Mrs. Peyton was silent, and the girl continued after a pause: "I suppose now it will be almost impossible for him to finish his drawings in time. It's a pity he had n't worked out the whole scheme a little sooner. Then the details would have come of themselves."

Mrs. Peyton felt a contempt strangely mingled with exultation. If only the girl would talk in that way to Dick!

"He has hardly had time to think of himself lately," she said, trying to keep the coldness out of her voice.

"No, of course not," Miss Verney assented; "but is n't that all the more reason for his friends to think of him? It was very dear of him to give up everything to nurse Mr. Darrow—but, after all, if a man is going to get on in his career there are times when he must think first of himself."

Mrs. Peyton paused, trying to choose her words with deliberation. It was quite clear now that Dick had not spoken, and she felt the responsibility that devolved upon her.

"Getting on in a career—is that always the first thing to be considered?" she asked, letting her eyes rest musingly on the girl's.

The glance did not disconcert Miss Verney, who returned it with one of equal comprehensiveness. "Yes," she said quickly, and with a slight blush. "With a temperament like Mr. Peyton's I believe it is. Some people can pick themselves up after any number of bad falls: I am not sure that he could. I think discouragement would weaken instead of strengthening him."

Both women had forgotten external conditions in the quick reach for each other's meanings. Mrs. Peyton flushed, her maternal pride in revolt; but the answer was checked on her lips by the sense of the girl's unexpected insight. Here was some one who knew Dick as well as she did—should she say a partisan or an accomplice? A dim jealousy stirred beneath Mrs. Peyton's other emotions: she was undergoing the agony which the mother feels at the first intrusion on her privilege of judging her child; and her voice had a flutter of resentment.

"You must have a poor opinion of his character," she said.

Miss Verney did not remove her eyes, but her blush deepened beautifully. "I have, at any rate," she said, "a high one of his talent. I don't suppose many men have an equal amount of moral and intellectual energy."

"And you would cultivate the one at the expense of the other?"

"In certain cases—and up to a certain point." She shook out the long fur of her muff, one of those silvery flexible furs which clothe a woman with a delicate sumptu-

# SANCTUARY

ousness. Everything about her, at the moment, seemed rich and cold—everything, as Mrs. Peyton quickly noted, but the blush lingering under her dark skin; and so complete was the girl's self-command that the blush seemed to be there only because it had been forgotten.

"I dare say you think me strange," she continued. "Most people do, because I speak the truth. It's the easiest way of concealing one's feelings. I can, for instance, talk quite openly about Mr. Peyton under shelter of your inference that I should n't do so if I were what is called 'interested' in him. And as I *am* interested in him, my method has its advantages!" She ended with one of the fluttering laughs which seemed to flit from point to point of her expressive person.

Mrs. Peyton leaned toward her. "I believe you are interested," she said quietly; "and since I suppose you allow others the privilege you claim for yourself, I am going to confess that I followed you here in the hope of finding out the nature of your interest."

Miss Verney shot a glance at her, and drew away in a soft subsidence of undulating furs.

"Is this an embassy?" she asked smiling.

"No: not in any sense."

The girl leaned back with an air of relief. "I'm glad; I should have disliked—" She looked again at Mrs. Peyton. "You want to know what I mean to do?"

"Yes."

# SANCTUARY

"Then I can only answer that I mean to wait and see what he does."

"You mean that everything is contingent on his success?"

"*I* am—if I'm everything," she admitted gaily.

The mother's heart was beating in her throat, and her words seemed to force themselves out through the throbs.

"I—I don't quite see why you attach such importance to this special success."

"Because he does," the girl returned instantly. "Because to him it is the final answer to his self-questioning—the questioning whether he is ever to amount to anything or not. He says if he has anything in him it ought to come out now. All the conditions are favourable—it is the chance he has always prayed for. You see," she continued, almost confidentially, but without the least loss of composure—"you see he has told me a great deal about himself and his various experiments—his phrases of indecision and disgust. There are lots of tentative talents in the world, and the sooner they are crushed out by circumstances the better. But it seems as though he really had it in him to do something distinguished—as though the uncertainty lay in his character and not in his talent. That is what interests, what attracts me. One can't teach a man to have genius, but if he has it one may show him how to use it. That is what I should be good for, you see—to keep him up to his opportunities."

# SANCTUARY

Mrs. Peyton had listened with an intensity of attention that left her reply unprepared. There was something startling and yet half attractive in the girl's avowal of principles which are oftener lived by than professed.

"And you think," she began at length, "that in this case he has fallen below his opportunity?"

"No one can tell, of course; but his discouragement, his *abattement*, is a bad sign. I don't think he has any hope of succeeding."

The mother again wavered a moment. "Since you are so frank," she then said, "will you let me be equally so, and ask how lately you have seen him?"

The girl smiled at the circumlocution. "Yesterday afternoon," she said simply.

"And you thought him—"

"Horribly down on his luck. He said himself that his brain was empty."

Again Mrs. Peyton felt the throb in her throat, and a slow blush rose to her cheek. "Was that all he said?"

"About himself—was there anything else?" said the girl quickly.

"He did n't tell you of—of an opportunity to make up for the time he has lost?"

"An opportunity? I don't understand."

"He did n't speak to you, then, of Mr. Darrow's letter?"

"He said nothing of any letter."

# SANCTUARY

"There *was* one, which was found after poor Darrow's death. In it he gave Dick leave to use his design for the competition. Dick says the design is wonderful—it would give him just what he needs."

Miss Verney sat listening raptly, with a rush of colour that suffused her like light.

"But when was this? Where was the letter found? He never said a word of it!" she exclaimed.

"The letter was found on the day of Darrow's death."

"But I don't understand! Why has he never told me? Why should he seem so hopeless?" She turned an ignorant appealing face on Mrs. Peyton. It was prodigious, but it was true—she felt nothing, saw nothing, but the crude fact of the opportunity.

Mrs. Peyton's voice trembled with the completeness of her triumph. "I suppose his reason for not speaking is that he has scruples."

"Scruples?"

"He feels that to use the design would be dishonest."

Miss Verney's eyes fixed themselves on her in a commiserating stare. "Dishonest? When the poor man wished it himself? When it was his last request? When the letter is there to prove it? Why, the design belongs to your son! No one else had any right to it."

"But Dick's right does not extend to passing it off as his own—at least that is his feeling, I believe. If he won the competition he would be winning it on false pretenses."

# SANCTUARY

"Why should you call them false pretenses? His design might have been better than Darrow's if he had had time to carry it out. It seems to me that Mr. Darrow must have felt this—must have felt that he owed his friend some compensation for the time he took from him. I can imagine nothing more natural than his wishing to make this return for your son's sacrifice."

She positively glowed with the force of her conviction, and Mrs. Peyton, for a strange instant, felt her own resistance wavering. She herself had never considered the question in that light—the light of Darrow's viewing his gift as a justifiable compensation. But the glimpse she caught of it drove her shuddering behind her retrenchments.

"That argument," she said coldly, "would naturally be more convincing to Darrow than to my son."

Miss Verney glanced up, struck by the change in Mrs. Peyton's voice.

"Ah, then you agree with him? You think it *would* be dishonest?"

Mrs. Peyton saw that she had slipped into self-betrayal. "My son and I have not spoken of the matter," she said evasively. She caught the flash of relief in Miss Verney's face.

"You haven't spoken? Then how do you know how he feels about it?"

"I only judge from—well, perhaps from his not speaking."

The girl drew a deep breath. "I see," she murmured. "That is the very reason that prevents his speaking."

"The reason?"

"Your knowing what he thinks—and his knowing that you know."

Mrs. Peyton was startled at her subtlety. "I assure you," she said, rising, "that I have done nothing to influence him."

The girl gazed at her musingly. "No," she said with a faint smile, "nothing except to read his thoughts."

## VI

MRS. PEYTON reached home in the state of exhaustion which follows on a physical struggle. It seemed to her as though her talk with Clemence Verney had been an actual combat, a measuring of wrist and eye. For a moment she was frightened at what she had done—she felt as though she had betrayed her son to the enemy. But before long she regained her moral balance, and saw that she had merely shifted the conflict to the ground on which it could best be fought out—since the prize fought for was the natural battlefield. The reaction brought with it a sense of helplessness, a realization that she had let the issue pass out of her hold; but since, in the last analysis, it had never lain there, since it was above all needful that the determining touch should be given by any hand but

## SANCTUARY

hers, she presently found courage to subside into inaction. She had done all she could—even more, perhaps, than prudence warranted—and now she could but await passively the working of the forces she had set in motion.

For two days after her talk with Miss Verney she saw little of Dick. He went early to his office and came back late. He seemed less tired, more self-possessed, than during the first days after Darrow's death; but there was a new inscrutableness in his manner, a note of reserve, of resistance almost, as though he had barricaded himself against her conjectures. She had been struck by Miss Verney's reply to the anxious asseveration that she had done nothing to influence Dick—"Nothing," the girl had answered, "except to read his thoughts." Mrs. Peyton shrank from this detection of a tacit interference with her son's liberty of action. She longed—how passionately he would never know—to stand apart from him in this struggle between his two destinies, and it was almost a relief that he on his side should hold aloof, should, for the first time in their relation, seem to feel her tenderness as an intrusion.

Only four days remained before the date fixed for the sending in of the designs, and still Dick had not referred to his work. Of Darrow, also, he had made no mention. His mother longed to know if he had spoken to Clemence Verney—or rather if the girl had forced his confidence. Mrs. Peyton was almost certain that Miss Verney would

## SANCTUARY

not remain silent—there were times when Dick's renewed application to his work seemed an earnest of her having spoken, and spoken convincingly. At the thought Kate's heart grew chill. What if her experiment should succeed in a sense she had not intended? If the girl should reconcile Dick to his weakness, should pluck the sting from his temptation? In this round of uncertainties the mother revolved for two interminable days; but the second evening brought an answer to her question.

Dick, returning earlier than usual from the office, had found, on the hall-table, a note which, since morning, had been under his mother's observation. The envelope, fashionable in tint and texture, was addressed in a rapid staccato hand which seemed the very imprint of Miss Verney's utterance. Mrs. Peyton did not know the girl's writing; but such notes had of late lain often enough on the hall-table to make their attribution easy. This communication Dick, as his mother poured his tea, looked over with a face of shifting lights; then he folded it into his note-case, and said, with a glance at his watch: "If you have n't asked any one for this evening I think I'll dine out."

"Do, dear; the change will be good for you," his mother assented.

He made no answer, but sat leaning back, his hands clasped behind his head, his eyes fixed on the fire. Every line of his body expressed a profound physical lassitude, but the face remained alert and guarded. Mrs. Peyton, in silence, was busying herself with the details of the tea-making, when suddenly, inexplicably, a question forced itself to her lips.

"And your work—?" she said, strangely hearing herself speak.

"My work—?" He sat up, on the defensive almost, but without a tremor of the guarded face.

"You're getting on well? You've made up for lost time?"

"Oh, yes: things are going better." He rose, with another glance at his watch. "Time to dress," he said, nodding to her as he turned to the door.

It was an hour later, during her own solitary dinner, that a ring at the door was followed by the parlour-maid's announcement that Mr. Gill was there from the office. In the hall, in fact, Kate found her son's partner, who explained apologetically that he had understood Peyton was dining at home, and had come to consult him about a difficulty which had arisen since he had left the office. On hearing that Dick was out, and that his mother did not know where he had gone, Mr. Gill's perplexity became so manifest that Mrs. Peyton, after a moment, said hesitatingly: "He may be at a friend's house; I could give you the address."

The architect caught up his hat. "Thank you; I'll have a try for him."

# SANCTUARY

Mrs. Peyton hesitated again. "Perhaps," she suggested, "it would be better to telephone."

She led the way into the little study behind the drawing-room, where a telephone stood on the writing-table. The folding doors between the two rooms were open: should she close them as she passed back into the drawing-room? On the threshold she wavered an instant; then she walked on and took her usual seat by the fire.

Gill, meanwhile, at the telephone, had "rung up" the Verney house, and inquired if his partner were dining there. The reply was evidently affirmative; and a moment later Kate knew that he was in communication with her son. She sat motionless, her hands clasped on the arms of her chair, her head erect, in an attitude of avowed attention. If she listened she would listen openly: there should be no suspicion of eavesdropping. Gill, engrossed in his message, was probably hardly conscious of her presence; but if he turned his head he should at least have no difficulty in seeing her, and in being aware that she could hear what he said. Gill, however, as she was quick to remember, was doubtless ignorant of any need for secrecy in his communication to Dick. He had often heard the affairs of the office discussed openly before Mrs. Peyton, had been led to regard her as familiar with all the details of her son's work. He talked on unconcernedly, and she listened.

Ten minutes later, when he rose to go, she knew all that she had wanted to find out. Long familiarity with the technicalities of her son's profession made it easy for her to translate the stenographic jargon of the office. She could lengthen out all Gill's abbreviations, interpret all his allusions, and reconstruct Dick's answers from the questions addressed to him. And when the door closed on the architect she was left face to face with the fact that her son, unknown to any one but herself, was using Darrow's drawings to complete his work.

Mrs. Peyton, left alone, found it easier to continue her vigil by the drawing-room fire than to carry up to the darkness and silence of her own room the truth she had been at such pains to acquire. She had no thought of sitting up for Dick. Doubtless, his dinner over, he would rejoin Gill at the office, and prolong through the night the task in which she now knew him to be engaged. But it was less lonely by the fire than in the wide-eyed darkness which awaited her upstairs. A mortal loneliness enveloped her. She felt as though she had fallen by the way, spent and broken in a struggle of which even its object had been unconscious. She had tried to deflect the natural course of events, she had sacrificed her personal happiness to a fantastic ideal of duty, and it was her punishment to be left alone with her failure, outside the normal current of human strivings and regrets.

She had no wish to see her son just then: she would have preferred to let the inner tumult subside, to repossess her-

# SANCTUARY

self in this new adjustment to life, before meeting his eyes again. But as she sat there, far adrift on her misery, she was aroused by the turning of his key in the latch. She started up, her heart sounding a retreat, but her faculties too dispersed to obey it; and while she stood wavering, the door opened and he was in the room.

In the room, and with face illumined: a Dick she had not seen since the strain of the contest had cast its shade on him. Now he shone as in a sunrise of victory, holding out exultant hands from which she hung back instinctively.

"Mother! I knew you'd be waiting for me!" He had her on his breast now, and his kisses were in her hair. "I've always said you knew everything that was happening to me, and now you've guessed that I wanted you to-night."

She was struggling faintly against the dear endearments. "What *has* happened?" she murmured, drawing back for a dazzled look at him.

He had drawn her to the sofa, had dropped beside her, regaining his hold of her in the boyish need that his happiness should be touched and handled.

"My engagement has happened!" he cried out to her. "You stupid dear, do you need to be told?"

# SANCTUARY

## VII

SHE had indeed needed to be told: the surprise was complete and overwhelming. She sat silent under it, her hands trembling in his, till the blood mounted to his face and she felt his confident grasp relax.

"You did n't guess it, then?" he exclaimed, starting up and moving away from her.

"No; I did n't guess it," she confessed in a dead-level voice.

He stood above her, half challenging, half defensive. "And you have n't a word to say to me? Mother!" he adjured her.

She rose too, putting her arms about him with a kiss. "Dick! Dear Dick!" she murmured.

"She imagines you don't like her; she says she 's always felt it. And yet she owns you 've been delightful, that you 've tried to make friends with her. And I thought you knew how much it would mean to me, just now, to have this uncertainty over, and that you 'd actually been trying to help me, to put in a good word for me. I thought it was you who had made her decide."

"I?"

"By your talk with her the other day. She told me of your talk with her."

His mother's hands slipped from his shoulders and she

sank back into her seat. She felt the cruelty of her silence, but only an inarticulate murmur found a way to her lips. Before speaking she must clear a space in the suffocating rush of her sensations. For the moment she could only repeat inwardly that Clemence Verney had yielded before the final test, and that she herself was somehow responsible for this fresh entanglement of fate. For she saw in a flash how the coils of circumstance had tightened; and as her mind cleared it was filled with the perception that this, precisely, was what the girl intended, that this was why she had conferred the crown before the victory. By pledging herself to Dick she had secured his pledge in return: had put him on his honour in a cynical inversion of the term. Kate saw the succession of events spread out before her like a map, and the astuteness of the girl's policy frightened her. Miss Verney had conducted the campaign like a strategist. She had frankly owned that her interest in Dick's future depended on his capacity for success, and in order to key him up to his first achievement she had given him a foretaste of its results.

So much was almost immediately clear to Mrs. Peyton; but in a moment her inferences had carried her a point farther. For it was now plain to her that Miss Verney had not risked so much without first trying to gain her point at less cost: that if she had had to give herself as a prize, it was because no other bribe had been sufficient. This then, as the mother saw with a throb of hope, meant that Dick, who since Darrow's death had held to his purpose unwaveringly, had been deflected from it by the first hint of Clemence Verney's connivance. Kate had not miscalculated: things had happened as she had foreseen. In the light of the girl's approval his act had taken an odious look. He had recoiled from it, and it was to revive his flagging courage that she had had to promise herself, to take him in the meshes of her surrender.

Kate, looking up, saw above her the young perplexity of her boy's face, the suspended happiness waiting to brim over. With a fresh touch of misery she said to herself that this was his hour, his one irrecoverable moment, and that she was darkening it by her silence. Her memory went back to the same hour in her own life: she could feel its heat in her pulses still. What right had she to stand in Dick's light? Who was she to decide between his code and hers? She put out her hand and drew him down to her.

"She'll be the making of me, you know, mother," he said, as they leaned together. "She'll put new life in me—she'll help me get my second wind. Her talk is like a fresh breeze blowing away the fog in my head. I never knew any one who saw so straight to the heart of things, who had such a grip on values. She goes straight up to life and catches hold of it, and you simply can't make her let go."

He got up and walked the length of the room; then he came back and stood smiling above his mother.

"You know you and I are rather complicated people,"

he said. "We're always walking around things to get new views of them—we're always rearranging the furniture. And somehow she simplifies life so tremendously." He dropped down beside her with a deprecating laugh. "Not that I mean, dear, that it has n't been good for me to argue things out with myself, as you 've taught me to —only the man who stops to talk is apt to get shoved aside nowadays, and I don't believe Milton's archangels would have had much success in active business."

He had begun in a strain of easy confidence, but as he went on she detected an effort to hold the note, she felt that his words were being poured out in a vain attempt to fill the silence which was deepening between them. She longed, in her turn, to pour something into that menacing void, to bridge it with a reconciling word or look; but her soul hung back, and she had to take refuge in a vague murmur of tenderness.

"My boy! My boy!" she repeated; and he sat beside her without speaking, their hand-clasp alone spanning the distance which had widened between their thoughts.

The engagement, as Kate subsequently learned, was not to be made known till later. Miss Verney had even stipulated that for the present there should be no recognition of it in her own family or in Dick's. She did not wish to interfere with his final work for the competition, and had made him promise, as he laughingly owned, that he would

# SANCTUARY

not see her again till the drawings were sent in. His mother noticed that he made no other allusion to his work; but when he bade her good-night he added that he might not see her the next morning, as he had to go to the office early. She took this as a hint that he wished to be left alone, and kept her room the next day till the closing door told her that he was out of the house.

She herself had waked early, and it seemed to her that the day was already old when she came downstairs. Never had the house appeared so empty. Even in Dick's longest absences something of his presence had always hung about the rooms: a fine dust of memories and associations, which wanted only the evocation of her thought to float into a palpable semblance of him. But now he seemed to have taken himself quite away, to have broken every fibre by which their lives had hung together. Where the sense of him had been there was only a deeper emptiness: she felt as if a strange man had gone out of her house.

She wandered from room to room, aimlessly, trying to adjust herself to their solitude. She had known such loneliness before, in the years when most women's hearts are fullest; but that was long ago, and the solitude had after all been less complete, because of the sense that it might still be filled. Her son had come: her life had brimmed over; but now the tide ebbed again, and she was left gazing over a bare stretch of wasted years. Wasted! There was

SANCTUARY

the mortal pang, the stroke from which there was no healing. Her faith and hope had been marsh-lights luring her to the wilderness, her love a vain edifice reared on shifting ground.

In her round of the rooms she came at last to Dick's study upstairs. It was full of his boyhood: she could trace the history of his past in its quaint relics and survivals, in the school-books lingering on his crowded shelves, the school-photographs and college-trophies hung among his later treasures. All his successes and failures, his exaltations and inconsistencies, were recorded in the warm huddled heterogeneous room. Everywhere she saw the touch of her own hand, the vestiges of her own steps. It was she alone who held the clue to the labyrinth, who could thread a way through the confusions and contradictions of his past; and her soul rejected the thought that his future could ever escape from her. She dropped down into his shabby college armchair and hid her face in the papers on his desk.

## VIII

THE day dwelt in her memory as a long stretch of aimless hours: blind alleys of time that led up to a dead wall of inaction.

Toward afternoon she remembered that she had promised to dine out and go to the opera. At first she felt that

## SANCTUARY

the contact of life would be unendurable; then she shrank from shutting herself up with her misery. In the end she let herself drift passively on the current of events, going through the mechanical routine of the day without much consciousness of what was happening.

At twilight, as she sat in the drawing-room, the evening paper was brought in, and in glancing over it her eye fell on a paragraph which seemed printed in more vivid type than the rest. It was headed, *The New Museum of Sculpture*, and underneath she read: "The artists and architects selected to pass on the competitive designs for the new Museum will begin their sittings on Monday, and tomorrow is the last day on which designs may be sent in to the committee. Great interest is felt in the competition, as the conspicuous site chosen for the new building, and the exceptionally large sum voted by the city for its erection, offer an unusual field for the display of architectural ability."

She leaned back, closing her eyes. It was as though a clock had struck, loud and inexorably, marking off some irrecoverable hour. She was seized by a sudden longing to seek Dick out, to fall on her knees and plead with him: it was one of those physical obsessions against which the body has to stiffen its muscles as well as the mind its thoughts. Once she even sprang up to ring for a cab; but she sank back again, breathing as if after a struggle, and gripping the arms of her chair to keep herself down.

# SANCTUARY

"I can only wait for him—only wait for him—" she heard herself say; and the words loosened the sobs in her throat.

At length she went upstairs to dress for dinner. A ghost-like self looked back at her from her toilet-glass: she watched it performing the mechanical gestures of the toilet, dressing her, as it appeared, without help from her actual self. Each little act stood out sharply against the blurred background of her brain: when she spoke to her maid her voice sounded extraordinarily loud. Never had the house been so silent; or, stay—yes, once she had felt the same silence, once when Dick, in his school-days, had been ill of a fever, and she had sat up with him on the decisive night. The silence had been as deep and as terrible then; and as she dressed she had before her the vision of his room, of the cot in which he lay, of his restless head working a hole in the pillow, his face so pinched and alien under the familiar freckles. It might be his death-watch she was keeping: the doctors had warned her to be ready. And in the silence her soul had fought for her boy, her love had hung over him like wings, her abundant useless hateful life had struggled to force itself into his empty veins. And she had succeeded, she had saved him, she had poured her life into him; and in place of the strange child she had watched all night, at daylight she held her own boy to her breast.

That night had once seemed to her the most dreadful

## SANCTUARY

of her life; but she knew now that it was one of the agonies which enrich, that the passion thus spent grows fourfold from its ashes. She could not have borne to keep this new vigil alone. She must escape from its sterile misery, must take refuge in other lives till she regained courage to face her own. At the opera, in the illumination of the first *entr'-acte*, as she gazed about the house, wondering through the numb ache of her wretchedness how others could talk and smile and be indifferent, it seemed to her that all the jarring animation about her was suddenly focussed in the face of Clemence Verney. Miss Verney sat opposite, in the front of a crowded box, a box in which, continually, the black-coated background shifted and renewed itself. Mrs. Peyton felt a throb of anger at the girl's bright air of unconcern. She forgot that she too was talking, smiling, holding out her hand to newcomers, in a studied mimicry of life, while her real self played out its tragedy behind the scenes. Then it occurred to her that, to Clemence Verney, there was no tragedy in the situation. According to the girl's calculations, Dick was virtually certain of success; and unsuccess was to her the only conceivable disaster.

All through the opera the sense of that opposing force, that negation of her own beliefs, burned itself into Mrs. Peyton's consciousness. The space between herself and the girl seemed to vanish, the throng about them to disperse, till they were face to face and alone, enclosed in their mortal enmity. At length the feeling of humiliation and

## SANCTUARY

failed her, and she had to stand still and press her hands against her heart. Then the weight on her breast lifted, and she went on again, upward and upward, the great dark building dropping away from her, in tier after tier of mute doors and mysterious corridors. At last she reached Dick's floor, and saw the light shining down the passage from his door. She leaned against the wall, her breath coming short, the silence throbbing in her ears. Even now it was not too late to turn back. She bent over the stairs, letting her eyes plunge into the nether blackness, with the single glimmer of the watchman's lights in its depths; then she turned and stole toward her son's door.

There again she paused and listened, trying to catch, through the hum of her pulses, any noise that might come to her from within. But the silence was unbroken—it seemed as though the office must be empty. She pressed her ear to the door, straining for a sound. She knew he never sat long at his work, and it seemed unaccountable that she should not hear him moving about the drawing-board. For a moment she fancied he might be sleeping; but sleep did not come to him readily after prolonged mental effort—she recalled the restless straying of his feet above her head for hours after he returned from his night work in the office.

She began to fear that he might be ill. A nervous trembling seized her, and she laid her hand on the latch, whispering "Dick!"

# SANCTUARY

Her whisper sounded loudly through the silence, but there was no answer, and after a pause she called again. With each call the hush seemed to deepen: it closed in on her, mysterious and impenetrable. Her heart was beating in short frightened leaps: a moment more and she would have cried out. She drew a quick breath and turned the door-handle.

The outer room, Dick's private office, with its red carpet and easy-chairs, stood in pleasant lamp-lit emptiness. The last time she had entered it, Darrow and Clemence Verney had been there, and she had sat behind the urn observing them. She paused a moment, struck now by a faint sound from beyond; then she slipped noiselessly across the carpet, pushed open the swinging door, and stood on the threshold of the work-room. Here the gas-lights hung a green-shaded circle of brightness over the great draughting-table in the middle of the floor. Table and floor were strewn with a confusion of papers—torn blue-prints and tracings, crumpled sheets of tracing-paper wrenched from the draughting-boards in a sudden fury of destruction; and in the centre of the havoc, his arms stretched across the table and his face hidden in them, sat Dick Peyton.

He did not seem to hear his mother's approach, and she stood looking at him, her breast tightening with a new fear.

"Dick!" she said, "Dick!—" and he sprang up, staring with dazed eyes. But gradually, as his gaze cleared, a light spread in it, a mounting brightness of recognition.

# SANCTUARY

*you* kept apart and did n't meddle or pry, the other, the you in my heart, seemed to get a tighter hold on me. I don't know how to tell you,—it's all mixed up in my head—but old things you 'd said and done kept coming back to me, crowding between me and what I was trying for, looking at me without speaking, like old friends I 'd gone back on, till I simply could n't stand it any longer. I fought it off till to-night, but when I came back to finish the work there you were again—and suddenly, I don't know how, you were n't an obstacle any longer, but a refuge—and I crawled into your arms as I used to when things went against me at school."

His hands stole back into hers, and he leaned his head against her shoulder like a boy.

"I 'm an abysmally weak fool, you know," he ended; "I 'm not worth the fight you 've put up for me. But I want you to know that it 's your doing—that if you had let go an instant I should have gone under—and that if I 'd gone under I should never have come up again alive."

## THE END